YELLOW CROCUS

YELLOW CROCUS

Laila Ibrahim

LAKE UNION
PUBLISHING

This is a work of fiction. Names, characters, organizations, places, events, and incidents are either products of the author's imagination or are used fictitiously.

Published by Lake Union, Seattle
www.apub.com

Amazon, the Amazon logo, and Lake Union
are trademarks of Amazon.com, Inc., or its affiliates.

Cover design by Laura Klynstra.

ISBN-13: 9781477824757
ISBN-10: 1477824758

Library of Congress Control Number: 2014935302

Printed in the United States of America.

For Kalin, Maya, and Rinda. And all the Matties in the world—past, present, and future.

PROLOGUE

Mattie was never truly mine. That knowledge must have filled me as quickly and surely as the milk from her breasts. Although my family "owned" her, although she occupied the center of my universe, her deepest affections lay elsewhere. So along with the comfort of her came the fear that I would lose her someday. This is our story. You will wonder if it is true; I can assure you it is, though my parents wish it were otherwise. This is as true a story as has ever been told: the story of my love for Mattie, and, I suppose, her love for me in return.

CHAPTER 1

APRIL 14, 1837

Mattie lay curled around the warm shape of her son when the unwanted messenger knocked. She stayed on her pallet, reluctant to end this precious time, and listened to the sound of quiet snores coming from her grandfather. She gazed at Samuel, pressed her nose close against his soft neck to take in his sweet baby scent. She gently wiped the glistening sweat away from his damp forehead and gave him a tender kiss upon his temple. Another intrusive knock struck the door. Mattie got up. Cradling Samuel so close that she could feel warm puffs against her breast, she shuffled across the packed dirt floor. Though she expected this visitor, had anticipated a knock for weeks, she dreaded this moment.

Once she opened the door, her life would forever be divided into before and after.

Mattie slowly pulled on the rough plank door and saw a lithe silhouette in the moonlight. There stood Emily, a skinny girl with pale-hazel eyes and skin the color of tea with milk. Mattie had seen her before but did not know her well. She appeared to be no more than twelve.

In contrast, twenty-year-old Mattie's skin was as dark as roasted coffee beans. She kept her jet-black hair twisted back into two tight braids that framed each side of her narrow face. A dingy white cloth tightly covered her head, as usual.

Without a greeting, Emily mumbled, "You got to come now. The baby gonna be here soon." With her news delivered, she turned back to the big house.

Mattie called after her, "I gotta pass Samuel over to my poppy."

"Be quick about it. They expectin' you."

As Mattie crossed to his pallet, Poppy sat up to receive his great-grandson. His old hands were swollen and twisted, and just a few teeth stuck out of his swollen gums.

"It time?" he asked.

Mattie nodded. Tears pushed hard against the backs of her eyes. She kissed Samuel tenderly on his round cheek. "I love you," she quietly whispered into her son's tiny ear, and pressed her lips against his bald head one last time. Biting her cheek, she carefully passed Samuel into her grandfather's scarred arms.

"Remember, Rebecca gonna feed him when he get hungry," she reminded him, though he was well aware of the plan.

He was patient with her as always. "Don' you worry 'bout him. You just be careful in there." He patted her dark-brown arm.

She stared into Poppy's eyes and hoped he understood all that she did not say. She wanted to know that her son would be well cared for, that he would be told she had not chosen to leave him, and that when she returned he would know that she was his mother. But Mattie said nothing. She did not scream in protest or plead for more time. Instead she turned away in silence, blinking back tears as she left her home and abandoned her son. She had no choice. She had to be strong, get through this separation, and return to Samuel as soon as possible.

Whether that would be in months or years, she had no way of knowing.

—

Mattie shivered as she followed the dim light cast by Emily's oil lamp. They walked toward the big house, a path she had learned to dread and which she rarely traveled.

"How long she been havin' pains?" Mattie asked as they passed the small brick cookhouse.

"Most of the day, I think. She start screaming after dinner."

"Her water show yet?"

"Don' know," the girl replied as they reached the rear of the big house.

They entered through a painted door and climbed up the worn back stairs to the second floor. Mattie had never been inside this building and had no reason to expect that she ever would be until a few days ago. Field hands did not go into the big house. She did not know why they picked her over her sister Rebecca to feed this new baby. It was not her place to ask or argue with the White folks. She did as she was told.

Nervously, Mattie stepped behind Emily along a soft, colorful rug. Going down the smooth white hallway past several polished doors, Emily stopped in front of the last door on the left.

"They waitin' in there for you," she informed Mattie, pointing. Mattie watched the girl's mouth open wide in a yawn. Then Emily turned and made her way back down the corridor.

Mattie's heart beat fiercely as she stood alone and uncertain in the long hallway. Suddenly the white door flew open. She jumped back in time to avoid being trampled by a figure rushing out.

Warm air tinged with the smell of sweat wafted out of the room. Hesitating at the threshold, Mattie peered into the dim chamber.

A petite White woman with skin the color of heavy cream lay in a large bed. Eyes closed to the world, she moaned loudly. Her damp, dark hair stuck to her sweaty, swollen face. The woman's features contorted and she cried out in pain. Her eyes squeezed shut so tightly that her lashes disappeared, and her mouth was pulled in so hard that her lips hid in the cave of her mouth.

"There you are," proclaimed one of the two women hovering around the bed. The large White woman with narrow blue eyes and gray hair pulled into a severe bun pointed to a chair in the corner of the room. "We are not yet in need of you. Complications . . ." She trailed off without a complete explanation. "Go sit in the chair, and do not do anything to upset your mistress."

Mattie moved into the room as quietly as possible and made herself small to avoid drawing the attention of the red-faced man looming over the foot of the bed. She lowered herself into a plush velvet armchair and unconsciously rubbed the smooth pile with the tips of her brown fingers. Her gaze flew around the room, taking it in. Mrs. Ann, the mistress of the house, was in the intricately carved four-poster bed that took up much of the space. Next to it sat a marble-topped washbasin covered with crumpled cloths. The man directed the two women poised on either side of the bed.

"Hold her down when I am ready to pull the infant out," he commanded. "Prevent all movement or they both may die."

The doctor pulled dirty metal forceps out of his bag and wiped them quickly with a bloodstained cloth. Then he bent over the bed.

"Now," he commanded.

The women pressed their pale hands against the patient's shoulders and arms, pushing her hard into the mattress. Mattie winced in sympathy and sucked in her breath as the doctor thrust the forceps deep into her thin body. "Ahh, ahhh, ahhh," screamed

Mrs. Ann. The doctor tugged hard on the metal handles, but there was no movement.

Repositioning himself with his legs braced wide apart, the doctor pulled again. His hands slipped off the end of the instrument, leaving it protruding from the woman's body. He muttered to himself and rubbed his sweaty hands on his pants, then firmly grabbed the forceps once again. Heaving on the forceps, the doctor's hands slowly slid backward; the instrument moved along with his thick fingers.

Sandwiched tightly between the triangle of the forceps, bulges of purplish scalp emerged between the mistress's thin white legs.

The doctor grunted. His left hand lost its grip again. "He is a stubborn one!" the doctor said.

He pulled on the forceps again just as the woman's uterus was contracting, and the infant's head emerged until Mattie could see the tips of ears. The contraction ended. When the doctor pulled again there was no movement. The next pull came along with a contraction, and this time the rest of the head, shoulders, torso, and limbs rushed out. A purple, motionless infant flopped onto the bed.

The doctor stared at the limp child. Mattie fought the urge to grab the baby, turn it over, and rub hard. Helplessly she waited for the doctor to do something.

Do it, she silently encouraged the child who was ruining her life. *Take a breath.*

The doctor tied off and then cut the pulsing cord as the infant lay still. The baby suddenly jerked, then tipped back its damp head, opened its blue mouth, and let out a raspy wail. Mattie gave a silent cheer. *You did it, little one!*

"Good thing I was here for the delivery," the doctor declared. "This one needed modern medicine to take her first breath."

"A girl?" asked the new mother.

"Yes," confirmed the doctor matter-of-factly.

The young woman craned her neck to see and reached out her arms for her daughter. The doctor carelessly bundled the infant in a receiving blanket and started to pass her to the woman in the bed.

"Not now. You are too weak to hold the girl," said the large woman with the bun. "Give her to the wet nurse," she directed the doctor.

The mother collapsed against the bed without argument. With a shrug of his shoulders, the doctor carried the damp bundle to Mattie. Handing the newborn over, he asked, "Is your milk in?"

"Yes, sir. My son, he born some months ago," replied Mattie, looking down at the oak floor.

"Then do what you came here to do," replied the doctor. He turned back to the bed to receive the afterbirth and stitch up his patient.

Mattie looked down at the nameless pink baby. The forceps had left blue and purple bruises around her smushed ears. The infant was already licking her lips and bobbing her head in search of food. Drawing up her shirt, Mattie exposed a full breast with a large nipple ready for an infant's mouth. She took her breast in hand and gently tickled the tiny lips with the raised nub until the baby opened her mouth wide. Then Mattie swiftly pulled the baby close until the infant's eager mouth covered her breast. The baby sucked vigorously and soon Mattie felt the familiar tug as her milk flowed. She settled back on the soft, cushioned chair, holding the baby girl against her heart. Gazing at this new life, Mattie thought about Samuel, asleep on a hard pallet in another world only two hundred steps away. Her body ached for him. She wanted to be holding him in her arms, not this strange child. She wondered if he was sleeping soundly next to Poppy or if he was stirring, hoping for his morning feed. It broke her heart to know he could not possibly begin to understand that their life together was now over.

Before the newborn finished suckling, the big White woman with the tight bun interrupted. "You will call the baby Miss Elizabeth. I am Mrs. Gray, the housekeeper. Follow me."

Mattie gently removed Miss Elizabeth from her breast and rearranged her own clothing. Using her pinky finger as a pacifier to soothe the newborn, she followed with the sticky baby in her arms.

Mrs. Gray led the pair along the dimly lit hall to a room at the back of the house. A green couch and two beige chairs sat around a fireplace on the right side of the room. Straight ahead, a small bed and a rocking chair nestled close to a long window. The housekeeper did not stop here, but crossed left to another door that led to a small, windowless chamber. A low bed, covered with a faded quilt, occupied most of the room, and a small cupboard took up what little space remained. On the far wall was another door.

Standing in the doorway between the two rooms, Mrs. Gray lectured, "The large room is Miss Elizabeth's. You will sleep in here. The rear door leads to the servant hallway and stairs. You are to take the front staircase only when you are accompanying Miss Elizabeth. When she is not with you, you will use the rear staircase. There are two sets of clothes for your use—two dresses and two nightgowns—in this wardrobe." Mrs. Gray pointed as Mattie struggled to follow her directions. "You will place one day gown and one nightgown in the chute each Monday morning—that is the day after the Sabbath. You may not have your clothes laundered more than once a week. You will not need that head rag any longer, so that will be thrown out. Emily, the second-floor maid, will bring you meals three times a day. If you have any questions, you may ask Emily; she is fully aware of the routines of the household. You will be told when Miss Elizabeth is to be taken outside her room."

Mrs. Gray stared at Mattie. "Becoming a house slave is a rare privilege. I trust you will not abuse it?"

"Yes, ma'am," replied Mattie.

"Warm wash water is on the stand by Miss Elizabeth's dresser," Mrs. Gray instructed as they returned to Miss Elizabeth's room. "Bathe her before the water is chilled."

After Mrs. Gray left, Mattie looked at the infant cradled in her arms and remarked, "Look like it just us, little girl. Don' know what I gonna do with you. Suppose we gonna figure it out together. First we look round your room; then we gonna wash you up."

Mattie walked Miss Elizabeth around the room and took in her new surroundings. Long strips of dark-green material hung on poles suspended across the wall a few inches below the ceiling. After crossing to touch the smooth silk, Mattie realized it covered something. Parting the drapes, she saw two long windows. Mattie had seen glass, knew the word for it, but had never touched it. She rubbed her rough fingertips up and down the cold, smooth surface. She gazed out, her breath catching at the sight of the slave quarters. It was still dark outside, but she could make out each small building.

Disoriented, viewing her home from above, she puzzled out which dwelling belonged to which family. When she found her own cabin, the fifth in the row with log benches in back, her heart leaped. She searched for Samuel and Poppy, but they were not in sight. She stared out the window, yearning for a glimpse of them. Her eyes welled up with tears and her heart tightened. No one was up out there, but she kept watching.

Miss Elizabeth's mewling brought Mattie's attention back to the baby. She gave the infant her finger and then looked around again. To the left of the windows, a newly made, tightly stitched patchwork quilt covered a narrow bed made of a rich cherrywood. The bright fabrics formed a pattern of flying geese set to take flight out the window. She sat upon the bed, marveling at its comfort and the feel of smooth fabric.

"You got yourself a fine place to sleep, baby girl, not that you gonna be usin' it anytime soon." Mattie said. For many months, the baby would sleep with her in the anteroom.

To the right of the window, in the corner, the brightly polished rocking chair waited. A matching chest of drawers with a quilted pad on top stood next to it. She laid the baby on top, next to the washbowl with warm water. Opening each drawer, Mattie found finely stitched baby gowns, socks, diapers, and bonnets rolled in tight packages like eggs waiting to hatch. Looking down at the infant, Mattie remarked with a shake of her head, "You already got more clothes than the field hands all put together."

She selected a set of smooth cotton clothes and laid them on the bed. She carefully unwrapped the floppy infant and dipped the girl in the shallow bowl of lukewarm water. Miss Elizabeth cried in protest as Mattie rubbed away white vernix and red blood, the last vestiges of the womb.

"Hush, hush. You gonna be all right. It not so bad," Mattie assured Miss Elizabeth. "We all done now. The worst of it over."

Mattie quickly tied a soft flannel diaper on the baby. She tugged a crisp white gown over the girl's downy-topped head, being careful to avoid the bruised and tender areas of Elizabeth's face; then Mattie pulled the thin, mottled arms through the gown's puffy sleeves and swaddled her tight in a flannel blanket. Then the newborn relaxed and stared intently up at Mattie.

"See, you all right now," Mattie murmured. "You all clean."

She stared at the newborn. She ran her finger over her red face and the light fuzz of brows that were barely visible. The eyes staring back at her were a strange muddy-blue color. Unlike Samuel, this little being seemed like a creature from another world. It was hard to believe she would ever be lovely to look at.

Despite her exhaustion and sorrow, Mattie was curious about this place. "We gonna see about the rest of your room now. What this over here?" She walked to the furniture near the fireplace and perched upon the green velvet davenport. She explored the movements of the springs by bouncing up and down. Next she shifted to each chair in turn and attempted to bounce on them, but they were hard and did not move.

Leaving a swaddled Miss Elizabeth nestled at the back of the davenport, Mattie knelt down to examine the intricate tile work on the hearth and around the façade of the fireplace. It was cold like the windows, but filled with rich colors in shades of green and gold. She traced the swirling colors with her finger, then stood up and was startled at the sight of movement in front of her.

"Hello!" she called out.

There was no reply. She leaned forward to get a better view of the scene. A woman came toward her. Mattie jumped back in surprise. The image retreated as she did. Cautiously she raised a hand to the glass. It felt cool and smooth. She peered in closely, then turned to examine the room, then turned back again. The room spread in front of her and behind her. This was like looking in water. She tilted her head left and right, opened her mouth, poked out her tongue, and studied her own reflection.

She looked carefully at her own round eyes, seeing them clearly for the first time. As a child, she'd been told they were like her mother's. In this reflection she now saw that was true. They were big and warm, dark-brown like her mama's. She reached up to touch her face, watching her own hand explore her cheeks, lips, and nose. Mattie searched for Samuel's features in her own. The nose, she decided. She and Samuel shared a nose. And maybe the ears.

"Little girl, this place sure is somethin'," Mattie spoke out loud, shaking her head as she retrieved Miss Elizabeth from the couch.

She turned a full circle, following the wandering flowers along the wallpaper until she was looking at the rocking chair once again. Mattie pulled the chair close to the window, sat with Miss Elizabeth in her arms, and looked out over the slave quarters. The sun was just rising and soon everyone would be emerging to go work the fields. Occasionally she glanced at the door to confirm no one was watching her. She stared and rocked, rocked and stared, as if desire alone could will her spirit across the divide.

Eventually Poppy came out of their cabin with Samuel in his arms. He turned away from the big house and headed toward Rebecca's for Samuel's morning feeding. Leaning close to the window, Mattie searched her son's face for any signs of distress. It was hard to make out clearly from this distance, but she could tell he wasn't crying. Samuel's little head poked above Poppy's shoulder, his placid face bobbing in rhythm with his great-grandfather's gait. Mattie stared hard as her son got smaller and smaller until he faded out of sight altogether, like a leaf floating down a river.

Washed over with yearning and loss, Mattie could not bear to watch her world any longer. She left the room with the window and sought out the strange bed in the little anteroom. She took the baby into the quiet, dark cave and closed the door behind them. After placing the infant in the middle of the old quilt, Mattie lay down and wept. She burrowed her head in her arms and her tears flowed and flowed, like a hot summer storm, down her cheeks into the fluffy feather pillow. She ached for her son with such force that she could hardly breathe.

When her sobs subsided, she raised her head to look at the stranger sleeping next to her. Tiny blue veins showed beneath translucent, pale skin in Miss Elizabeth's eyelids. The fragile and dependent baby lay unaware of the world around her. Mattie touched tiny eyes, nose, lips; her hand trailed across the infant's soft chin, her small, vulnerable neck.

A wave of hatred washed over her.

Mattie laid her hand across the tiny mouth and pressed down until it covered two small nostrils as well. Her heart pounded fiercely behind her rib cage. In a few minutes this could be over.

The infant squirmed, her lips parted, and a loud, sudden cry escaped from the small body.

Mattie jerked her hand away.

"I trapped here, but I ain't so desperate, little one," she whispered fiercely. "I ain't gonna hurt you, little miss," reassuring herself and God, not the oblivious child.

Mattie collapsed onto the bed. Exhausted, she longed to sleep, to escape into her dreams, but as she lay flat on her back, her mind filled with images. She pictured Samuel screaming in Rebecca's arms, his back arched in utter protest. She wondered if Rebecca would remember to swaddle him just right, with his arms bent up, if he cried hard. She replaced the image of screaming Samuel with an image of him utterly satisfied on Rebecca's breast. That was not much more of a comfort.

She rose and went by herself back to the other room with the window. Pressing her ear hard against the glass, she listened for sounds of her son. Nothing. She heard only the loud swoosh of her own pulse.

"Rebecca know how to take care of a baby," she whispered to herself. "She real good and she love Samuel. Rebecca and Poppy gonna take good care of him."

Mattie prayed out loud: "Dear God, it me, Mattie. I know it mornin' and I mostly only talk to you at night, but today I need extra help. Please watch over my Samuel. Make him happy to get food from Rebecca, but not so happy he forget about me. Help me to treat this here little baby good. And make her not need me for so long, so I can get back to my family. Thank you for listenin' to me extra. Amen."

Mattie crossed back to her little room. She lay down in her bed and turned her back to the infant she had left there. She sang to herself as she lay there, hoping that the comforting words of a familiar lullaby would lull her to sleep.

When she awoke a few hours later to the sounds of a hungry baby, she found herself curled around Miss Elizabeth, like a mother cat encircling her kittens. Her heart sank when she remembered where she was and why she was here. But she did her duty, and gave this baby what she needed.

CHAPTER 2

Two days later the housekeeper intruded into the large bedroom just as Mattie settled in the rocking chair to nurse Miss Elizabeth. Mattie rose like a soldier coming to attention.

"Your mistress is recovered enough to see her daughter," Mrs. Gray declared. "Bring the infant to madam's chambers at two o'clock."

"Yes, ma'am," responded Mattie. "Excuse me, ma'am. I don' know what you mean by *two*."

Mrs. Gray sighed and shook her head. She scowled. "That is a time," she declared sharply, rolling her eyes. "Have you not noticed the chime from the clock in the sitting room?"

"Yes, ma'am, I hear a sound every so often."

"Every fifteen minutes there is a short song. Each hour it strikes according to the time. Can you count?"

Mattie nodded, working to hide her confusion, and replied, "Yes, ma'am. Up to ten."

"Well, you shall have to learn more, or at least come to understand the partitions of an hour. You will be given a time to do your tasks and know when to do them by the clock," Mrs. Gray explained.

Mattie did her best to follow Mrs. Gray's complicated instructions. She was used to marking chores and time by the sun. She understood that she needed to count each time the clock struck. The number of strikes would be an hour. An hour was when she would be somewhere or do something.

"So," Mrs. Gray went on, "when the clock strikes two times, it is two o'clock and time for you to return to the room where Miss Elizabeth was born. It is straight down the hall, the third door on your left. Do not sit unless you are invited to. Remember to answer *ma'am* each time you are spoken to."

"Yes, ma'am."

"And do not exhaust her," Mrs. Gray insisted. "She is still recovering from the ordeal of childbirth."

"Yes, ma'am."

Mattie fed the baby and listened carefully for the sounds of the clock. It made a little music but nothing she could count. During a change of diaper it made a short song again, but still no sound she could count. She feared she was missing something but was more afraid to arrive too early. She rocked Miss Elizabeth and waited, hoping it would be clear. Then she heard the short song followed by a distinct single chime. It was followed by another chime. Then it was silent. *One, two*, Mattie thought to herself. Mrs. Gray said to come out when there were two chimes. She carried the newborn to the door, turned the knob, and looked out into the hallway. No one was there. She stepped out, praying she was doing the right thing.

———

Bobbing in a sea of pillows and fabric, Ann eagerly waited to meet her daughter. Open draperies let in the warm sunlight and made the room bright. The bedside table supported a bouquet of colorful flowers. Whorls marked the marble top: white and black swirling in an intricate dance, pushing close, mixing in some places, staying distinct in others.

Smiling down at a small pillow, Ann held it like an infant, rocking it back and forth. In her mind she practiced a greeting: *Hello. I am your mother. You are my daughter, Elizabeth.* She was excited and nervous to meet her daughter. She had never held a newborn before, and felt uncertain and young. At the sound of a knock, she hastily set down the pillow and once again smoothed down her covers.

"You may enter," Ann called out. "Good day, Mattie," she added, her hungry eyes intent on the bundle in Mattie's arms.

"Good afternoon, ma'am," Mattie spoke deferentially from the doorway.

Every time someone called her ma'am, Ann Wainwright felt a fraud. Nine months after her wedding, she was still adjusting to the fact that she was married and living on a Tidewater plantation hours away from her real home. And now she was a mother and did not quite know what was expected of her. Conceiving on her honeymoon had pleased both her husband and her mother-in-law. That the child was a daughter was a disappointment they expected her to remedy soon enough. She wanted to be a good mother, but did not know what that meant. So far she was told to rest and leave the care of her child to the wet nurse.

As Mrs. Jonathan Wainwright, she was the mistress of the house, in theory. But she was hardly involved in the running of the plantation: Mrs. Gray handled day-to-day matters, and her mother-in-law was loath to relinquish her role as hostess of Fair Oaks. Ann had had few opportunities to socialize either as a host or as a guest, since her confinement had begun almost immediately after she arrived. She had yet to make the important social connections that were essential for establishing herself in this place.

Ann beckoned Mattie over with a wave of her hands. She studied her daughter in Mattie's arms.

"She is not so beautiful, is she?" Ann stated matter-of-factly.

"She young yet," replied Mattie.

"I suppose," Ann responded. "I have never seen one so young before. Is everything going as it should?"

"Yes, ma'am. She strong. She a good baby."

"Let me hold her," Ann directed. She reached her arms out wide.

Mattie handed the child to her. Ann held the baby's head in one hand, but did not know what to do to support the rest of her wrapped-up body. The infant started to flop down sideways. Ann jerked to catch her. This was much harder than holding a pillow.

"Perhaps, ma'am, it be easier if'n you hold her close to your body," Mattie suggested.

Ann held the bundle closer. That was better. She relaxed a bit.

"She is quite light. I imagined her heavier. Are they normally so red?"

"I don' know, ma'am. This the first White baby I ever seen," Mattie said.

"You have experience with babies?"

"Yes, ma'am. I been at births. I always take care of the babies around; I watched the young ones while their folks worked the tobacco when I little." Suddenly self-conscious about saying so much, Mattie stopped speaking.

"Mrs. Gray chose well when she selected you." Ann studied Mattie. Her dark hands were rough and scratched. It was obvious she had been a field hand. Mother always said field hands made the richest milk, so she was not disappointed when the rented hand died.

"Thank you, ma'am," Mattie replied.

Ann asked, "You have a son? Am I correct?"

"Yes, ma'am. He three months."

"A son. How nice for you."

Having run out of questions and answers, an uncomfortable silence filled the space between the two women. Ann hated being alone with the hands. She preferred to ignore them, but it was hard in this situation. The two women stared at the baby held in an awkward embrace. After a few minutes Elizabeth started squirming. Ann jiggled her daughter up and down against her chest. The infant turned her head toward her mother, opening her mouth wide, bobbing her face into her mother's breast. Startled, Ann jerked her baby away.

"What is the matter with her?"

"She turning her head for food. She hungry, ma'am," replied Mattie.

Ann felt a tingle in her breast; then some moisture leaked out. She was repulsed by the sensation. She hoped her breasts stopped making liquid soon.

"Well, I cannot be of any help to her. Here, you give her what she needs," Ann directed as she handed her daughter over to Mattie.

The woman took the infant. She stood next to the bed, uncertainty written on her face. The infant turned her head into Mattie's body, and the field hand slipped her pinky into the baby's eager mouth. Ann watched the woman sway from side to side, comforting the infant but making no move to suckle her.

After a long, strange silence, Ann spoke. "You may sit in that chair. I wish to see you do it."

"Yes, ma'am."

Settling into the seat where she'd first held and nourished Elizabeth, Mattie gave the baby her breast. Ann was fascinated and horrified. They were so close to each other. She could not imagine holding a child against her naked breast like that. It would make her so uncomfortable, and yet the two of them looked so calm as they were doing it. Ann observed her baby suckling for a while; then she spoke again.

"Yes, that is unseemly. Leave as soon as you are finished. I have seen enough."

CHAPTER 3

All the residents of Fair Oaks honored the Sunday Sabbath, though the house slaves did not forgo their duty to keep their owners fed and comfortable. After gathering in the sitting room to listen to a reading from the Bible, the house slaves prepared for the Sabbath dinner while the Wainwright family worshipped with the Episcopalian congregation in Charles City. The field slaves were given a day of rest from sunset on Saturday until sunrise on Monday, except during the harvest.

One Sunday afternoon, just past Miss Elizabeth's three-month mark, Mrs. Gray and skinny Emily interrupted the quiet of the nursery.

Mrs. Gray spoke crisply from the doorway. "Miss Elizabeth is old enough to be away from you for a few hours. As you are fortunate enough to live near your family, you may visit with them on Sunday afternoons beginning today. Instruct Emily on how to care for Miss Elizabeth when you are away."

"Yes, ma'am. Thank you, ma'am," Mattie responded, hiding her excitement from the housekeeper.

"You must return by supper, though you may always be called in earlier," Mrs. Gray commanded before she left the room.

"Yes, ma'am."

Mattie's heart raced. She was anxious to touch and caress Samuel. She yearned to hold him, feed him, and be his mother for a time. Each day she had spent hours staring out the nursery window tracking her people. Once or twice a day over the last months she had briefly seen her son coming and going. She watched as his cheeks grew fatter and bits of black fuzz formed on his head. She searched for hints of his personality, studying the way he moved his head or looked around. Of course he never saw her. He might not know her at all. He was nearly twice the age he'd been when she left him.

Though Mattie longed to rush out to the quarters, she attended to Miss Elizabeth's needs first. Settling into the rocker to nurse, Mattie unbuttoned her dress. Miss Elizabeth arched her back, flapped her arms, and squealed in excitement and anticipation when she saw Mattie's movements. As she nestled against Mattie's breast, the baby's deep-blue eyes gazed intently into Mattie's dark-caramel irises. Her pink fingers patted and stroked soft brown skin. She grinned up at Mattie, causing milk to dribble out the sides of her mouth.

"Silly girl," Mattie admonished the baby, tickling and teasing her. "You gotta pick: eatin' or smilin'."

Turning her attention to Emily, Mattie gave directions for the infant's care. "She don' like to be in a wet diaper, so get her a dry one right away. If she fussy, sometimes she satisfied with my finger. She like to be walked round the room, lookin' out the window and lookin' at herself in the mirror."

Clearly irritated, Emily replied, "I cared for babies before. How much trouble can she be?"

"She no trouble," declared Mattie. "She a good baby."

"She a baby. A baby just a baby. They all alike," said Emily.

After Miss Elizabeth had her fill, Mattie brought the child up to her shoulder and slowly rubbed the girl's back. Years of experience had taught Mattie that there was no rushing a baby. It only took longer if you tried to make it go quick. Rocking the baby, acting like patience itself despite her intense yearning to be with Samuel, Mattie sang a soft song.

Go to sleepy, little baby
Go to sleepy, little baby
Your mama's gone away and your daddy's gone to stay
Didn't leave nobody but the baby

A soft belch escaped from Miss Elizabeth's tiny mouth.

Go to sleepy, little baby
Go to sleepy, little baby
Everybody's gone in the cotton and the corn
Didn't leave nobody but the baby

Miss Elizabeth grew heavy, melting against Mattie's body.

You're a sweet little baby
You're a sweet little baby
Honey in the rock and the sugar don't stop
Gonna bring a bottle to the baby

Mattie moved Miss Elizabeth down into her arms and cradled her close, rocking back and forth.

Don't you weep, pretty baby
Don't you weep, pretty baby

She's long gone with the red shoes on
gonna meet another lovin' baby

The little one's eyes glazed over; her eyelids slowly blinked shut and then open, shut and then open, then shut.

Go to sleepy, little baby
Go to sleepy, little baby
You and me and the devil makes three
Don't need no other lovin' baby

Mattie continued the gentle song, rocking slowly, confident of lulling Miss Elizabeth to sleep.

Go to sleepy, little baby
Go to sleepy, little baby
Come and lay your bones on the alabaster stones
And be my ever-lovin' baby

Miss Elizabeth lay with her silky soft head against Mattie's warm arm. Her pink mouth glistened with saliva and breast milk, and her limp arms flung back at her sides. Mattie gently wiped away the pooled milk in the corners of Miss Elizabeth's mouth before deftly transferring her to the bed they shared in Mattie's small anteroom. Miss Elizabeth tipped her head back to protest. Bending over the baby, Mattie rested her hand on the girl's back to settle her back into a deep sleep and waited patiently until she heard the sound of rhythmic breathing. After a last pat, Mattie turned away to go to her family.

An unbroken string of Mattie's ancestors going back to her great-great-grandparents had lived at Fair Oaks since its founding in 1690. The plantation, which sat on the northern bank of the James River, was part of the Virginia Company's westward expansion. As was customary, land grants were given in proportion to the number of people a grantee imported to tame the land. Commander Theodore Pryne had the funds to bring thirty Europeans and Africans as indentured servants, so he received fifteen hundred acres to plant. All indentured servants, both European and African, agreed to work off their debt for seven to fifteen years. After that, they were to be released and given five acres of land each, a bushel of seed, and the freedom to pursue their own fortunes in the New World.

Quickly the landed gentry realized that their plantations would not be profitable if they paid their workforce. Thus Mattie's African ancestors were not turned free or given the means to farm for themselves, but held in perpetual bondage after the Virginia Assembly passed a law in 1705 clarifying once and for all the status of Africans in the colony. It declared "all servants imported and brought into the Country . . . who were not Christians in their native Country . . . shall be accounted and be slaves. All Negro, mulatto, and Indian slaves within this dominion . . . shall be held to be real estate." In addition, social status for slaves transferred from mother to child rather than from father to child, so regardless of your father's status, you would be a slave if your mother was enslaved. Those changes in social codes ensured eighteenth-century planters of Virginia a steady supply of workers.

Family lore held that Mattie's paternal great-great-grandfather would have been free had the assembly waited but two months to pass this law: his indenture was to be complete later in 1705. As it was, none of her ancestors had secured their freedom from the peculiar institution known as slavery. Naturally they all imagined living as one of the free Africans in Charles City County, Virginia, with varying degrees of envy and rage.

Mattie hurried down the muddy footpath to her family's cabin. Though it had been her home for her entire life until three months ago, she was nervous. She had never been away from the quarters before. Would she be accepted back after being "brought in"? No one she knew had ever moved to the big house; there was a wall between the two worlds that was rarely scaled. She hoped she could make a gate in that wall.

Anxious and excited, Mattie arrived at the unfinished plank door and took a deep breath before pushing it open and saying, "Hello." There was no response. Her eyes quickly adjusted to the darkness; no one was there. Her heart dropped and she sighed. She went back outside to look for her son and Poppy. Hoping to find them quickly, she headed toward Rebecca's cabin.

Rebecca was a strong, substantial woman who was always on the move. She and her husband, Lawrence, took pride in their cabin and their three children, all kept as clean and tidy as possible. Always ready to offer an opinion—asked for or not—Rebecca had readily volunteered to feed Samuel as soon as word came that Mattie was being brought in. Deeply grateful Rebecca had milk to spare for her son, Mattie had accepted.

For all purposes Rebecca was Mattie's sister, though they did not come from the same parents. Rebecca was born in a barn two counties away, on the land of a newly freed White indentured servant. He had purchased Rebecca's mother, Millie, as his first step in becoming part of the owning class. But Millie and Rebecca did not live in the barn for long. The mistress of the farm soon realized that her husband had fathered Rebecca and insisted that the "whore and her bastard" be sold.

The large plantation they were sold to was Rebecca's home until she was eight. Born with her left leg wrapped around her neck, Rebecca was late to walk and did so with an obvious limp. This decreased her owner's ability to sell her individually, so she became part of a lot of ten slaves sold to fund a grand tour of Europe. Millie was not part of the sale. Fortunately Rebecca was assigned to Mattie's cabin, where she found a warm welcome in Mattie's family and became the big sister that four-year-old Mattie longed for.

Mattie knocked at the rough plank door. Rebecca swung it open and screamed at the sight of Mattie. Surprise and delight shone in her eyes. Pulling Mattie into her large arms, Rebecca held on tight. Sudden tears streamed from Mattie's eyes as she sank into her sister's warm embrace.

"There, there, girl. Let it all out. You home now. You okay," Rebecca murmured as Mattie sobbed into her chest.

Slowly her tears subsided until Mattie caught her breath and pulled away. She managed to squeak out, "Samuel here?" through her tight throat.

Rebecca pointed across the room. Samuel sat on Poppy's lap. Shaking, Mattie rushed across the room to scoop him up. She held her son tight against her heart, taking in his smell as she swayed and murmured endearments into his ear. Her salty tears dropped onto his half-bald head. Samuel arched his neck back to look up at the woman holding him.

Mattie took Samuel in. He had changed so much. His cheeks were filling in and his hair was a row of black puff down the middle of his head. She watched him out the window every day, so it wasn't a complete surprise, but seeing him up close and feeling him in her arms was different from watching him from across the way. She had already missed half of his life.

"I been tellin' him all about you so he gonna know you," Rebecca told Mattie. "We ain't gonna let him forget you or think you forgot him."

Mattie started to cry again. Poppy walked to her, kissed her cheek, and said, "Glad to see you, Mattie. Welcome home."

Samuel leaned away from Mattie to get to Poppy.

Mattie said to her son, "Uh-uh. You gotta stay with me while I'm here." She stepped away from Poppy, turned Samuel to face the other way and bounced her son. Soon enough he was smiling at her. It was a start.

Word flew that Mattie was visiting, and folks stopped by to pay their regards, hear about life in the big house, and to see what transformation might have been wrought in one of their own. They gathered outside in the sticky July air on the four wooden benches that formed a square behind Rebecca's cabin.

Sarah, Rebecca's daughter, showed off a newfound skill. A round-faced, cheerful baby with an easy smile, she took great delight in crawling back and forth to the people who waited for her with open arms and proud smiles. Samuel, on the other hand, sat on Mattie's lap, staring intently at the faces surrounding him. Whenever he asked to go to Poppy or Rebecca, Mattie stood up to distract him.

Mattie was sorry that Emmanuel, her man, was not there too. This was his usual visiting time of month, but he had not come from Berkeley Plantation. No one knew why. Now she would worry about him until next month. He missed his visiting time a lot, but she never liked it. He might only be working extra, but she feared he was sick or worse.

Poppy asked about the big house. Few of the field hands had ever been inside it—though they were all familiar with, and somewhat afraid of, the exterior of the large white building visible through the hedges. The most dreaded ritual of the year occurred on the grounds in front of the imposing, columned façade of that building. On New Year's Day, after the Big Times, all the workers from the house and the quarters gathered while Massa and the overseer called out the names of the people who had been sold or rented out for the year.

"It all bright-white inside like the outside," Mattie told Poppy, "with big stairs in the front of the house for the White folks and small stairs in the back for us to use. I don' see many people, just Emily, that skinny, high-yellow girl; Mrs. Ann, she Miss Elizabeth's mama; Mrs. Gray, she always tell me what I supposed to do; and, of course, Miss Elizabeth. She a pretty good baby. Don' get me wrong, she not so dear as my Samuel here," she said as she bounced him up and down on her knees, "but she a good eater and she don' cry much. I gonna start doing laundry soon now that Miss Elizabeth old enough to be tied to my back. Then I gonna get to know more folks."

Mattie pointed. "See that window there? The one on the corner up highest from the ground? I think that Miss Elizabeth's room. I watch out of it when I get the chance."

"You see us?" Poppy asked.

"Mm-hm. I see you carrying Samuel to Rebecca and coming in from the fields and such."

Poppy nodded his head. "Good to know where you at. I gonna stop and wave from now on. Just in case you there."

"I gonna be waving back. Even if you don' see me. Every mornin' and every evenin' I stand there watchin' you all. Samuel look like he pretty happy," Mattie ventured.

Rebecca jumped in. "He confused at first, but now he used to it. I sing to him. That helps."

"He sleepin' all right?" Mattie wondered.

"He a real good sleeper," Poppy said. "Hardly ever get me up."

"Cook say Mrs. Ann gonna try at havin' another one. That true?" Rebecca asked.

"That what I hear. They got her eatin' meat at all her meals. Massa be wantin' a son, just like most menfolk."

"Guess they gonna be keepin' you busy for a while," Rebecca said.

Mattie sighed. "I wanna finish up with Miss Elizabeth and be done with the big house, but I gonna be doin' whatever Mrs. Gray tells me. I s'pose they gonna have me feed this next one. I hopin' for a boy too. Maybe they send me back out if they done with the babies."

"Bet you likin' all the food and fancy clothes," someone declared.

With heat in her voice she replied, "The food good, the clothes nice, but I rather be out here with Samuel."

At the sound of his name, Samuel fussed. He reached for Rebecca. Mattie got up to distract him. She bounced him up and down, but he kept turning for Rebecca. Mattie's heart skipped a beat.

"You think he hungry?" she asked her sister.

Mattie wanted to feed him while she could, while she was here, but she was afraid he might refuse her. Samuel twisted hard away from her to get to Rebecca. He started crying.

Rebecca nodded. "He hungry. Go ahead. You offer it to him. That all you can do," Rebecca said gently. "Take him to your cabin where he ain't gonna see me or smell me."

Mattie carried Samuel away. He continued to fuss. She lowered herself onto a hard pallet and slowly undid the top buttons of her dress and pulled the fabric aside. Then Mattie laid Samuel across her lap, tucked his right arm behind her waist and pulled him toward her left breast. He arched his back, jerked his head away, and scrunched up his face in preparation to let out a wail.

"You okay," Mattie said gently. "I got the good stuff too. You used to love it right here."

Samuel stopped protesting when Mattie spoke. She rubbed the back of his head and leaned over to kiss his forehead. "We got time."

She gazed into his eyes, rocked back and forth, and sang to him:

Go to sleepy, little baby
Go to sleepy, little baby
Your mama's gone away and your daddy's gone to stay
Didn't leave nobody but the baby

Eventually Samuel relaxed. Mattie cautiously, slowly brought his head toward her breast. He parted his lips a little. She squirted a bit of milk into his mouth. He licked his lips, smiled up at her, and opened his mouth. She gently placed her nipple into his waiting mouth. His body tensed, but he didn't pull back. She squeezed her breast to bring out more milk. Samuel licked her nipple. She did it again and he licked some more. They sat frozen, her breast against his mouth, with him neither pulling away nor latching on. Mattie held her breath and silently said a prayer: *God, please give me this.*

She inhaled slowly and calmly breathed out. Tenderly she rubbed the bits of tight curls on his head. He pulled away, but she kept her hand behind his head. He pushed back against her flesh as he attempted to pull away. She rubbed his hair again. He quickly turned his head slightly from left to right, opened his mouth wide, and then pulled her nipple deep into his mouth, sucking with vigor. Her milk rushed out into him.

"That right, baby boy. That right. You know. You know what to do."

Mattie breathed a sigh of relief. They hadn't taken her son away from her completely. Sitting on the edge of the pallet, she was determined to enjoy this moment, this precious time with her son.

CHAPTER 4

Miss Elizabeth sat comfortably against Mattie's left hip as they came down the front stairs. When Mattie turned to enter the formal sitting room, their bodies tensed in unison. Mattie gently patted Miss Elizabeth's leg as she quietly whispered, "You all right," into the eleven-month-old baby's small pink ear. "I ain't gonna leave you today."

Grandmother Wainwright and Mrs. Ann sat in waiting for this Saturday afternoon ritual. Mrs. Ann perched uncomfortably at one end of the blue upholstered couch in the center of the large, high-ceilinged room, a brown muslin dress pulled taut across her large, round abdomen. Nodding absently at the words coming out of Grandmother Wainwright's mouth, Mrs. Ann gazed away from her mother-in-law. Grandmother Wainwright fully occupied one end of the blue couch. Volumes of black fabric from her skirt covered the seat cushion. Her pale eyes stayed fixed on Mrs. Ann's face as Mattie and Miss Elizabeth hovered in the entryway of the room.

"Of course you shall not suckle this one either," she said.

Mrs. Ann said, "You know many women are feeding their own children now. The Ford family does not use a wet nurse."

"I do not care if it is the fashion. It is unseemly for a woman of your stature to feed a child. Your heartbreak would only be greater should they die. I know from experience, it is best not to love your children too deeply, as it only causes pain."

Mattie figured Grandmother Wainwright thought that because she had lost two children. Miss Rose fell from a fever when she was young long before Mattie was born. Folks said that Grandmother Wainwright changed after that. She got selfish and angry, and never came back. Mourning did that to some folks. When Mr. Alistair died just three years ago, she got even worse. He was the massa after the old man died, but not for so long. He broke his neck falling from a horse. Mattie could feel the anger and the sorrow from the big house all the way out in the quarters. Mr. Wainwright moved back from Richmond to be the new massa. It didn't make much difference to the folks in the quarters who was the massa. But it mattered to Grandmother Wainwright.

"Elizabeth is to be weaned to goat's milk," Grandmother Wainwright said. "We do not want her to become attached. It serves no one. As soon as my grandson is born, she can start with him."

Mrs. Ann nodded. Mattie's heart stopped. Wean this baby girl? Now that she cared for her and was adjusted to her new life, she was going to be forced to tear herself away again.

Grandmother Wainwright looked over at Mattie and said, "Bring the child over to visit her mother."

As they crossed the room, Mattie felt Miss Elizabeth slip her hand under the fabric of her dress. Pudgy pink fingers traveled along Mattie's collarbone until they grasped the shells of the necklace that nestled there. The toddler rested her head in the crook of Mattie's neck, hiding her face from the two women on the couch.

Rubbing the child's back with her free arm, Mattie resisted the impulse to kiss the top of Miss Elizabeth's head or whisper words of comfort into the little girl's ear. When they reached the couch, the child tightened her grip on the shell necklace as Mattie started to pull her away from her body. Tears filled Miss Elizabeth's deep-blue eyes, and her bottom lip quivered as she clung tightly to Mattie.

Mattie pulled at Miss Elizabeth, bent over by Mrs. Ann to pass the baby to her mother. But Mrs. Ann did not reach for the girl. She shook her head. Mattie was relieved, but did not show it.

"Keep her on your lap for today." Resignation tinged Mrs. Ann's voice. "I am too big to hold her comfortably."

"You spoil that child." Grandmother Wainwright made no attempt to hide the contempt in her voice. "She needs to know she is not in control."

"She will learn soon enough," Mrs. Ann said. "I am too tired for tears today."

Mattie, careful not to make eye contact with either of the women, sat on the chair next to the divan, getting as close to Mrs. Ann as possible. Miss Elizabeth kept her face hidden in the crook of Mattie's neck, though she tentatively peeked out at her mother. Mattie encouraged her to turn around. When Mrs. Ann tickled her leg, Miss Elizabeth shyly smiled at her mother. Slowly Mattie shifted Miss Elizabeth until the baby faced her mistress.

"Patty-cake, patty-cake," Mrs. Ann began. She chanted the familiar rhyme and clapped her daughter's warm hands together. She moved both of their hands through the gestures, and they both smiled when they got to the end. Miss Elizabeth turned around to make sure Mattie approved of the game as well. Mattie nodded and smiled reassuringly at the child. It pained Mattie that Miss Elizabeth was not very fond of her own mother. But they hardly had any time together. Mattie did her best to encourage Miss

Elizabeth to be comfortable with Mrs. Ann, and hoped that in time Miss Elizabeth would come to care for her mother.

Grandmother Wainwright interrupted the game. "As soon as my grandson is born, you will suckle him. We have purchased a new girl to be with Elizabeth."

"Yes, ma'am," Mattie replied. "I can feed 'em both if you like. It no problem for me."

"No," Grandmother Wainwright declared. "In our household each child has their own nurse."

"It will not be for a number of weeks yet," inserted Mrs. Ann. "And it may not be a son."

"Yes, ma'am."

"Of course it shall be a son," Grandmother Wainwright declared without hesitation.

Mattie looked composed through the rest of the visit, but she was deeply shaken. She had anticipated suckling the new baby, but she did not think they would force her away from Miss Elizabeth. As much as she had desired to keep her special feeling only for Samuel, this caring little White girl had captured her heart.

And she was going to lose her too.

The next weeks felt like the days leading up to Miss Elizabeth's birth, when Mattie waited to leave Samuel. Each morning Mattie wondered if this would be her last day with the baby. And then each night she thanked God for the gift of that day and asked for one more.

Though it would be an easier transition for Miss Elizabeth—and for herself—if they nursed less in preparation for the change, Mattie did not deny the one-year-old child her breast. Whenever they settled in for a feeding, Mattie had a heavy heart, knowing this might be the last time she held Miss Elizabeth so close.

Late on a Sunday evening, Mattie stared out the window of the nursery, hoping to catch sight of Samuel. She had been standing there since she returned from her visit to the quarters. For many hours on that lovely May afternoon Samuel had squealed in delight as Mattie ran after him. His tight-fisted hands pumped back and forth as she chased him; then he would suddenly freeze, allowing himself to be caught in his mother's arms and twirled around. After a few spins he used his limited vocabulary to ask for "Mo, mo," and she happily began the game all over again.

Miss Elizabeth sat near Mattie's feet. She pulled herself up on Mattie's long skirt, proud of herself for her new accomplishment. Mattie tossed a ball across the room. The baby crawled after it and then brought it back in her mouth. Mattie laughed at her. Miss Elizabeth dropped the ball at Mattie's feet. Mattie was about to strike the ball with her foot when the door to the nursery opened. Miss Elizabeth reached her arms up, and Mattie scooped the child onto her hip.

"Good evening, ma'am," Mattie said.

"Labor has begun," declared Mrs. Gray. "No need for you to come to the birthing room. When the child is born Emily will bring him to you and take Miss Elizabeth to her new room."

"Yes, ma'am. Thank you, ma'am."

With that, Miss Elizabeth and Mattie were alone for the last time. Mattie collapsed onto the rocking chair with the girl on her lap. Her voice shook as she explained to the child, "You gotta be with that Charlotte now. I gonna be with your baby brother or sister. Charlotte was brung over to take care a you. She seem fine enough." Her voice caught. "You gonna be all right."

Mattie pulled Miss Elizabeth close for a cuddle, but the active girl wanted none of it. Miss Elizabeth pushed her body away and slid her legs down to the ground. The child crawled to the ball by the window, transitioned to a sitting position, and threw the ball toward Mattie. It rolled past her. With a sad smile Mattie lowered herself to the ground to retrieve the ball from behind the rocker. She turned around to see Miss Elizabeth gazing at her expectantly, eyebrows arched upward and head cocked sideways in a hopeful question.

"Ba?"

Mattie blinked away her tears and said, "All right. We gonna do it your way." And she threw the ball back to the baby. Miss Elizabeth crawled after it and brought it back to her nurse.

The night was long and tense. Mattie listened for sounds from the hall, but did not get any more clues or information before going to bed. She and Miss Elizabeth went to sleep in her small anteroom curled next to each other, as they had done every night since the baby's birth.

Hours later, Mattie was woken by a sound. Half-asleep, she rolled over to pull Miss Elizabeth close, but something was wrong. Mattie sat up. Miss Elizabeth was gone. A newborn baby was lying in her place.

Outrage poured through Mattie. She didn't get even one last kiss. Hot, unshed tears stung her eyes. She refused to touch or even look at this new baby, knowing there was no point in caring. The baby lay there screaming, wanting to suckle, but Mattie ignored it until she could no longer stand it.

Miss Elizabeth woke up in a strange room in a strange bed. Her heart raced in her chest as she looked around in panic. Where was her Mattie? She cried out, "Ma-ie, Ma-ie," but Mattie did not come. Her cries got louder and more desperate, but still Mattie did not come. A not-Mattie came in.

The not-Mattie picked her up and walked with her. The not-Mattie offered her food. The not-Mattie shook her. Still Miss Elizabeth cried for her Mattie. She screamed until she slept.

When she awoke Mattie was still gone. In a small, anxious voice Miss Elizabeth pleaded, "Ma-ie?" The woman with her said something Miss Elizabeth did not understand. Miss Elizabeth waited. She comforted herself as best she could with her own thumb, rocked herself back and forth, and stared at the white door watching for her Mattie.

Sometimes she ate, sometimes she slept, but mostly she waited for her Mattie to come back.

And then she got hot. The heat came and did not go away. Miss Elizabeth got too hot to eat, too hot to move, too hot to drink. Voices came in and out of the room. People touched her body. Lots of not-Matties wanted her to drink. But Miss Elizabeth was tired and did not want to do anything but sleep. She dreamed. She dreamed of her red ball and a toe. She dreamed of brown eyes and a rocking chair. She dreamed of sweet milk and shells to hold on to.

Mattie heard Miss Elizabeth's cries echo down the hall. She paced the room nervously with the new baby in her arms as Miss Elizabeth cried out her name: "Ma-ie, Ma-ie." It took all of her self-control to stay in the nursery as the panic rose in Miss Elizabeth's voice. More and more desperately, the girl yelled for her.

For hours on end Mattie nursed and rocked, paced and wept as she listened to Miss Elizabeth's desperate sobs. She waited, hoping and expecting to be ordered to go to Miss Elizabeth. Two days after Master Jack's birth, the cries became intermittent and the girl's voice grew hoarse. Two days after that, her cries stopped. The silence was worse than the wailing. Now Mattie knew nothing of Miss Elizabeth.

She asked Emily when she brought lunch, "Lisbeth all right?"

"Don' let none of them hear you callin' her that. Miss Elizabeth not eatin', but she finally stopped cryin'. I never heard such carryin' on for so long. You'd think that Charlotte was stickin' pins in her from the way she yelled."

"What she doin' now?"

"When I brung them some lunch, she didn' head out the door like before. She just layin' in bed. Guess she gettin' used to it."

"She sleepin' all right?"

"It ain't my place to keep track of that little girl and tell you. And she ain't yours no more neither."

Mattie knew not to ask Mrs. Ann, Mr. Wainwright, or Grandmother Wainwright during their visits with baby Jack. However, she did dare to speak to the housekeeper about the situation. Mrs. Gray rejected Mattie's timid offer to care for both Master Jack and Miss Elizabeth with a curt reply: "That girl is learning that she cannot always have things her way. There is no need to give in to her now."

Dr. Jameson returned to Fair Oaks for a second time that week. In addition to examining the newborn baby and the birthing mother, he looked in on Elizabeth. Ann and Mrs. Gray hovered nearby as he examined the listless child. Racked by a high fever for three consecutive days, the toddler lay motionless in bed. He listened carefully to her shallow breathing, noted that her eyes were sunk into her head, and pulled at the skin on the back of her hand. The skin stayed pinched up in a fold for a few seconds before lying flat again. "Dehydration has set in," Dr. Jameson informed Ann and Mrs. Gray. "She must take in liquids or she will not survive this fever. It is the only treatment."

He paused at the door. "This is extremely serious. You must do whatever you can to hydrate this child or she will die. I am sorry to be so forthright. But the situation is dire. I can show myself out."

Stunned, Ann stared blankly where the doctor had been standing. Then she spoke. "Charlotte, as quickly as you can, get a concoction of salt, sugar, and water from Cook. Do not hesitate to explain the urgency of this situation. She must stop whatever she is doing to get you what I need."

Ann waited silently by the bed for Charlotte's return. Mrs. Gray hovered behind. Charlotte delivered the liquid and retreated to a chair in the corner. With a shaking hand, Ann brought the spoon to her daughter's parched lips.

"Open her mouth," she commanded Mrs. Gray.

"Perhaps sitting her up would be more effective?" suggested the housekeeper.

"Oh, yes, of course," replied Ann, confused. Riddled with childbirth hormones, tired from labor, and anxious about her daughter, it was hard for her to think. Her arm retreated back to the bowl, spilling liquid along the way.

Mrs. Gray grabbed the child under her armpits, pulled her into an upright position, and rested Elizabeth against the bed pillows. She stepped back. The girl slowly slid sideways in an arc until her head met the bed. Ann stared at Elizabeth.

"Perhaps my lap," she said. "Place her on my lap."

Mrs. Gray hauled the child up and roughly set her on Ann's thin legs. Ann struggled to balance Elizabeth on her lap. She juggled the floppy body of the dozing child like a sack of potatoes. She resumed her attempt to follow the doctor's order. With one arm she cradled her daughter behind the neck while the other arm traveled to and from the vessel of liquid. Drops of fluid spilled off the shaking spoon onto the girl's gown, neck, and chin. By the time it arrived at Elizabeth's lips, it was nearly empty. Ann, determined to save her daughter, kept the spoon moving back and forth, stopping occasionally to wipe away the liquid dribbling down her child's skin.

"Is she swallowing? I cannot tell!"

"Hmmph," Grandmother Wainwright broke in from the doorway, where she watched Ann's feeble attempts to hydrate Elizabeth. "I cannot see what good you are possibly doing. Either the fever will break or it will not," declared the elderly woman. "It is in God's hands. You must pray for your daughter."

Ann's hand froze at her mother-in-law's words. Like a scared bird uncertain which direction to fly, she clenched the spoon tightly. Closing her eyes and retreating into herself, she took a deep breath before silently resuming her task. Grandmother Wainwright muttered something about a "fool's attempt" as she left the scene.

Though the cup was only half-empty, Elizabeth started snoring, and Ann could no longer pretend she was feeding her daughter. She set aside the liquid concoction and returned Elizabeth to her bed. Little of the liquid had made it into Elizabeth's body. This was not working. With nothing else to do, but grateful to have something to occupy her troubled mind, Ann silently recited the Lord's Prayer over and over until she was so exhausted that she rested her head against the bed and joined her daughter in slumber.

Hours later, in the dark, Ann awoke to the sound of shallow, labored breathing. She uncovered the small, hot body, and then covered it again. Helpless and uncertain, she stared at her daughter's chest rising and falling in a jerky rhythm. Fingers tapping against her lips, standing, then sitting again, Ann considered sending for more sugar water, then rejected the idea. She thought of sending for cool rags to wipe her daughter down, but rejected that idea also when another possibility struck her.

She stood up, looking thoroughly around the room to confirm she was alone. She crossed to the door and turned the key to the right until she felt a satisfying click as the lock engaged with the doorframe. Returning to her daughter, she lifted the child, limp as a rag doll, onto her lap. Heart pounding, she unbuttoned her bodice. Elizabeth flopped off her lap and bumped her head on the seat of the chair. Ann returned the small body to the bed, finished the task of unbuttoning her bodice, and peeled her chemise over her head like the skin off a grape.

Her breasts free to the air, she looked around again before pulling her daughter across her lap. She leaned over Elizabeth and brought her breast over the baby's face. A droplet of white liquid seeped from the dangling nipple and hung from the tip until the force of gravity caused it to drop onto Elizabeth's eyelid. Both lids slowly rose to reveal glassy blue eyes. Elizabeth gazed at the pink nipple suspended over her head, then at her mother's hopeful face peering down at her. Ann hoped her daughter knew what to do with the proffered breast, and held her breath in anticipation. She leaned down closer, and another drop of milk landed on Elizabeth's cheek and rolled to her lips. The girl's tongue crept out and tasted the liquid. Hope rushed through Ann's body. She waited nervously. Elizabeth looked into her mother's eyes again and then at the offered nipple. Then the baby closed her eyes and turned her head away.

Ann sat back hard in the chair with a sigh. Shame and humiliation radiated through every pore. She felt foolish for even trying. She looked down at her fevered daughter and considered her options. She wiped away the sweat from Elizabeth's damp forehead. With another sigh, Ann returned her daughter to bed. Blinking away tears, utterly defeated, she slowly pulled her chemise over her body and buttoned up her gown. She was not going to let her daughter die. Ignoring Mrs. Gray and Charlotte, who had been hovering outside the locked door, she left the room to fetch Mattie.

When she found her, Ann spoke urgently. "Elizabeth has burned with a high fever for three days. She has not taken a drink since then." Desperation in her voice, she pleaded, "Come now. See if she will drink from you. She must drink something or . . ." She left the rest unspoken.

Mattie followed Ann down the long hallway. Mrs. Gray stood in the doorway like a sentry.

"I do not believe this is wise," stated Mrs. Gray. "She will not become used to the new arrangement if we bring Mattie every time she fusses."

"I am not concerned with my daughter becoming accustomed," Ann declared. "The doctor made it quite clear she must drink something. Let Mattie through. Now!"

Mrs. Gray stood aside. A bitter, metallic smell hung in the room. Elizabeth's small form lay under a light sheet. Mattie rushed to Elizabeth's side. She reached her hand to the girl's hot forehead and brushed damp hair away from her face.

Ann could barely hear Mattie whisper into Elizabeth's ear, "Mattie here now. I here now, beautiful girl. You gonna be all right."

Then Mattie carefully lay down next to Ann's daughter and gently pulled the baby into the crook of her arm, rubbing her back with one hand while caressing her face with the other.

Mattie murmured repeatedly, "I here now. You gonna be all right."

The child slowly opened her eyes and reached a hand up to Mattie's face. A weak smile drew up the corners of her mouth, and her eyes closed again. She buried her face into Mattie's chest. A croaky "Ma-ie" came out of Elizabeth's dry lips.

Mattie smiled at the sick child and gave her a tender kiss. "That right. It me. Mattie here. Let see about gettin' you somethin' to drink, baby girl."

Filled with a mixture of relief and sorrow, Ann interrupted their private reunion. "I will leave you two alone then."

She turned to Mrs. Gray and spoke definitively. "Elizabeth will move back in with Mattie. See to it that her belongings are returned and a wet nurse is secured for Jack immediately."

"Yes, ma'am. As you wish," replied Mrs. Gray, making it clear she questioned Ann's judgment.

CHAPTER 5

MAY 1839

Mattie nestled behind her husband as they lay in bed. She loved the feel of Emmanuel against her body. Her hand rubbed his strong chest, her knees spooned into the valley of his legs, and her cheek rested against his back. She planted kisses on his spine and took in his musky smell. Left alone in Samuel and Poppy's cabin, they basked in two glorious days together, a rare treat given by Emmanuel's overseer and agreed to by Mrs. Gray. Mattie expected that Massa hoped she would produce another child, but she would not give him one. This was not her fertile time, and if it were, she would have taken precautions. Though she longed for more babies, she was not going to have more children only to be separated from them.

Mattie met nineteen-year-old Emmanuel soon after her sixteenth birthday. She had been at a dance held in a musty old barn during the one week of the year the field hands did not have to work, the "Big Times" between Christmas and New Year's. She was sitting on a hay bale, taking in the sights and sounds around her and giggling with Rebecca. Mattie clapped along to the pounding drum while the folks around her sang:

Juba this and Juba that,
Juba killed a yeller cat,
Juba this and Juba that,
Hold your partner where you at.

She leaped in surprise when a handsome stranger from an unknown plantation walked up to her. He had deep-brown eyes, smooth coffee-colored skin, and strong muscles from years of physical labor.

"Can I sit?" he asked.

Mattie nodded and introduced herself.

"You work tobacco?" he asked her.

"Uh-huh. You too?" she asked back.

"Uh-uh," he said proudly, "I work the shop . . . metal and wood. Whatever they tell me to do. Sometimes I help with the horses."

Mattie was impressed. "I 'magine that hard?"

"Better than tobacco. Though I got burns from the fire." He showed her his marked-up arms.

"Sorry I don' have my pokeweed salve. It'd take care of those sores."

"Well, I guess I just gonna have to come get some from you soon. How you learn to make salve?" he asked.

"Grandma Washington teaching me everythin' she know about plants and herbs. She the nurse and midwife for us. I gonna take her place when she gone."

"I 'magine that hard?"

"Better than tobacco," she replied. Mattie smiled at him and he grinned right back.

They danced and laughed and talked all night, hardly paying attention to anyone else. It was hard to say good-bye at the end of the party. They went outside and Mattie got her first kiss. Emmanuel promised this would not be the last time they saw each other. Mattie sure hoped he was right.

A few weeks later he made the trek to Fair Oaks to get that pokeweed salve. He came back the next month and the next month, and the month after that.

One month Emmanuel told Mattie his fondest dream: "Someday I gonna get free. You gotta know that about me if'n we gonna be together."

Mattie had never thought to leave her home and family to head out into the wilderness, but she did not tell him that. She heard most men talk about freedom, but not many took their chances. So she just listened to his tales of freedom land.

"My pa ran," he told her.

"He got free?" she asked.

Emmanuel shook his head. "Nah. He ran twice. First time he just a boy, not much more than twelve. He working out in the fields when suddenly he seen there weren't nobody around him. He just dropped his sack of tobacco and tore off. Made it nearly to the next county when they caught him. His own overseer got him and brung him back. They cut off the top of his ear and he went back to work the next day."

"That musta hurt," Mattie said.

"He always say it was worth that bit o' his ear for that taste of freedom," Emmanuel told her. "The next time he run he was older, but not old enough. He planned it, but God was against him that time. A sudden storm made the river flood. He made it all the way to the banks of the Pamunkey—two counties away—but then couldn' go no farther. He knew he'd die if he went in that river so's he sat down on the bank and waited. The dogs found him first. He had the scars on his arm to prove it.

"They cut off his toes so's he could work good but not run. So he taught me what to do to get to freedom: Wait till you be a full man and run in May or June. It ain't so cold, but the big thunderstorms ain't come yet."

Mattie said, "You sure thought 'bout this."

"Yep," he said. "I gonna be free someday."

A few months later Mattie and Emmanuel jumped the broom, committing themselves to each other in the eyes of their families and God. For more than four years, once a month Emmanuel made the three-mile walk over to Fair Oaks for a visit. Mostly he came on a Saturday for the night, but a few times a year he got a Friday off too.

Emmanuel rolled over to face Mattie. "Been thinking this might be the spring to head out."

Mattie sighed. "Thought we already agreed. Samuel too young."

"I been thinkin' I can go on ahead. Then you two join me next year or the year after when Samuel big enough."

"You crazy!" Mattie cried out. "There ain't no way I can travel through the forest all alone with a little one his age. He too loud and active to run now. You leave us and you leavin' us for good. This my home. It ain't perfect, but we alive and we get to be together some of the time. You run off to God knows where and maybe we never gonna see you alive again."

"But Ohio ain't that far," Emmanuel insisted. "I gonna make it. I know it."

"Ohio gonna be there in a few years, when Samuel big enough to make the trip. You just hold on a little longer," Mattie said. "It ain't so bad in the meantime."

Every winter he made plans for the next spring. Each year she suggested it was too soon. Mattie hoped that Emmanuel's talk was just that. But he was sounding more and more like he was going to do it. She desperately hoped her love and their son would make Emmanuel stay. But this time of year, Mattie said a final good-bye in her heart whenever they parted. She expected that one day he would not return.

"Forget about Ohio," Mattie cajoled, pressing her body into his. "You in Virginia right now, with me, all alone, in this here bed. What you gonna do about that?"

She moved in closer, bringing her mouth so close that she could feel his breath. Emmanuel smiled, gazing through the dim light into her eyes, and ran his large hands across her back. He kissed her tenderly on her full lips. She parted her mouth, darting the tip of her tongue out to explore his mouth.

Pulling back, he asked, "Do you suppose that little girl gonna interrupt us again?"

"Her name Lisbeth," replied Mattie, "and no, I don' suppose she will. She fine when I left. I don' imagine I gonna be called in 'cause she be gettin' sick."

"Good. I don' want to get all hot and bothered jus' to have you disappear on me," he teased.

"Let's see about gettin' you all hot and bothered."

Pushing him onto his back, she climbed over him, straddling his belly. She kissed him deeply, bringing his tongue into her mouth. She pressed against him until he forgot all of his plans to leave Virginia.

After making love, Emmanuel kissed Mattie, rolled over, and fell asleep. Mattie wrapped her arms around him and nestled in close, her body humming with joy. A good man was hard to come by and she knew she was lucky to have this one.

She'd be fully satisfied if she knew she could keep him.

In the sitting room, after Sunday supper, Ann sat with Elizabeth, a book of nursery rhymes open before them. Jonathan read by the fire. Muttering to himself at regular intervals, he clearly disagreed with the author of this particular text. Grandmother Wainwright sat on a chair, attempting to look busy with crewelwork.

"Mat-tie come?" demanded the anxious two-year-old.

"Elizabeth, you must not speak to me in that tone," admonished Ann.

"Lisbeth want Mat-tie," declared Elizabeth plaintively.

"Elizabeth wants Mattie," Ann corrected. "Well, you must wait. You have no choice. She will be here when she will be here. Now listen to this poem, and be patient."

Elizabeth stared hard at the door, as if willing the knob to turn. Ann read the next rhyme:

Hey diddle diddle,
The cat and the fiddle,
The cow jumped over the—

Jonathan interrupted. "Listen to this outrage: 'As men, as Christians, as citizens, we have duties to the slave, as well as to every other member of the community. On this point we have no liberty. The eternal law binds us to take the side of the injured; and this law is peculiarly obligatory when we forbid him to lift an arm in his own defense.' I cannot believe he has the audacity to speak for Christians when he has clearly announced he is a Unitarian."

"Whatever are you reading?" inquired Grandmother Wainwright.

"Reverend William Ellery Channing's pamphlet *Slavery*."

"I cannot understand why you bother to read such nonsense. It only serves to confuse," declared Grandmother Wainwright.

"Staying informed is my duty as the head of this household, Mother. I need not remind you of that."

"Some arguments are not worth bothering with."

"Abolitionists are using these very words as a weapon against our way of life. They are out to take away all that we have created."

"Ridiculous!" declared Grandmother Wainwright. "I have heard that my entire life. This country was founded with the understanding that we shall be allowed to hold slaves. It was a condition of the formation. That shall not change regardless of the rhetoric coming from the North."

Ann's husband ignored his mother. "This is what Channing says about the government: 'It must regard every man, over whom it extends its authority, as a vital part of itself, as entitled to its care and to its provisions for liberty and happiness.' He is implying that Jefferson intended the Constitution to bestow civil rights to Africans. Utterly ridiculous. Our forebears were quite clear on the matter: slaves are only three-fifths of a man. They are not entitled to the same rights as Christians."

Ann was weary of these conversations. Every few months her husband would take it upon himself to read and then share the arguments coming from the North. She agreed with his frustration, but did not believe it was important for her to pay attention to such matters. She attempted to entertain her daughter while keeping her quiet.

Jonathan continued, "Only someone who has never actually lived with a Negro could romanticize their capacities so. Without slavery they would all be starving heathens. We have no pauperism in the South, which is more than Channing can say about his beloved Massachusetts. He does not understand all that we provide for the Negroes: basic security for life."

A knock at the door interrupted his tirade.

"You may enter," Grandmother Wainwright called out.

"Mat-tie!" screamed Elizabeth as she ran over to her nurse, arms out wide, a huge grin splitting her face. "Mat-tie back!"

The nurse squatted down in the doorway, arms outstretched, ready to embrace her charge. Ann watched her daughter hurtle toward the other woman. She could hardly fathom the joy they found in each other, but it was obvious in Elizabeth's eyes. Even though it was a mystery, Ann found it amusing to witness, whereas her mother-in-law seemed to find it unpleasant.

"Elizabeth," reprimanded Grandmother Wainwright, "return here at once!"

Elizabeth halted her rush toward the door. With stooped shoulders and her head down, she swung around slowly and returned to sit on the couch.

"Now ask your mother if you may be excused," commanded her grandmother.

Eyes cast down, her voice quiet, Elizabeth inquired, "I be 'scused?"

Ann smiled. Patting Elizabeth's chubby leg and kissing the top of her head, she reassured her, "Yes, dear, you may go. Good night."

Elizabeth scrambled down from the couch and hurried across the room to her nurse. Mattie scooped her up and the little girl wrapped her arms tight around her nurse's neck, squeezing hard with her small arms. Then she patted Mattie's cheeks with her pudgy hands, pushed her nose into the woman's face, and exclaimed, "Missed you! Lisbeth missed Mattie."

"I missed you too, Miss Elizabeth." Turning to her owners, Mattie said, "Good night, Massa. Good night, ma'ams."

When the door closed Grandmother Wainwright said, "They are entirely too attached."

"I do not believe it is hurting anyone," Ann said, surprised to hear herself standing up to her mother-in-law. "They will be separated soon enough. There is no need to hurry the process. I find it charming, actually."

Grandmother Wainwright asked her son, "Do you agree with me that they are too attached?"

"It is Ann's decision, Mother," he replied.

Ann was grateful that Jonathan did not take his mother's side against her. It had taken time, but she was starting to have some authority in her home.

Climbing the stairs was difficult with Lisbeth clutching Mattie's leg. After nearly tripping over the girl, Mattie picked her up and carried her to their rooms. They walked down the hall, the girl's head bobbing back and forth, planting kisses on Mattie's cheek in rhythm with their steps. Lisbeth burrowed her face into Mattie's neck when she saw Emily, who was putting away clothes in Lisbeth's room.

"How she do?" inquired Mattie.

"Nothin' much happened. Mostly she stood by the window and watched. She squeaked like an animal the few times she saw you. She asked me to get you, but I told her she stuck with me. She gonna be tired soon, 'cause she didn' sleep long in the afternoon."

After getting ready for bed, Mattie led Lisbeth to the window. They watched until the sun set. Then Poppy brought Samuel out to wave good night. Mattie blew him an unseen kiss. Lisbeth blew a kiss of her own to the folks outside. Mattie laughed and kissed Lisbeth on the temple.

"Good night, Samuel. Good night, Poppy," Mattie said to the window.

Lisbeth waved. "Good nigh.'"

"That a good girl. Now we gonna say our prayers."

The pair walked to the bed in the anteroom, where Mattie knelt. "Stand here by me," Mattie directed. "That right, good girl. Now what you happy about today? What you want to thank God for?"

"Mattie back!" exclaimed Lisbeth.

Mattie laughed, "Okay, we say, 'Thank you, God, for bringin' Mattie back.' Anyone special you thinkin' about you want God to watch over?"

"Mattie!"

"All right, Mattie. But who else?"

"Baby Jack."

"Uh-huh."

"Moter."

"Yeah," encouraged Mattie.

"Fater."

"Mm-hmm."

"Granmoter."

"Yeah, thas right. We say, 'God, please watch over Baby Jack, Mother, Father, and Grandmother. And if'n we die before we wake, take us straight to heaven, dear Lord. Amen.'"

"A-meh," echoed Lisbeth.

Before Mattie rose, she made her own prayer. "Lord, thank you for my time with my family. Please keep watch over Samuel and Emmanuel and Rebecca and Poppy and Miss Lisbeth here. Thank you. Amen."

"A-meh," echoed Lisbeth once again.

CHAPTER 6

MARCH 1841

Lisbeth tried to be good. She was a big girl, nearly four years old. She knew she needed to sit still and not talk too much. She tried to keep her pretty blue dress neat and tidy, and she pretended to eat the food on the big white china plate in front of her. Mattie did not come with her to Saturday-night supper. Lisbeth wanted her to, but Mother said, "You are a big girl. You do not need Mattie all of the time. I will help you at supper." Lisbeth was surprised, because Mother did not help her very often.

She could just see over the top of the large, rectangular table. She liked looking at herself on the edge of the table, because when she tipped her head up and down and wiggled her mouth around her reflection changed in the dark, shiny wood. She had to be sneaky about it or Grandmother would command, "Elizabeth, sit," even though she was already sitting. Father filled the large chair at the head of the table, and Mother perched on a chair next to Lisbeth. Lisbeth knew some of the other grown-ups, but not most of them. None of them spoke to her except to say, "Hello," and, "Good evening," and, "My, you are becoming quite the young lady." Sometimes she tried to follow what the grown-ups were saying to one another, but mostly she did not understand them.

When Lisbeth got tired of looking at herself in the reflection of the shiny table, she scooched down low to look at the grown-ups' shoes. She studied the stitching and buckles and buttons on feet of all sizes. From above, the adults looked as if they were not moving, but the view from under the table showed otherwise. The adults stretched their legs and wiggled their feet from side to side. Unfortunately Grandmother Wainwright noticed this game and commanded Lisbeth to "sit up straight."

So Lisbeth sat up but swung her legs back and forth. She swung them, making her legs go higher and higher. She held her body still so Grandmother Wainwright would not scold her for wiggling around. Accidentally she bumped the table with her leg. She stared straight ahead, hoping no one noticed. No one had. The water in her glass wiggled a bit, but nothing else happened. She tried it again. Swinging her leg forward, she kicked the table just a tiny bit to make her water dance. It worked. She did it again. But this time she kicked the table too hard.

Lisbeth watched as the water glass tipped sideways into the bowl of potatoes, filling it with clear liquid before landing on the table and rolling around, dribbling the last bit of water in a circle on the tablecloth.

Father yelled in his big voice, "Behave, Elizabeth," his eyes boring into her.

Grandmother glared at Lisbeth with her scrunchy, angry face.

Scared, Lisbeth started crying and called out, "Mattie, Mattie."

Father insisted, "No, Elizabeth, you may not run to Mattie. You must stay at the table and eat."

Mother patted Lisbeth's small white hand as she shushed her. "Be quiet now. Hush up. It is over. Stop your tears."

Mother was trying to be kind, but she was of little comfort. Lisbeth wanted Mattie. She sat in her chair, looked at her lap, and held back her tears. Her stomach clenched tight, so she didn't eat anything, but Father didn't care. He only wanted her to sit quietly until the grown-ups finished their meal and left the table.

In bed that night, lying side by side under the covers after prayers, Lisbeth told Mattie about the evening. "I made the water fall over and Father got mad. I cried for you. I said, 'Mattie, Mattie, Mattie,' over and over and over again. But Mother and Father made me stay. It was awful."

"Lisbeth, honey, when you miss me you jus' sing our special song real quiet to yourself. You gonna feel like I with you even when I far away."

Mattie sang the familiar lullaby in her clear, strong voice; Lisbeth's sweet, high voice joined in. Snuggling into the warmth of Mattie's body, Lisbeth reached up to rub the shells on the string in the hollow of Mattie's neck. Singing and rubbing, humming and touching, Lisbeth drifted off to sleep during the third verse:

You're a sweet little baby
You're a sweet little baby
Honey in the rock and the sugar don't stop
Gonna bring a bottle to the baby

CHAPTER 7

The heavy, oppressive August heat drove Mattie and Lisbeth to take their afternoon rest in the shade of a large willow tree. The old tree, which grew between the big house and the quarters, was a favorite spot for both of them. Lisbeth loved the private world the enormous green canopy provided them. Mattie appreciated the opportunity to view her son. She always settled them on the side facing the quarters, so she might get a glimpse of the tall and lanky boy bringing drinks to the sweaty workers in the tobacco fields beyond the cabins. At five years old, Samuel had lost his toddler roundness and was full of energy, toting water up and down the lines of workers.

Lying next to Mattie on an old quilt, Lisbeth traced the pattern of the fabric with her finger. She lifted her head off the blanket and asked, "Mattie, who do you suppose made this quilt?"

"Don' know. A bondwoman who lived here long ago. It older than you or me. I bet it even older than your grandmother."

"Is she dead?"

"Who?"

"The slave."

"Imagine so," Mattie laughed, amused at the little girl's question.

Lisbeth looked puzzled until she finally asked, "Do you think slaves and people go to the same heaven?"

Shocked and offended by the question, Mattie took a breath before answering, "Slaves is people. Never heard 'bout more than one heaven, so I 'magine there only the one."

"Who does the work?" wondered Lisbeth.

"There ain't no work in heaven," declared Mattie.

"What if you do not get into heaven?"

"As far as I concerned, God loves ever'body so God forgives ever'body so ever'body gonna get to heaven."

Lisbeth looked like she was full of more questions. She pondered Mattie's answer for a while before asking, "Do you miss your mama, Mattie?"

"Ever' day. But I know she watchin' over me, from heaven."

"Is she watching over me too?" Lisbeth asked, yearning in her voice.

Mattie thought for a minute, then nodded slowly. "Yes, Lisbeth, she watchin' over you. She watchin' all the people I love."

Lisbeth replied confidently, "You will see her again when you get to heaven. And I can meet her. Did she take care of you all the time?"

"Until she got sold away."

"Did you cry when she left? How big were you?" Lisbeth inquired.

"Just past eight years. 'Course I cried. Every night I cried in bed. Poppy or Rebecca sat with me, but it ain't the same."

"You will not let them sell you, will you?" implored Lisbeth as she clutched tight to Mattie's skirt. "I will cry real hard if they sell you."

"I got no choice. Your father decide such things. I ain't gonna make you no promise I don' get to keep."

Tears formed in Lisbeth's eyes. "I shall ask Mother to give you to me when I am grown, and then you will be with me forever," Lisbeth declared emphatically. "Then no one can sell you away."

Flattered and insulted, Mattie did not respond to Lisbeth but lay in silence, willing the child to fall asleep soon. Lisbeth laid her head down on the quilt and closed her eyes while Mattie slowly and gently rubbed her back. As she held on to the folds of Mattie's dress, Lisbeth rubbed the material between her thumb and her forefinger.

"What was your mama like?" Lisbeth asked.

"She had a real pretty voice. She sang all the time. Her favorite lullaby same as you, 'Didn't Leave Nobody but the Baby.' Yellow her favorite color. Every spring we go on a hunt for yellow crocuses."

"Crocuses?"

Mattie replied, "It a flower that come out first in spring. It kinda little and don' last for so long. But it tell you spring come."

Lisbeth sat up. "Oh, Mattie, can we do that? Hunt for crocuses? I love hunts."

"Yes, honey." Mattie smiled. "Next spring we can look for the crocuses."

"Mattie, did your mama have a name?" Lisbeth asked.

"Of course she had a name!" Mattie scoffed. "Everybody got a name! She called Naomi, from the Bible. Now, that enough about my mama. You lay back down and you go to sleep. I gonna tell you more about her later."

Mattie sang as Lisbeth drifted off to sleep. While her young charge breathed in deep and long, Mattie sat up and scooted toward the low-hanging branches. She parted the branches slightly to get a better view. As she watched for her son she thought about the last time she saw her mother.

January first was accounting day on the plantation. After a delicious week of resting and visiting came the most dreaded day of the year for the field slaves. Following the midday meal of black-eyed peas, thought to bring good luck in the coming year, Massa and the overseer gathered everyone to announce sales and rentals. Pleading or arguing did no good. If your name was on the list, you left the next day. A rental at a nearby plantation was the best of a bad situation. That meant visits most Sundays if it was close by or, if it was farther away, a visit once a year at the Big Times, the winter holidays. A sale to a slave trader heading into Georgia or Louisiana was devastating news. It meant never seeing your family again and likely an early death, though no one knew for certain: news of family sold south rarely made it back to Fair Oaks.

On New Year's Day, 1825, all the anxious slaves had gathered on the grounds in front of the big house. Those good-luck peas sat hard in their churning stomachs as they listened to Massa Wainwright's announcement. Mattie stood up tall, wrapped in her mother's strong arms. Nearly eight, Mattie was old enough to be rented or sold. She felt the tension running through her mother's body as the overseer read the list, his deep voice showing no hint of emotion.

"Benjamin, Olivia, and Miriam to be rented to Berkeley. Young James, Daniel, and Frances to be rented to Willowbrook. Louisa, Sugar, and Willametta rented to White Pines."

Mattie's mother, Naomi, pulled her tighter as Massa moved on to the sold list.

"Willamena sold to Westover. Benny sold to Cumberland. Naomi sold to Hopewell."

"No!" Mattie cried out. Her mother's fingers flew over her mouth hard and fast. Smothered by the rough hand, her protest did not make it to Massa's ears.

Fingers clawed deep into Mattie's shoulder. Though the names went on, Mattie did not hear them. Her mother's name was on the list, and hers was not. She did not know how far Hopewell was, whether it meant weekly or yearly visits, but she knew her mother was leaving her.

That afternoon and night, sorrow hung as heavy as a burial. Early the next morning, before the sun fully rose, her mother packed up her few belongings. She untied the necklace from her own throat and bit off a single shell with her teeth. Then she placed the necklace on Mattie's neck, keeping the single shell for herself.

"You keep this safe till I come back. This came from my mama who got it from her mama, all the way back. I gonna keep one. You always gonna be connected through these shells, not jus' to me, but to all the womenfolk that came before us. We are strong women, Mattie. You one of us, so you strong too."

Mattie nodded silently, her throat too full to let words pass.

They joined the other families outside waiting to be torn apart. Mattie wrapped her arms around her mother and clung tight.

Naomi cupped Mattie's small chin and stared intensely into her eyes. Fiercely she whispered, "Mama loves you. Mama always gonna love you. You carry me in your heart for always. I gonna be back next Big Times." Then she broke away from Mattie's embrace and climbed into the wagon.

Flanked by Poppy and Rebecca, Mattie had watched her mother grow smaller and smaller as she was driven away. In her mind, Mattie shouted, *Mama, don' leave me! Take me with you!* To the world, she appeared sturdy and calm, like a thick tree trunk planted firmly in the ground.

She might have protested more if she had known that her mother would not be returning for the Big Times. Soon after she departed Fair Oaks, Naomi died of an infection and was placed in the earth without ceremony. When word of her death came three months after she took her last breath, her family erected a plain wooden cross in her honor in the Fair Oaks Negro cemetery. Her empty tomb sat amidst the graves of Mattie's great-great-grandparents, great-grandmother, grandmother, grandfather, and father overlooking the James River.

Sitting under the shade of the willow tree, unconsciously stroking Lisbeth's hair, Mattie made a promise to herself and her son: if the overseer ever sold either of them, she was taking Samuel and running.

That evening, the Wainwright family was gathered in the sitting room. Father was reading as usual. He occasionally read something out loud to Mother. Mother embroidered a new pillowcase. Lisbeth hoped it might be for her bed, because she liked the colors. She would ask for it when Mother was nearly finished. Jack was already in his room. Lisbeth played with a porcelain doll on the couch.

"What was your mother like?" she asked her mother.

"What a question, Elizabeth," Mother replied, looking surprised at her daughter's inquiry.

"What did she look like?" Lisbeth wondered.

"Actually, you favor her. Your eyes are very similar to hers. Though I hardly remember my mother."

"Why?" Lisbeth asked, concerned.

"I was quite young when she died, perhaps eight or nine. I hardly remember her at all."

The five-year-old's curiosity was undaunted. "What was her favorite song?"

"Goodness. I have no idea." Mother laughed.

"Did she sing to you?" Lisbeth asked.

"No." Mother shook her head.

"Did she have a favorite flower?"

"Favorite flower?" Mother considered the question. "No, I cannot say that she did. Or if she did, I did not know about it."

"What was her favorite color?"

A small smile passed over Mother's face. "Blue. Deep blue. She favored that because she thought it brought out her eyes."

Satisfied with that one nugget of information, Lisbeth's mind flitted to a new topic. "Mother, can Samuel come in? Mattie would be happier if Samuel lived here. I shall share her with him."

Mother laughed. "You are a sweet one, Elizabeth. It is very kind that you care about Mattie. She is very fortunate to be with you. I can assure you, though, that it is best for Samuel to stay in the quarters and for Mattie to stay here caring for you."

"But—" Lisbeth started.

Mother went on without pause. "Do not argue with me, Elizabeth. There are many things you do not understand. You must trust me. Samuel would not be at all comfortable in the house. There is nothing for him to do here. They can visit with one another every week, which is more frequent than most workers can visit with their families."

Mother was very clear. There was no point in talking about it further. Although Lisbeth did not understand her mother's reasoning, it was settled: Mattie would stay with her. Samuel would stay outside. That was for the best for everyone.

CHAPTER 8

SPRING 1843

"Can I come with you?" Lisbeth pleaded with Mattie.

"Why you want to come with me?"

"I do not want to be with Emily. And I like seeing everybody. It's been such a long time since I went with you," Lisbeth replied.

When she was little she often went to the quarters on Sunday mornings, but she rarely got the chance since she became old enough to sit through church. But now Lisbeth had been confined to her bed for several days with a head cold, and she was left behind when the Wainwrights left for church after Mother declared her unfit to sit for hours in a cold, damp building. Lisbeth started asking to venture out to the quarters with Mattie as soon as her family's carriage pulled away. Her pleading eventually worked, and Mattie finally agreed. Lisbeth was excited as they walked down the dirt path to the shanties.

Mattie prepared her for the visit: "We gonna see Samuel, of course, and Poppy. We also gonna visit with Rebecca and all of her family: Lawrence, Sarah, Henry, and Frank. You remember Sarah; she a bit older than you."

"I remember everyone," Lisbeth said. "You do not have to remind me."

Lisbeth knew these people from her window. She watched each day as they left for the fields and returned to their cabins. She saw them cook, and wash, and play games. She imagined their conversations with each other. And she heard stories from Mattie about them on Sunday evenings.

However, when they arrived at the quarters Lisbeth was suddenly uncertain and nervous. Watching this place was familiar. It had been so long since she was out here that being here felt strange. Lisbeth hid her eyes in the folds of Mattie's long skirt as they approached Poppy and Samuel's cabin. Murmurs from the people gathered on the benches outside floated over to them. Mattie smiled when she made out the sound of her son's voice. Samuel's face broke into a wide grin as soon as he saw his mother come around the corner from behind the cabin.

"You lost both your top teeth!" Mattie exclaimed, and cupped his chin in her hand to take a close look at Samuel's gap-toothed smile. "You throw 'em on the roof and make a wish?"

"Uh-huh. And it come true. Look!"

Lisbeth followed the trail of Samuel's pointing finger to see a man smiling at Mattie.

"Emmanuel!" cried Mattie. They rushed to embrace, with Lisbeth trailing close behind. "What you doin' here? It ain't your visiting time till next week."

"They needed some horses brung over, so I told 'em I take 'em."

"It so good to see you." Mattie beamed up at the man.

Lisbeth clutched onto Mattie's skirt while the two adults hugged hello. When Mattie stepped back from Emmanuel's embrace, she stumbled over Lisbeth.

"For goodness' sake," cried Mattie. "Lisbeth! Come out here and say hello. You 'member Samuel and Rebecca and Poppy and Sarah and everyone else. This here my husband, Emmanuel. You heard me talk about him, but it been a long time since you seen him in person."

Lisbeth stared at the man before her. She was so surprised to meet Emmanuel that she was at a loss for words.

"Cat got your tongue?" Emmanuel teased.

"No, it is right here," Lisbeth responded, and without thinking she stuck it out. The instant her tongue poked out, she realized her mistake. Horrified, her eyes popped open wide as her hand rushed to cover her mouth. Everyone else laughed. After she realized that nobody was mad at her, she laughed too.

Gathered on the benches attached to the outside of the cabin with Lisbeth and Samuel pressed close on either side of her, Mattie reported to her son, "Four, five, two, seven, nine, two, and eight."

"No, Mattie, it was six on Friday," Lisbeth corrected.

"She right!" exclaimed Samuel. He turned sharply and scowled at Lisbeth with hard, narrowed eyes. "You watchin' through the window too? With my mama?"

"Yes," Lisbeth said uncertainly. "We both count the number of fingers you put up each morning. You cannot see me standing there as well?"

"No," Samuel muttered.

"They can' see in, Lisbeth," Mattie explained.

Lisbeth turned around to look at her window to see the truth of it for herself. The glass reflected the sunlight.

Samuel glared at Lisbeth, and then at his mother. He jumped off the bench and ran away. Mattie flew after him.

Left at the bench, Lisbeth watched Mattie cajole Samuel. She kissed the top of his head, tickled him under the arms, and hugged him from behind. Samuel ran from Mattie; Mattie chased after him. He allowed himself to be caught, then squirmed away from his mother's attention.

Lisbeth had grown up on Sunday-evening stories of Samuel and Emmanuel and everyone else. She had watched their comings and goings out the window twice a day since she was a baby. First thing in the morning and just before supper she stood beside Mattie to count Samuel's fingers and check on his world. She knew these people. But today Lisbeth saw something else. Seeing Mattie here with them, she understood that this was Mattie's family. Mattie belonged here; this was Mattie's home.

A pit opened in Lisbeth's stomach. Suddenly she did not want to be here anymore. She longed to be an observer of this place, looking down upon it from her room with Mattie by her side.

Sarah, Rebecca's long-limbed daughter, bounded up to Lisbeth on the bench. "Miss Lisbeth, Auntie Mattie says to teach you somethin'."

"Oh, that is all right," Lisbeth stammered, blinking away tears. "Thank you, though."

"She says I got to!"

Mattie yelled across the way, "Learn somethin' new, Lisbeth—Sarah gonna teach you."

"All right," Lisbeth acquiesced, though she was uncertain.

"It go like this—put your hand up, fingers open by your shoulders, like this."

Lisbeth followed Sarah's directions and mirrored the posture of the girl across from her. Sarah pounded out a rhythm in a complicated pattern, alternately clapping her hands together and slapping them against her own knees or Lisbeth's hands.

Sarah chanted while her hands flew:

Little Sally Walker, sitting in a saucer,
Rise, Sally rise, wipe your weeping eyes,
Put your hands on your hips and let your backbone slip,
Shake it to the east, shake it to the west,
Shake it to the one that you love the best.

"You are so fast!" Lisbeth exclaimed when Sarah finished.

"Everyone always sayin' how fast I go," Sarah boasted. "I the fastest tobacco picker for my age."

"I could never clap like that."

"'Course you can! I show you slow now."

Sarah's calloused palms clapped against Lisbeth's smooth skin. Over and over Sarah moved her hands slowly, chanting out the song until Lisbeth sang along. After a while Lisbeth dared to move her hands along with the rhyme, often making mistakes. The girls burst out laughing whenever Lisbeth missed a step and clapped up into Sarah's face instead of her own knees or hands.

"You gettin' it," Sarah encouraged.

"Not as good as you."

"Just practice, you gonna get better."

"I have no one to practice with."

"Auntie Mattie real good at this one. Practice with her."

Lisbeth jerked her head in Mattie's direction. "Mattie knows this game?" Lisbeth's eyebrows furrowed as she stared at her nurse.

"Oh, yeah. Auntie Mattie know lots of hand-clapping games. She taught me some good ones."

Lisbeth studied her nurse playing with Samuel and Emmanuel in the distance. There was so much about Mattie that she had not seen before. Mattie's head was thrown back, her mouth open wide in hard laughter as her son and husband ganged up to tickle her. Lisbeth felt her understanding of the world come apart and slowly re-form. A sickening realization dawned: Mattie loved her life here, away from Lisbeth.

Sarah studied Lisbeth studying Mattie. Waiting patiently, Sarah stood in front of Lisbeth ready to resume the game whenever the young mistress of the plantation wished.

Eventually Mattie and Samuel came over to Lisbeth at the bench.

"Lisbeth, Samuel got a surprise for us," Mattie said. Samuel pulled Mattie toward the river.

"What is it?" Lisbeth asked as she followed them down a narrow path along the water.

Mattie shrugged.

"You gotta see for you self," Samuel told them. "I already showed ever'body else."

He stopped a few hundred feet down the path and pointed at a clump of grass. Lisbeth was confused. She didn't see anything special. And then the wind moved the grass and she saw it.

"A crocus!" she exclaimed. "A yellow crocus."

"Where?" asked Mattie.

Samuel said, "She right. There a crocus in that grass."

Mattie knelt down and parted the green blades. The littlest bit of yellow showed in a still blooming crocus.

"Why looky at that yellow—how lovely," Mattie declared. "Thanks for showin' us that bit of spring, Samuel."

At the same time Samuel and Lisbeth said, "Black-eyed peas!"

Mattie laughed and nodded, "Guess my Mama's tradition is carryin' on. We all gonna eat some black-eyed peas to celebrate."

The Ford family, the oldest White family in the valley, was in attendance for supper that night. Though they were not prosperous by Tidewater standards, as founders of the valley they enjoyed high social status. The six members of the family—mother, father, three boys, and a girl—shared similar looks: pale skin with ruddy cheeks, soft-blue eyes, and sandy-blond hair. The sons, ages ten, eight, and seven, were a blur of motion. Mary, the youngest at six, was a calm contrast to her brothers.

Lisbeth kept glancing across the table to watch her friend seated next to Jack. Adorned in a stiff pink dress with white lace at the collar, Mary quietly ate her food, hardly looking up from her plate. Lisbeth found no entertainment in her at the moment. She was not very much fun when adults expected her to behave. Situated between the two "Berts," Albert and Robert, Lisbeth played tap the table. Having made her own water dance, she tried out her skills on her neighbors' glasses. She stretched out her right foot ever so slowly and gently touched the table, making a slight shiver in Albert's water. He did not notice her sly movements. She switched to her left foot, knowing she needed to be more cautious. Robert would tattle simply to make the dinner more interesting. Carefully she positioned her left knee at an angle and raised her leg. Her toes were nearly at the table when Robert accidentally struck her leg hard with his knee, causing Lisbeth to smash against the table. Robert's water glass, along with Jack's, fell over. Instantly water rushed off the table all over Grandmother Wainwright, who screeched loudly, drawing the attention of everyone at the table.

Grandmother Wainwright leaped up, fury written all over her face. Lisbeth braced herself for a scolding, but Grandmother did not look at her. Instead she towered over Jack with a large spoon gripped tightly in her hand. He cowered from her.

Grandmother Wainwright struck Jack on the head with the spoon as she screamed at him, "You careless, careless boy! You are not fit to eat at a table. If you do not learn your manners, you will never grow up to be a gentleman. Apologize to me at once."

Shaking all over, Jack squeaked out an apology to his grandmother.

Father broke in, "Now apologize to our guests for intruding upon our fine meal too."

"I am sorry," he said, though his face showed anything but remorse. He stared at the table, his eyes flashing with anger and his lip curled in frustration at the injustice.

"No need to apologize," Mr. Ford replied. "With these three boys, we have spills ten times a week at our table. If I had a nickel for every upset glass I would be as wealthy as Cunningham."

"We do not put up with such behavior in this household," declared Grandmother Wainwright. "If you will excuse me, I shall take my leave to put on a dry gown."

Lisbeth felt horrible that Jack was blamed, but relieved she was not in trouble. She did not mean to make a mess that would get Jack scolded. Rather than risk further upset, she sat quietly and finished her food.

After supper, the two families gathered in the parlor. Lisbeth, finally next to Mary on one end of the couch, confessed into her friend's ear, "I knocked the water over, not Jack. Robert struck me with his knee and then I struck the table."

"Poor Jack," Mary declared. "He was punished though he did nothing."

"I wished to say so, but I did not want to be punished as well."

"The spoon must have hurt! I would have cried."

"Me too. But Jack doesn't cry when he gets struck; it only makes Grandmother Wainwright more cross and she hits him all the more. It is best simply to stay clear of her," Lisbeth said. "Now I have something to show you. Put your hands up, like this."

Mary did as she was told. Lisbeth showed Mary the game Sarah had taught her that morning. She whispered the words of the chant as her hands moved in rhythm. The two friends, in their own private bubble, startled when Father broke in.

"Whatever are you doing?" he inquired.

Lisbeth replied quietly, "I am only teaching Mary a game that Sarah taught me today."

"Who is Sarah?"

"Mattie's niece. She calls Mattie 'Auntie.' It sounds strange, 'Auntie Mattie.'"

Father looked at Mother. "Do you think it wise to let her play in the quarters?"

"I used to play with the pickaninies as a child. It did me no harm. In fact, I believe it is good for her to be exposed to them. She needs to understand their ways."

Mr. Ford spoke up. "I absolutely agree. Our children must be familiarized with them in order to be successful masters and mistresses."

Lisbeth watched Father's face, waiting for his approval. When it came, as a nod, she turned back to her friend.

Lying in bed, Lisbeth thought about the day while Mattie sat nearby humming a tune. Her own voice broke into the calm night. "Mattie, did you ask Cook about black-eyed peas for tomorrow?"

"Uh-huh. She say yes. She gonna cook up a whole batch and we gonna take some for a picnic under the willow with some corn bread."

"Can Samuel come too?" Lisbeth asked.

"That sweet thinkin', but he gonna be working."

"He can sneak under there with us. No one can see us under the willow, and who is going to tell?" Lisbeth pushed back.

"Tomorrow be too soon for such a thin'. Maybe we gonna plan that for another time," Mattie replied.

Satisfied with someday, Lisbeth had another question: "When I lose a tooth, can I throw it on the roof and make a wish?"

"Don' see why not."

"You think Samuel and Poppy will let me use their roof? Mine is too high to reach."

"I can ask 'em. I 'magine they gonna say yes."

"Do you think the wish will come true if it is not on my own house?" wondered Lisbeth.

"I don' suppose I know all about wishes, but I don' see why not. Now you hush up and go to sleep."

Mattie rocked in the chair close by while Lisbeth lay still in bed. After some time, Mattie spoke into the quiet. "Lisbeth, when we invite Samuel to be with us under the willow, what you think about you teaching Samuel a bit of what you been learnin' about books and numbers? Maybe?"

"Yes," Lisbeth replied in a dream-coated voice, innocently agreeing to betray her parents.

CHAPTER 9

SPRING 1845

Mattie relished Tuesday and Thursday afternoons. All felt right in the world as she sat under the broad willow tree sandwiched between Lisbeth and Samuel, listening to them practice the shapes and sounds of letters and words. The anxiety she had felt when Samuel first joined them evaporated as weeks turned into months, and then into years without any hint of discovery. Under the willow between the quarters and the big house proved to be a perfect place to meet. Weather permitting, Mattie and Lisbeth had been going there most afternoons since Lisbeth was a toddler, first for naps and then for studying. None of the White folks suspected that Samuel joined them under the willow two afternoons a week. The wispy green branches hung so low that they weren't visible from the quarters or the fields, and the wide dark-brown trunk hid them from the big house too. It took some doing, getting Samuel away without the overseer knowing, but in nearly two years he had hardly missed a lesson.

Rebecca, Lawrence, and others worked extra to cover Samuel's share of planting or picking while he was away. The overseer didn't pay much attention to the comings and goings of a young boy, so long as all the work was getting done. Samuel brought his knowledge back to the cabins, and by scratching into the dirt, he taught Sarah and other children to unlock the mystery of letters. Everyone knew this could be a ticket to freedom. Itinerant preachers had been whispering about the Underground Railroad. Nobody knew who might try, but knowing something about letters could be important someday.

Having mastered Lisbeth's reading primers, Samuel now read from the Holy Bible. Mattie loved hearing her son's lips form the words of the Lord. On a hot late-summer day, sheltered by the cool of the tree, resting her head against the smooth bark of the trunk, she closed her eyes and listened to the soft sounds of the eight-year-old children. Samuel sat to her left, Lisbeth sat to her right, and the Bible was open upon her lap. Samuel easily read most of the book and needed assistance from Lisbeth only when a particularly difficult word came along. Occasionally they worked together to sound out a word that was beyond even Lisbeth's vocabulary. They delighted when they found names of friends and family members, such as Rebecca, Mary, or Sarah, and chuckled over unfamiliar names like Enoch.

"Eeenooooch," Samuel drew out in a silly voice. The three of them laughed hard and long until they had stitches in their sides.

Recently the lessons began to include writing. Even Mattie learned to write her name, though she refused Lisbeth's offer to teach her any letters beyond *M-A-T-T-I-E*, arguing, "I don' see how I ever gonna have any use for writin' my own name, much less any other letterin'. I jus' glad to know the shape of it. You jus' keep on learnin' Samuel his letters. You young folks need readin' and writin', not me."

Samuel had mastered writing capital letters and was moving on to lowercase. Using the ground as a chalkboard, he copied the shapes Lisbeth wrote in the dirt. Again and again Samuel formed careful loops and lines while his mother listened. The children teased her that she fell asleep during the lessons, but Mattie insisted she was "jus' resting her eyes."

"All the letters are correct except the *q*. See how the loop is to the back?" Lisbeth pointed out to Samuel. "You are making a *g*."

Samuel tried again. "Like this?"

"No, this direction." Lisbeth drew again in the dirt.

Samuel tried again.

"You are still making it backward. This is a *g*," Lisbeth reached over Mattie to guide Samuel's hand with her own to form the distinct letters, "and this is a *q*."

"Don' do that!" Mattie sat forward quickly. She leaped up, grabbed Samuel by the arm, and jerked him onto his feet. "Never touch a White girl! Never! Do you hear me?" Spit flew from her mouth as she yelled at him. "You gonna get yourself killed!"

The two children stared at Mattie.

Trembling with rage and adrenaline, Mattie hissed into Samuel's face, "Go! Back to the fields. You done learnin' for the day."

Her hand dug into Samuel's arm as she spun him around toward the quarters and shoved him hard between his shoulder blades. His back hunched over, Samuel rubbed his arm and walked away from the trunk without a word.

"Get your hat!" Mattie ordered. Samuel always returned to the fields with his hat on his head. The head covering was his excuse for being away from the fields if the overseer noticed him. He parted the willow branches and peered around before he left their cool shelter.

"Stupid boy. Stupid, stupid, stupid," Mattie mumbled to herself.

"I am sorry, Mattie," Lisbeth's small voice apologized. "I was only trying to teach him. I did not know it was dangerous."

"Well, your not knowin' might get my son killed someday. He can never touch a White girl. Never."

CHAPTER 10

MARCH 1847

Lisbeth sat all alone in the shade of her beloved willow tree, reading. Now that she was nearly ten years old, she was expected to take care of herself during the day while Mattie attended to other chores. This afternoon Mattie was ironing sheets. Samuel, his reading and writing lessons complete, no longer joined her under the tree either. Those conspiratorial afternoons were a part of the past, though Lisbeth still gave Mattie books to sneak to Samuel.

Lisbeth was surprised to hear the sound of jeering intrude upon her quiet. It was rare that anyone came near her private fortress. She listened as taunting voices got louder and louder. She made her way to the edge of the tree and parted the branches. Her brother and his friends were in the clearing behind the quarters. Lisbeth was appalled when she realized what she was seeing. Jack was showing off for some of his older friends—Edward

Cunningham, Nathaniel Jackson, and William Anderson—by harassing one of the Negroes. They made a ring around their victim, taunting and threatening him with a rope that swung from Jack's hands. Lisbeth threw her book aside and stormed down the rise toward her brother and his friends. She hated the way they tormented the field hands for sport. As she got closer, her breath caught. Their victim was Samuel! His head bowed, he did not see her approaching. Shame and rage poured through her, but she covered her feelings quickly. She knew she must handle this correctly or she would only make things worse, because Jack was not inclined to take directions from his older sister.

When she walked up to the boys she did not look at Samuel, lest she betray that he mattered to her. Mustering as much self-righteous indignation as possible, and doing her best to mask her fear, Lisbeth haughtily declared, "You are disturbing my reading. You know you are supposed to let me study."

"Study elsewhere," Jack taunted without taking his eyes off Samuel.

"I do not wish to," Lisbeth stated. "You know this is my preferred place to learn. What are you doing?"

"Teaching this nigger to show us respect."

"Father does not approve when you interfere with the niggers," she replied.

"He does not care about this one," Jack replied with a sneer. "He is to be sold. We do not need another buck around here." Jack turned his gaze to Lisbeth and stared hard.

Stunned by the news, but not wanting to reveal anything to her brother, Lisbeth lied, "Well, I do not care about him either. I simply want to study in peace. Now go elsewhere."

Jack kept staring at her. Lisbeth stared right back. She felt the eyes of the onlookers pass back and forth between the two of them. Her hands were moist, but she did not make a move to wipe them dry.

Finally Jack snorted and looked away. "Come on," he said to his friends, "there are frogs down at the creek. I bet I catch the biggest one."

The tension broke the instant the boys, playing at being men, walked away without a backward glance, their minds on their next task. The gang frolicked like a pack of puppies, bumping into one another as they made their way down the path.

Lisbeth sighed with relief and rubbed her damp hands on her gown. She had done it—she had driven off her brother and his friends.

With Jack gone, she dared to look at Samuel as he glared after Jack. Rage burned on his face. His tormentors played with one another, not giving him another thought.

When they were entirely alone, Lisbeth quietly, shamefully spoke, "I am sorry, Samuel. I will tell Mattie what Jack said. It will be all right."

Samuel stared at Lisbeth, fury beaming from his eyes. Her eyes welled up; her chest tightened.

"It will be all right," she insisted, trying to convince herself as much as Samuel.

A cold, hard look crossed Samuel's face. Without a word, he shook his head, turned, and walked away.

Counting her steps as she walked—one . . . two . . . three—Lisbeth returned to the willow. She sat down, picked up her book in her shaking hands, and pretended to read. She willed her heart to slow down, taking deep breaths. After she calmed herself, she ran to Mattie.

Mattie was in their rooms, waiting to dress Lisbeth for supper. A breathless Lisbeth blurted out, "Mattie, Jack says Samuel is to be sold! He might only be teasing, but it may be true."

Mattie sank into the rocking chair. Lisbeth stared intently at her nurse, waiting for a response.

Lisbeth broke the long silence. "Mattie, he will be fine. They will sell him to someone nice."

"Hush!" Mattie snapped as she stared blankly. "Let me think."

That night Lisbeth and Mother sat in the sitting room with embroidery hoops in their hands. Mother occupied one side of the divan while Lisbeth sat at an angle to her in an upholstered chair.

"Let me see your stitches," Mother commanded.

Lisbeth passed her work into judging hands. Mother studied the needlework carefully.

"Much improved, Elizabeth. Although you still tend toward carelessness in your transitions. Right here, the transition from sky to cloud is too tight; see how the material puckers? And here it is too loose. Tear out these areas. But the rest is quite acceptable."

A timid knock interrupted them.

"Enter," Mother called. "Oh, Mattie, it is you." She smiled. "Time for bed, Elizabeth."

Lisbeth finished snipping out a stitch and left the unfinished pillowcase bound in the hoop in the basket next to her chair. "Good night, Mother," she said as she stood.

"Kisses, dear," reminded Mother.

Lisbeth returned and kissed her Mother's smooth, pale cheek before joining Mattie.

Before the pair departed, Mattie spoke, her voice shaking with emotion. "Mrs. Ann, I . . . uh . . . got somethin' to ask you, ma'am. I need a favor real bad. I cared for your daughter all these years and now I, uh, need your help."

"My goodness, Mattie," declared Mother, "come out with it."

"My son, Samuel, is to be sold, ma'am. Please," Mattie begged, "please see to it he gets sold to where his daddy live—over at Berkeley. They need some men there. Please, ma'am."

Uncomfortable witnessing her nurse's despair, Lisbeth looked away. Standing by the door, she longed to leave yet wanted to hear her mother's response. She pretended not to listen as her eyes followed the trail of gold flowers on the rug.

"Mattie, as you well know, I have nothing to do with the field hands. They are Mr. Wainwright's affair."

"Yes, ma'am."

"But I will pass on your request. He is not an unreasonable man. If he can get a fair price . . ." Mother hastily added, "I am making you no promise, you understand?"

"Yes, ma'am. Thank you, ma'am." Mattie nodded as she left the room.

A week later, her mother gave Mattie an answer when the nurse came for Lisbeth in the sitting room. "Mattie, I am sorry, but Mr. Wainwright was unable to fulfill your request. Samuel will be going to the Andersons. Their estate is only three miles away. He will be able to visit with you on Sundays. You can be consoled by that."

Lisbeth stared at the stony face of her nurse as they walked to her room in absolute silence. Mattie radiated an emotion that Lisbeth could not name. Each step up the staircase and down the long hallway weighed heavily.

Once the door to their rooms closed, Lisbeth cried out, "I am sorry, Mattie. But he is not going far. You will get to see him once a week, just like you do now."

"I get to see my son every day, twice a day or more, out that window. It ain't much, but it been enough. Ain't nothing you can say that is gonna make this better for me, Lisbeth. Don' even try."

Mattie and Emmanuel were alone in Poppy and Samuel's cabin for their monthly visit. They whispered in the dark, making plans in response to the news that Samuel would be leaving for the Anderson estate.

Mattie was finally ready to take their chances on freedom.

"It too soon," Emmanuel insisted. "The rain might come still."

"You saying you want Samuel just to stay there? All alone?"

"He strong. He smart. He gonna be all right for a while."

Mattie started to cry. "What if they—"

"I know some folks there. I gonna tell them to keep an eye on him. Six weeks after the first sign of spring, that the best timing. You know I thought about this—lots. We got to plan careful and not rush if we want any chance to make it."

Mattie nodded silently.

Emmanuel went on, "We got to set things up with the right folks."

"How you know we can trust them?"

Emmanuel shrugged. "Got no choice but to trust strangers. They say it their Christian duty."

Mattie had nothing else to say. She rested her head against Emmanuel's warm chest and let her tears fall against his skin. His comforting pats led to slow, sweet lovemaking.

CHAPTER 11

Mattie did not cry as she gave Samuel final instructions. They were in his cabin for his last night at Fair Oaks. Mrs. Gray had given her thirty minutes to say good-bye during family dinner. He stood before her, trying to look brave, but she knew he was scared, nearly as terrified as she was.

"They gonna put you with all men, young and old. If someone nice to you, offer you some of his food, you stay away from him. Find an old man, as old as Poppy, and stay close. Keep to yourself if you don' find an old man. Sleep with your back to the wall if you can."

Samuel looked confused, but he nodded.

Mattie went on, "Hold tight till you hear from us. Your daddy say it gonna be in six weeks or so. Don' worry if it longer. We ain't gonna forget about you, I promise. We got to wait for a sign of spring."

Mattie pulled out a piece of paper with a drawing. "Here the map he drew up. Study it good, but keep it hidden inside your shoe. Make it look like it part of the shoe. We gonna meet by this tree when the time come. But that not for a while. I gonna see you next Sunday. They gonna let you walk here. Go on the main road. Keep the river to your left and you find your way back. It gonna take you half the morning to get here so start early—just at sunrise."

She helped him pack up his belongings. He was getting too old for hugs, but when it was time for her to go back to the big house, he let her wrap her arms around him. She clutched him against her body, savoring the feel and smell of him.

"I gonna see you Sunday. You smart and strong. You gonna be just fine," she said.

"Good-bye, Mama," Samuel said.

"Good-bye, Samuel. Your mama love you. Never forget it," Mattie said to her son.

Mattie returned to her room in the big house, sat down on her bed, and let the tears flow. Salty water streamed down her cheeks, soaking into her dusty skirt. Her shoulders jerked up and down in rhythm with her breath. She collapsed onto the bed, burying her face in the covers to muffle her cries.

When she stopped crying, Mattie went down upon her knees to pray. "Please, Lord, please watch over my son tonight and all the nights to come. Take care o' him for me. Make 'em treat him right; keep him warm and fed. Don' let no harm come to him. Please, Lord, keep him safe."

She stayed on her knees and repeated her prayer again and again. She was so intent on her petitions that she neglected to fetch Lisbeth from the sitting room, and eventually the girl was sent upstairs on her own. Mattie did not acknowledge Lisbeth when she walked into the room or when the girl knelt beside her with prayers of her own.

After a night of tossing and turning punctuated by fitful dreams, Mattie rose before the sun. She quietly made her way to the window by Lisbeth's bed. Staring out into the still-dark morning she stood rigid, waiting for a last look at her son. Before the sun finished making its way over the horizon, a wagon pulled up. Samuel, followed by Poppy, walked out of their cabin and climbed into the wagon. Though he could not see her, he looked up at his mother, knowing she was there.

Mattie muffled a cry into one hand and waved through the cold, damp glass with the other. Dropping her hands to her sides, she stood stiff as a board as she watched her son ride away, growing ever smaller in the distance until she could not make him out anymore.

While she stood there, frozen, staring at an empty road, small, sticky fingers slipped into her hand.

Lisbeth's little-girl voice broke into the horrible morning, "It is all right, Mattie. I will not leave you. You still have me."

With no other way to help her son, Mattie prayed for him as she went about her duties. Sometimes she spoke her prayers out loud, but mostly her petitions were spoken in her heart. Distracted and bereft, Mattie was barely able to care for Lisbeth's physical needs, and paid little attention to her charge otherwise. Lisbeth, in a futile attempt to cheer up her nurse, took to the habit of sneaking up some dessert in her pocket. But Mattie did not eat it.

Samuel's Sunday visit did nothing to diminish Mattie's anxiety. In less than a week, he had lost weight and gained a panicked look. He did not say much about his time at the Anderson estate, but it couldn't be good.

"I don' wanna go back," he pleaded to Mattie on Sunday evening. "Don' make me. Hide me here!"

"Samuel, that just gonna make things worse. Hold on for jus' a few more weeks," Mattie attempted to reassure him. "Then we gonna all be together."

—

On a bright March afternoon, ten days after Samuel's departure, Mattie was waiting in Lisbeth's room with their midday dinner when Lisbeth bounced in. Excitement shone in her eyes as she proudly proclaimed, "Mattie, come see! I found the first crocus. It is spring. I asked Cook to make us a picnic: corn bread and black-eyed peas! It will be ready soon."

Mattie snapped, "Lisbeth, I know you tryin' to make me feel better. But ain't no little flower gonna do it." Her voice rose as she continued, "Ain't no little bits of your leftover dessert gonna make me feel better neither. I scared for my son, child. Ain't nothin' gonna make me feel better but to see him again."

Lisbeth's face fell.

More gently, Mattie went on, "Now you go on and have that picnic without me."

Lisbeth stared at Mattie, confusion written all over her face.

"But Mattie . . ." the girl started to say. Then she stopped and ran out of the room. Mattie considered going after her, but could not stir herself to action.

She wasn't entirely surprised when Emily sought her out later that afternoon to tell her she was wanted in the sitting room. Someone must have seen that the girl was upset. Mattie knew Lisbeth would not complain about her.

Mattie tapped gently on the sitting room door. The calm expression she forced onto her face belied the activity in her heart. She was never comfortable in Mrs. Ann's presence, though these meetings were typically short and to the point.

When she entered the room and saw both Mr. Wainwright and Mrs. Ann waiting to speak with her, she feared the worst. She stood before them, eyes turned down, rubbing her sweaty palms on her dress.

"Mattie, we have news from the Andersons," Mrs. Ann stated. "It seems Samuel has disappeared. They want to know if you know anything about it."

Mattie's heart skipped a beat; blood rushed away from her head, making it impossible to focus on the words coming toward her. A hot, nauseous wave swept through her body. It was too soon! They were not supposed to leave for weeks yet!

"My baby," escaped from her lips.

Then she staggered, working to hold herself up while trying to make sense of the words coming out of Mrs. Ann's mouth.

Eventually Mr. Wainwright broke in loudly, "Mattie, answer the question. Do you know where Samuel is? Is he being hidden anywhere? He is too young to have gotten far on his own. Apparently he has been gone for several days now."

"I don' know nothin' 'bout my son. Ask the good Lord if you want to know where he at."

"Now Mattie, angry words are not called for," Mrs. Ann said. I am certain the Andersons made him welcome. They are good people. He did not give it enough time. It takes a while to adjust to a new home."

Mattie had no response.

"They will want to speak with you directly. I will bring you over in the morning. Good night," declared Mr. Wainwright.

Early the next morning, Lisbeth stood in the doorway adjoining her room to Mattie's. She watched as Mattie pulled a clean dress over a crisp white slip. Mattie carefully and efficiently buttoned up the front of her bodice.

"Mattie, how long will you be gone?" Lisbeth inquired as Mattie adjusted her necklace.

"Don' know."

"But you will be home to eat dinner with me?" implored Lisbeth.

"Don' know."

"Oh, Mattie, I am scared for you."

"Ain't nothin' they can do gonna be worse than my son gone missin'," Mattie said, though horrible visions of whips, humiliation, and pain ran through her head.

Mattie fixed her hair in silence while Lisbeth watched.

"You missed some," Lisbeth pointed out as Mattie pulled her hair into a bun. Lisbeth reached up to put the stray lock into Mattie's hand.

"Thank you, honey."

She gave Lisbeth's hand a quick squeeze as she took the hair. She turned to her charge. Cupping the girl's chin in her hand, Mattie tipped Lisbeth's head back until they were looking at each other eye-to-eye. Staring at the girl wordlessly, Mattie gave a small shake of her head, sighed, and pulled Lisbeth into a tight hug. Lisbeth clutched Mattie's warm body until the older woman pulled away. Mattie looked down at Lisbeth, their arms still wrapped around one another, and said, "I gonna be all right."

Mattie rubbed Lisbeth's soft cheek with her thumb, kissed the top of her head, and stepped back. "Now you get on," she told her.

Lisbeth watched Mattie's skirts disappear through the back door. After a moment she crossed the room and opened the door to the dim hallway that led to the back staircase. She could no longer see

Mattie, but she heard her steps echoing down the stairs. To calm her nerves she counted—one . . . two . . . three—up to thirteen, until she could no longer hear Mattie descending away from her.

She went over to the window so she could watch what happened next. Two horses were hitched up to a wagon, waiting to go. Father appeared and climbed up to the front. He looked tall and imposing in the driver's seat. Father going on this errand meant it was very important. Mattie perched on the back rail. She looked uncomfortable and gripped tight.

With a jerk the wagon started to move. She waved, but knew that Mattie could not see her. Lisbeth's heart clenched tight. She wanted to run after them, to give Mattie a last hug and tell Father to make sure she was all right. But she didn't. She simply stood there watching as they drove away.

She went to her lessons in the sitting room but had difficulty paying attention to Bible passages and arithmetic tables. After lessons she usually ate her midday meal with Mattie, but today she ate with Mother and Jack. Mother acted as if it were common for her to have dinner with her children, but Lisbeth did not go along with the pretense. She met Mother's inquiries with brief replies and stared obviously out the window looking for Mattie. Jack, on the other hand, happily shared every detail of his day, oblivious to the tension in the room.

While she tried to stomach tasteless barley soup, Lisbeth heard the sound of wheels against gravel. She peered out the window, but she could not get a good view of the road. Mother heard the sound too, but made no mention of it.

From the clamor in the entryway, Lisbeth knew Father was home. But the sound of his footsteps retreating down the hall to the study dashed any hope of news from him. As quickly as possible, Lisbeth finished her meal and went to her rooms to find Mattie.

She did not find her in either her own large room or Mattie's small adjacent one. Although Lisbeth wanted to search for Mattie, she did not. She imagined Mattie was in the kitchen or laundry, and she expected Mattie would be back to get her ready for supper. In the meantime, Lisbeth had to go to her lessons at the Cunninghams' with her mother.

When she set out for the Andersons' Mattie was terrified but didn't show it. Mr. Wainwright said only one thing to her: "Tell them what you know. It will go easier for you . . . and the boy."

As soon as they arrived at the grand plantation, the overseer, a dark-haired White man, led Mattie away. Mr. Wainwright did not come with her. She followed the overseer to an isolated cabin set apart from the quarters. Pointing to a bench outside the lonely hut, the man growled, "I'll deal with you later."

Mattie sat for hours without food or water as the sun rose higher and higher in the sky. Sweat from fear as well as from the heat poured down her back. Her lips moved in a silent litany of prayers: *Dear Lord, it me, Mattie. Please watch over my son and make sure he all right. And, dear Lord, if it not too much, give me the strength to make it through this day.*

In the middle of the day, Mattie saw Mr. Wainwright's carriage drive away. A hot wave of fear washed over her, sucking away her breath. Her hands gripped the bench she sat on. She had been left behind.

The comportment teacher, Miss Taylor, had been educating the daughters of plantation owners along the James River for as long as anyone remembered—she had tutored most ladies under the age of forty. Etiquette, table manners, elocution, and dance were perfected under her tutelage. She transformed young girls, starting at the age of nine, into young ladies in order to facilitate the most advantageous marriages.

Lisbeth's twice-weekly lessons rotated on a monthly basis among the homes of the girls taking them. This gave all the mothers the ability to observe the lessons, see one another's homes, and play hostess for the other women as they waited for their daughters. It also gave them the opportunity to assess their own daughter's standing in relationship to the other girls.

Lessons this month were at White Pines, the largest Tidewater estate east of Richmond. Like the Wainwrights, the Cunninghams had the distinction of being one of the area's older families and also were thought to be the wealthiest. Their daughter, Emma, ten years old like Lisbeth, was preparing for her debut in the same year. But of more interest to the debutante families was Emma's fourteen-year-old brother, Edward. As the eldest son he stood to inherit the entire family estate.

Miss Taylor started lessons with a dinner course to impart table manners and proper use of cutlery. The girls needed to know about all the courses of a meal, so they learned a different course at each lesson. All the girls agreed that the dessert course was their favorite lesson. Soup was the least favorite because there were so many opportunities to warrant a scolding.

Comportment followed the meal portion of the lesson.

"Young ladies may speak to young men about the weather, meals, clothing, and their relatives. Avoid conversation concerning politics, finance, or religion. Though a gentleman may bring up such topics, and a lady must follow where a gentleman leads, a skilled lady will return the conversation to an appropriate topic."

The girls feigned interest as Miss Taylor went on, "When speaking with a lady who is older than you, you must follow her lead. Occasionally, though, you will be required to initiate conversation. Fashion, the weather, and inquiries about relations are always appropriate topics among ladies. Do not allow a gentleman to overhear you speaking about courtship, literature, or politics."

With so many rules about what to say and what not to say, Lisbeth's head spun. Her mind drifted to Mattie as Miss Taylor gave instructions about speaking with elderly men. When they practiced their conversation skills, Lisbeth was paired with Camilla Anderson, who remarked loudly enough for all to hear, "Elizabeth, you must have misunderstood. A lady does not speak about relations with an older gentleman!"

Lisbeth was relieved to move on to dance and away from Camilla.

"Girls, line up across from your dance partner," Miss Taylor commanded. "Today we learn the Virginia reel. As always, begin by honoring your partner."

The "ladies" curtseyed as the "gentlemen" bowed.

"Miss Ford, that was a perfect curtsey. You all would be wise to follow Miss Ford's lead," Miss Taylor said. "Now, repeat after me: forward two steps, back two steps."

The girls chimed, "Forward two steps, back two steps."

"Very good. Begin when I return to one. One, two, three, four. One . . ."

Miss Taylor plodded through the steps. In truth, she danced terribly with little sense of rhythm. But none of the parents cared; she served her purpose well, preparing their daughters for their debuts.

The girls would begin attending dances after their twelfth birthdays. Although eighteen or nineteen was the traditional debutante year—the year courting began in earnest—the early years on the dance circuit allowed the families of eligible young men plenty of time to observe the girls and make a decision about whom to invite into their families. Of course, in such a small community, they had already been speculating for years about potential matches among the Tidewater plantations and which families might look beyond.

Lisbeth felt grateful her dear friend Mary Ford was present at these lessons. Still as cooperative as she was as a young child, Mary paid close attention, so Lisbeth needed only to follow her cues. Although Mary never disrupted class, she happily joined Lisbeth afterward to complain about the arrogant Camilla Anderson or to laugh at the awkward Edith Framington.

"Mary, they took Mattie away today," Lisbeth whispered.

"Who took her? Where?" Mary asked.

"Father took her to the Andersons'. We sold Samuel, Mattie's son, to them, and then he ran. They want her to tell them where he went."

"That explains Camilla's attitude toward you today," Mary said.

"She does not need an excuse to be rude. I wish to know what will happen to Mattie, but I dare not ask. Mother had dinner with us today and did not speak of it at all."

"How long will she be gone?"

"I do not know," Lisbeth complained. "No one has told me anything. I expect she will be home when I need her tonight."

But Mattie was not waiting to dress Lisbeth for supper. Sullen Emily stood ready to assist. With her usual efficiency, Mrs. Gray had ensured that the household continued to function properly, but no one provided answers to a young girl's unspoken questions.

No answers came during supper or in the sitting room after their meal. That night, as Lisbeth stared out the window, she said an extra fervent prayer: "Dear Lord, please watch over Mattie tonight and bring her home soon. And bless Mother, Father, Jack, and Grandmother. Amen."

As the sun descended toward the horizon, long shadows marked the earth like a stain. Just as Mattie felt some relief from the beating of the sun, the overseer came to deal with her.

"In," he said sharply as he pointed to the cabin door beside the bench. Mattie fumbled with the metal latch to open the door. The young overseer did not follow behind, but rather pulled the door firmly closed, leaving Mattie alone in the dark, empty cabin. She heard the sharp echo of metal against wood as the door locked behind her.

This space felt familiar, but somehow wrong. It was constructed like the quarters at Fair Oaks, with walls made from unfinished split logs and a dusty dirt floor. The eight-by-eight-foot-square dwelling was entirely empty, with no window openings. Bits of light shone through the cracks in the boards, illuminating the particles of dust floating like stars in the empty space. The hard-packed dirt floor had a tight, circular path worn in the middle—likely made by the pacing of earlier occupants.

When Mattie's eyes adjusted to the dark, she noticed carvings and dark-brown images on the walls: stick figures, stars, animals, and abstract patterns. Her eyes snaked over a particularly compelling pattern of five circles surrounding a center circle, like a flower. The pattern traveled around the entire room, snaking up and down across the boards. The artist must have taken days to complete it. It was beautiful. She moved closer to examine the image. A slow, painful realization crept over her: it was drawn in blood. Images of cut flesh and severed limbs filled her mind.

Mattie sank down onto the ground, curled up her body, pressed her eyes hard into her knees, and struggled to breathe. She rocked back and forth, mumbling a quiet prayer, asking for strength and faith.

Hours later, in the middle of the night, her dreams were interrupted by the kick of a well-worn black boot.

"Stand up."

The light of the moon came through the open door, throwing the man into silhouette. He towered over her as she struggled to awareness. Before she managed to get herself up, he grabbed her arm and roughly pulled her up.

"Unbutton your dress."

The acrid taste of fear filled Mattie's mouth, a cold sweat sprang from her pores, and her heart pounded so loudly she could hear the swish, swish, swish of her own blood. She willed her arms to move, to do as the man staring at her asked, but they were frozen by her side.

"Do it now!" he raged at her.

Large and imposing, the overseer bored his gaze into Mattie. Reaching toward her neck with shaking hands, she clumsily undid the buttons along her gown. He focused harder as she exposed more of her dark, shiny flesh in the moonlight. She heard the sounds of his deep breath and saw a bulge in his pants.

"Stop!" he yelled suddenly when she reached the button at her navel. "Turn around."

She turned slowly. The instant Mattie faced the wall, the man grabbed the neck of her gown and jerked it off her shoulders. Suddenly he lashed her three times, cutting into the skin at her shoulder blades. She screamed. Her back burned with a pain more intense than she had ever felt.

Tensing her shoulders, she prepared for more blows. Frozen in fear in the dark room, she waited for what would come next. Her ears filled with the frantic beating of her own heart so that no other sounds penetrated. The sweat ran down her back, stinging the freshly made cuts. She took in a shaky breath.

Listening for the sound of his breathing, she willed her heart to slow down so she could hear beyond its pounding. She dared a slight turn of her head. Nothing. She turned her head farther. Nothing. She turned around completely and saw that the room was empty. She was alone. A gasp of relief rushed from her body. She closed her eyes and leaned back against the wall to steady herself. Sharp pain forced her to jerk away. Turning to face the wall, she pressed her forehead against the boards. Tears fell from her eyes.

Mattie wedged herself into a corner of the shanty and leaned forward into the walls. Her mind reeled. He had not even asked her a question. Reaching to her shoulder, she touched the warm moisture on her back with her finger. She scooped up a small pool of blood and examined the crimson drops shimmering on her skin. Then she wiped the blood on the wall. In the dark she could barely make out the mark, but she knew she added her stain to the board. She reached back to get more blood, marking the board again and again. Working fast to complete her undertaking before her blood stopped flowing, she added her name to the wall of pain: *M-A-T-T-I-E.* Then she buried her name under even more blood.

She had found a use for her lettering after all.

Over breakfast the next morning, Lisbeth asked, “Mother, when will Mattie be home?”

Mother replied, “This is nothing you need be concerned about. We are handling this issue.”

“Is she all right?” Lisbeth asked.

“Elizabeth!” Mother scolded. “I told you, you need not be concerned about her.”

“Why did Father take her to the Andersons’?”

“They have questions for her that she needs to answer.”

“Are they hurting her?”

“I am confident your father forbade them from doing any permanent harm.”

Lisbeth looked at her mother in horror. “What do you mean, *permanent*?”

“No more questions, Elizabeth!” Mother commanded. “I know you are fond of Mattie, but that feeling cannot translate into protecting her when she steps out of place. We have been forced into this situation none of us wishes to be in. If she had controlled her son, we would not be having this conversation."

"But how can—"

"Enough, Elizabeth!"

Confused and hurt, Lisbeth sat at the table holding back tears. She did not ask about Mattie again, but she listened attentively for any clues about her. Coming into supper that night, she heard Father telling Mother, "Anderson is reluctant to send her back until she tells them something."

Lisbeth thought he must be talking about Mattie. She did not understand why Mr. Anderson was making decisions about her, but Father did not say any more that night.

Lisbeth's stomach churned in anxiety. It was hard to eat and even harder to sleep. At night she lay in bed wondering when Mattie would ever return and if there was anything she could do or say to help. She prayed for Mattie and hoped that, at least, was doing something for her nurse.

Two days later, in the afternoon, Lisbeth heard a wagon draw up to the back door when she was in the sitting room with Mother. *Please let that be her*, she prayed. Although she wanted to, Lisbeth did not leap up to look out the window. Instead she sat with Mother and worked on her embroidery.

"Elizabeth, the Cunninghams are coming for supper. You will be seated by Edward," Mother explained. "Can you make interesting conversation, please?"

"Certainly," Lisbeth replied.

"They had a trip to Williamsburg recently. You can ask him about that."

"I will," Lisbeth agreed.

"It is not too soon to start making a favorable impression upon his family. Be sure to greet his parents warmly. And after supper you can ask Mrs. Cunningham about her mother. She has been ill. It will show that you are a caring person to make such an inquiry."

Lisbeth nodded. She looked calm on the outside, but inside Lisbeth was anxious to get upstairs.

Mother went on, "After supper you can show Emma some of your clapping games. And this embroidery—that will make a nice impact. Do you agree?"

"I do," Lisbeth said.

Clearly Mother cared about impressing this well-respected family. Lisbeth only cared to find out if Mattie was home. She was relieved when Mother sent her upstairs to get dressed. Wearing a calm mask, she climbed the wide, front stairs and walked down the hallway to her rooms.

Mattie stood by the window. A wave of relief rushed over Lisbeth. Mattie was back, and she looked fine. Maybe a little tired, but nothing dramatic. Mother was right.

"Oh, Mattie! I missed you. I worried so much, but no one told me what became of you," Lisbeth burst out. "Is Samuel home now?" Without waiting for an answer, Lisbeth threw her arms around Mattie in an exuberant embrace. The older woman flinched.

Lisbeth pulled away. "What is the matter? Are you hurt?"

"They gave me some lashin's. It sore," Mattie replied. She moved her body very carefully.

Lisbeth gaped. "But why? How could they?" Mother bragged that they did not whip slaves at Fair Oaks. She stated that only cruel or undisciplined households required the lash. She had told Lisbeth that Mattie would not be hurt.

"We have to tell Mother and Father what they did to you," Lisbeth exclaimed.

"Child, they sure didn' give me these without askin' your father first. I gotta get you ready for supper on time or there gonna be more trouble for me," Mattie said, looking anxious and weary.

"All right, Mattie." Lisbeth knew that despite her outrage, the best way to be helpful was to just do what Mattie asked.

A lavish spread covered the table: veal cutlets with mushroom catsup, beefsteak pie, oyster soup, parsnips, young greens, wine, and apple pudding for dessert. Surrounding the table were the five well-dressed members of the Wainwright household and their four guests: Mr. and Mrs. Cunningham and their children, Edward and Emma.

Edward sat to Lisbeth's left and Emma was across from her next to Jack. Lisbeth meant to make interesting conversation for Edward, as Mother had asked, but she was distracted by the adult conversation.

"Did you get the little darky returned?" asked Mr. Cunningham.

"No. Turns out his buck ran away from Berkeley as well. They may have gotten quite far by now. They had a pass," Father replied.

"Where did they get such a thing?" exclaimed Mrs. Cunningham.

"We do not know," Father replied. "We did not learn anything from Mattie. Looks like some fool is teaching the niggers how to write!"

Fear rushed through Lisbeth. Her heart beat hard. She started to reach for her water, but her fingers shook noticeably. Quickly she hid her hand in her skirt, looking around to see if anyone had noticed her nerves, but no one was paying any attention to her. She could only imagine Father's fury if he learned that she was responsible for Emmanuel and Samuel's escape.

"It is such a shame," Mother broke in. "We made certain he went to a good family and this is what happens. Mr. Anderson will never buy one of our darkies again."

Grandmother Wainwright spoke up, "You know you are too lenient with them. Before you know it we will have lost them all."

"Who have they got looking for them?" asked Mr. Cunningham.

"Ron Reynolds and Geoff Bloom. We want them returned alive."

The word cut through Lisbeth. Alive! Father wanted them back alive. She considered the alternative. Samuel might be dead? Suddenly she understood Mattie's distress. She listened carefully to the adult conversation. Discussions about escaped slaves were as much a part of the ritual of supper as grace, and she generally paid it about the same attention. It had never seemed important before, but this mattered to her.

"Elizabeth," Mother interrupted her train of thought, "I believe you were curious about Edward's travels to Williamsburg."

"Oh, yes." Lisbeth perked up. She interrupted the conversation between Edward and Jack to ask the boy seated next to her, "Edward, did you have a nice visit?"

"It was fine," he said.

"What was the purpose of your trip?" she asked in a cheery voice.

"My aunt lives there." Edward turned back to Jack to resume their discussion about the game of King's Domain they played earlier in the week. Mother made eyes at Lisbeth to indicate she needed to keep making conversation.

"Edward, were you the champion of the game?" Lisbeth asked.

Jack smirked. Edward gave him a look and said, "Yes, I was."

Jack said, "But he cheated."

"It was not cheating," Edward replied. "My foot did not go over the line."

"Albert says it did."

"Well, I say it did not," Edward insisted.

"Perhaps you should have a judge for these sorts of disputes," Lisbeth offered.

Jack said, "Albert Ford was the judge."

"But he was biased in favor of his brother, Robert," Edward said. "He ruled that Robert won the round rather than me, but he was wrong. My foot did not go out. So I stayed in the ring and beat all comers."

Jack shook his head and the pair starting bickering quietly over nonsense that did not include Lisbeth. In order to please her mother, she smiled and nodded to make it look like she was part of their conversation. She was glad when it was finally time to leave the table and her charade could end.

In the middle of the night, Lisbeth woke from a dream in a rush. Father had been pushing a whip into her hand, repeating, "It is for the best. It is for the best. You will see." As she lay in the dark, frightened and alone, her heart beat fast while tears seeped from the edges of her eyes. She was scared all the way through, but she did not know why. Then she did something she had not done for many years. She climbed out of her warm bed and made her way to the small anteroom where Mattie was sleeping.

"Mattie?" Lisbeth whispered as she shivered by the bed.

Half-asleep, Mattie stirred and shifted to make room for Lisbeth. Her arms spread open to allow Lisbeth to snuggle in close.

Lisbeth lay in the dark, held in Mattie's arms. She rubbed the shell necklace in the hollow of Mattie's throat just as she had as a little girl. The warm bed and body enveloped Lisbeth, driving away her demons. The comfort of Mattie worked its magic and lulled Lisbeth to sleep.

CHAPTER 12

The morning after Mattie's return, a disoriented Lisbeth found herself in Mattie's bed, Mattie deeply asleep next to her. Lisbeth gazed intently at the still form. Curled up on her left side, her head wrapped in a cotton scarf, Mattie's cheek rested on the arm protruding from a white gown. Lisbeth laid her pale arm alongside Mattie's dark one. The smooth skin on her young limb was in sharp contrast to the strong muscles, puckered scars, and rough calluses of Mattie's arm. Lisbeth's eyes followed the trail of Mattie's arm up to the white material of her gown bunched up near the shoulder. Spots of dried blood, dark and round, peppered the light fabric. Lisbeth shuddered in fear and anger.

Lisbeth sighed and carefully slipped out of bed. She was accustomed to being woken up by Mattie after a fire had been lit, the warm wash water fetched, and her clothes prepared. But today she decided to let Mattie sleep and take care of these duties for herself.

She passed through the door that led to the back stairs, an unfamiliar passageway, to fetch warmed water from the kitchen. Despite the fear running through her body, she approached Cook, the imposing, stern woman who scared Lisbeth.

"May I have the wash water, please?" Lisbeth requested.

Cook scowled silently at Lisbeth without making a move.

"Mattie is sleeping," Lisbeth explained timidly. "I am fetching the water today."

Cook gave a quick nod and brought Lisbeth a bucket filled with warm water. She patted Lisbeth's hand after she passed over the bucket.

"May I have some salve too?"

After another silent nod, Cook found the pokeweed salve. Tears glistened in her eyes as she handed Lisbeth a remedy of pokeweed and lard.

Lisbeth tiptoed quietly up the creaky stairs, but Mattie was already awake. A tired smile passed over her face when she saw the salve in Lisbeth's hand. Mattie reached out to take it, but Lisbeth shook her head.

"Let me put it on."

Mattie sat on the edge of her bed with her gown around her waist. Tenderly Lisbeth spread the soothing balm on Mattie's wounds. With the index finger of her right hand, Lisbeth slowly traced each mark from top to bottom across Mattie's back: nine neat slices in all, three from each night she had been gone. Despite her care, Lisbeth broke open the scabs in some places. Bright-red blood stood in contrast to the dark-brown crust, pale-white finger, and coffee-brown back. When all the wounds were covered, Lisbeth had blood on her hands. As she stood to examine her work, she wiped it into the fabric of her dress.

CHAPTER 13

Mattie was exhausted. She went about doing her chores as best as she could, but she lagged behind on her duties. Cook, Emily, and the other household workers picked up the slack in the laundry and kitchen. None of them wanted to see Mattie get in more trouble. Lisbeth was kind enough to prepare herself for bed, and in the mornings she often left Mattie to sleep while she fetched wash water, lit the fire, and dressed herself. Mattie was grateful for the support from all of them. She thanked them, but they would not hear of it.

Weeks later Mattie was still tired. She missed her monthly bleeding but thought it was because of the lashings. When she missed it for a second time and her breasts became very tender, she realized she might be carrying a child. She remembered this feeling from years ago when she was growing Samuel. It was early yet. She could end it with pennyroyal. But when she prayed and thought about it, she realized she wanted this child, this piece of

Emmanuel. Mattie wasn't going to give up this new infant. Instead of ending a life, she wanted a whole new one. If this was a baby, and it was born alive, she would take this child to join Samuel and Emmanuel, or die trying.

Mattie kept the idea to herself and waited for bleeding that did not come. Once Mrs. Gray knew she was expecting a baby everything would change quickly. She wanted to enjoy these last few weeks with Lisbeth and get good food for this little one before they sent her back to the fields. She held off saying anything as her body changed shaped and her belly started to protrude. One day Cook gave her tummy a pat and she knew she could not keep her secret any longer. That night, while they were preparing for bed, Mattie looked over at Lisbeth. It was going to be hard to leave her.

She took a deep breath. "I got some news. You know how I been so tired? Well, it 'cause I gonna have a baby."

Lisbeth laughed. "A baby? You're too old!"

"Old?" Mattie exclaimed with feigned outrage. "Thirty ain't so old to be havin' a baby!"

"Do you think it will be a boy or a girl? Too bad Samuel will not get to meet the baby. I shall help you take care of it." Lisbeth smiled.

"Lisbeth, honey, you know it don' work that way." Mattie shook her head. "Ain't no one gonna let me stay in here with a baby of my own."

"Where will you go? Will they sell you?" Lisbeth said, unable to hide the distress in her voice.

"I 'magine they gonna send me back outside."

Fat tears slid down Lisbeth's face. She did not look at Mattie, but gazed instead at her clenched hands. "What will I do? Who will be with me? Who will take care of me?" She looked up at Mattie, saw tears in her nurse's eyes too, and cried harder.

"You gonna be fine, Lisbeth. You can come see me in the evenings. Remember how I always have my mama's love in my heart?

Well, you gonna always have my love in your heart to guide you. You smart and you strong and you have a good heart, Lisbeth. You gonna be all right."

The next morning Mattie told Mrs. Gray about her condition. By noon, Mattie had moved out to the quarters and Emily moved into the room adjacent to Lisbeth's.

At supper, Mother commented on Lisbeth's puffy, red eyes. "Have you been crying, Elizabeth, dear?" she inquired, looking genuinely concerned.

"No, Mother, I'm fine, only tired, that is all," Lisbeth replied politely. She did not tell her mother the truth, because she knew Mother would only chastise her for being too attached to Mattie.

In bed that night, Lisbeth sang herself to sleep.

Go to sleepy, little baby
Go to sleepy, little baby
Everybody's gone in the cotton and the corn
Didn't leave nobody but the baby

In the early evening on Tuesdays and Thursdays, the time tucked between tea and supper, Lisbeth sneaked in visits to Mattie. Like so many aspects of plantation life, these visits were a widely known secret.

On one of these visits, when Mattie's swollen belly looked ripe as a watermelon ready to burst, Mattie asked Lisbeth for a favor.

"I got to pick out a name or the overseer gonna do it. I got it down to a few," Mattie explained, "but I want to know if it gonna be good for the eye as well as for the ear. Can you put them down for me?"

Using the end of a burnt stick, Lisbeth scratched out each one on the hearth: *Matthew*, *Jeremiah*, *Jordan*, *Naomi*, and *Aurelia*.

"Those are all nice names, Mattie."

"I like the look of that letter," Mattie pointed. "What that one called?"

"That is a *J*. This one says Jeremiah. This one is Jordan."

Mattie declared, "That good. Jeremiah if it a boy. Jordan for a girl."

On a clear, crisp November evening in 1847, after a good day of hard labor, Jordan arrived into the world. She was born in Mattie and Poppy's small cabin on the same pallet where Mattie had birthed and suckled Samuel nearly eleven years before. Rebecca caught the infant, cut her cord, and passed her to her mother's eager arms. Mattie's heart opened wider, making room for yet another child to love.

Mattie rested in bed with her daughter cradled in her arms, spent but so satisfied. Jordan latched to Mattie's breast, mastering the skills of sucking and swallowing. Whenever the infant stopped for too long, Mattie tickled her chin to keep her going. Mattie's heart filled with joy as she took in the beauty of this new miracle. A fierce swelling of protection rose in her.

Gazing down at her daughter, she spoke quietly and clearly. "I ain't never gonna let 'em take me away from you. Never. I promise you, I ain't goin' nowhere without you and you ain't goin' nowhere but with me. Soon, baby girl, we joinin' your father and your brother. We gonna be free."

Mrs. Gray came into the breakfast room the next morning with an announcement. "The newest addition to the quarters was born last night."

"Mattie had her baby?" Lisbeth exclaimed. "What name did she choose? Is it a boy or a girl?"

Turning a disdainful gaze to Lisbeth, Mrs. Gray responded laconically, "I do not know."

Lisbeth returned her attention to her soft-boiled egg, hiding the sting of embarrassment and her fury at Mrs. Gray's attitude.

That afternoon Lisbeth ran eagerly to Mattie's cabin. She had a present to bring to Mattie's baby. When she got to the door, standing in the fading sunlight, Lisbeth hesitated to knock. Maybe Mattie did not want to see her. Perhaps they were resting and did not want to be disturbed. Then she heard the infant mewling and Mattie cooing. They were not asleep. Timidly she knocked.

Rebecca opened the door. "Come on in, honey."

Lisbeth hung by the threshold, looking at Mattie and the new baby from across the room.

Rebecca laughed. "You can get closer. She ain't gonna bite ya."

Slowly Lisbeth crossed the room, her eyes never straying from the tiny newborn. Mattie beamed at Lisbeth as the girl grinned in wonder at the small form in Mattie's arms.

"Look at the little fingernails. They are so sweet." Lisbeth pointed. "Is it a girl? Mother did not know."

"Uh-huh," Mattie confirmed.

"Did you pick Jordan for a name?"

Mattie nodded. "I really like the look of that one."

"Hello, Jordan, I am Lisbeth. It is nice to meet you."

"She glad to meet you too." Mattie smiled. "You wanna hold her?"

"Are you sure?" Lisbeth asked with wide eyes and a big grin.

"I trust you, Lisbeth. You gonna take good care of Jordan," Mattie said. "You sit; it easier that way."

Lisbeth set the bundle in her hands on the bed and sat down. Mattie carefully placed Jordan on Lisbeth's lap and showed her how to cradle the baby's head in one arm. She was so warm and light. Lisbeth smiled at Mattie. Lisbeth gently felt the smooth skin on Jordan's hand, and she carefully stroked each tiny nail. "She is so soft."

"Uh-huh. They got special cream in there that keep 'em so soft."

"Look at the present I brought for her," Lisbeth said. "Mother said I may give this to you. It is my first quilt. I made it baby size. It is not very good, but Mother says I am getting better at my stitches."

Mattie unfolded the quilt. "Thank you, Lisbeth." She gave Lisbeth a careful hug with Jordan sandwiched between them; then she spread the quilt over the baby. "I think it beautiful. This gonna keep her nice and warm when it get cold out here. We gonna treasure this for always." Mattie continued, "What fine stitches you made. This some corn?"

"Yes! I wanted you to be able to tell. Mother thought the stitches were too sloppy. It is from the song. You know: 'Everybody's gone in the cotton and the corn,'" Lisbeth sang. "See the cotton? And over here is a shoe. It is the wrong color because I did not have red fabric."

Mattie hummed the familiar lullaby, and Lisbeth joined in with the words:

Your mama's gone away and your daddy's gone to stay
Didn't leave nobody but the baby

Rebecca and Mattie joined in:

Go to sleepy, little baby
Go to sleepy, little baby
Everybody's gone in the cotton and the corn
Didn't leave nobody but the baby

The three of them gathered around the new baby, singing loud and clear to welcome her to their world. Holding this new life, singing with Mattie and Rebecca, Lisbeth felt as if she belonged.

Throughout the winter and into spring, Lisbeth slipped away to visit Mattie and Jordan many times a week. In the afternoon, instead of reading under the willow tree, she headed down to the edge of the fields. There she often found Grandma Washington tending to Jordan while Mattie worked the fields.

Perched on Grandma Washington's lap, Jordan broke out in a grin and reached her arms out eagerly as soon as Lisbeth arrived. Lisbeth beamed back at the child and scooped her up into her arms. She sat down next to the old woman to play with the little baby. Grandma Washington liked to tell tales about her own life to anyone who would listen, and she found a willing audience in Lisbeth. She often repeated the same stories over and over again, but Lisbeth did not tell her that she had heard them before. Lisbeth liked knowing details about the people at her home. Especially from long ago. No one in her own family would tell her anything about the past.

"You know, I so old no one knows when I born, but this weren't a real country yet. I seen a lot over these years. Ever'body call me Grandma Washin'ton, but that only 'cause I take care of the little ones. My children ain't growed up to have children. No. God didn' give me that." The old woman shook her head.

Lisbeth did not have much to say back, but she liked listening and she often asked questions.

"How many children did you have?" Lisbeth asked.

"God gave me three. My first girl, Marie, never had one real breath, but I got a chance ta hold her in my arms and she got a good name. My second girl died from a fever afore she made four.

My William made it to manhood. But he run with his love after he all growed up. He die in the river."

The old woman watched as Lisbeth played patty-cake with Jordan. Jordan reached up to give Lisbeth a hug and rest her head against the young woman's shoulder. The baby patted Lisbeth's back. It was the sweetest feeling ever for Lisbeth. Spending time with Jordan, caring for this little girl, was the best part of her life.

"I declare. I ain't never seen nothin' like that," the old woman said with a shake of her gray-haired head. "A White girl huggin' on and carin' for a Negro baby."

CHAPTER 14

APRIL 1849

Two weeks before Lisbeth's twelfth birthday, she sat with her family in the sitting room after dinner, stitching on her last piece of "practice" work before she began in earnest on her trousseau.

Mother broke the quiet. "Elizabeth, I have news. We know the date of your first dance. The Parkers have announced they will be hosting at Willowbrook on the first of May."

Lisbeth blurted out, "We only have a month to prepare. What shall I wear? Mother, I am so nervous!"

"Do not be silly, Elizabeth," Mother said without looking up from her embroidery. "You are well prepared to do what is expected of you. Your father and I are counting on you to make a marvelous impression. As for your dress, I have arranged for the seamstress to come here tomorrow to take measurements. Be prepared to choose a fabric and style."

"Mother, can Mattie come in to dress me?" Lisbeth asked cautiously.

"Elizabeth, it is sweet that you are still so attached to Mattie, but Emily will make you presentable for the dance. You were fortunate to have your mammy until you were so old. Most of us give up our nurses long before you did. Why, I was only four years old when my nurse was sold." Mother went on, "Mattie is like your old baby quilt: she was important to you when you were little, but you have outgrown her now. I hope we did not make a mistake in letting her stay with you so long."

Lisbeth wanted to impress her mother and behave like a young lady. She also did not want her mother to forbid her to visit Mattie, so she said, "No, Mother. I understand. What color do you think I should wear?"

"Deep blue is my first choice, if the seamstress has one in the right fabric. Such an elegant color will accentuate your eyes and make your skin appear to be fair. I can tell you have not been wearing your hat when you go out of doors."

"I will now. I promise. I want to be as beautiful as I can for the dance."

Mother corrected her, "Focus on bearing, and beauty will follow. Your looks will not remain with you for life. But your bearing will go with you to the grave, Elizabeth."

"Yes, Mother," Lisbeth agreed with her mouth but not in her heart. She very much wanted to be beautiful.

The seamstress carried a red-and-beige carpetbag bulging with swatches of fabric and patterns of dresses into the sitting room. Lisbeth watched eagerly as she pulled out small rectangles of material and sorted them by material and color. Bright blues followed paler blues that transformed into deep and pale greens, then reds, yellows, and finally, boring white, black, and brown. Lisbeth yearned to touch the smooth silks, but did not dare take such a liberty.

Mother had no such hesitation and fingered each of the fabrics in turn, inquiring about the cost and content when she found one she might choose.

"Printed cotton is quite in style for the young ones this year," the seamstress informed them. "These are twenty-four cents a yard, and these are twenty-eight cents per yard."

"They are lovely, but I prefer something more elegant for Elizabeth. Have you taken the order for Camilla Anderson?" asked Mother.

"Yes. They chose this silk chiffon in a pale yellow." The seamstress pointed out the fabric.

Mother fingered it idly. "How much is the silk?"

"The domestic chiffon is eighty-eight cents and the imported is one dollar per yard."

"This is terribly thin. She would have to be very careful not to tear it. Elizabeth, can you manage that?"

"Absolutely, Mother. It is very lovely," Lisbeth enthused. "I would be very happy in a gown from this material."

The seamstress suggested, "This taffeta is heavier and only slightly more expensive than the domestic chiffon at ninety-two cents per yard."

Lisbeth reached out to touch the material. "Oh, Mother, this is so lovely!" Lisbeth dared not say more. She watched as Mother made social as well as financial calculations.

The seamstress broke the silence. "If you prefer, this linen, which has a heavy texture and will wear well, is fifty-five cents a yard. However, your color choices will be limited."

"No. We shall go with the silk taffeta. In the deep blue, I believe. What do you think, Elizabeth?"

"Oh, thank you, Mother!" Lisbeth beamed. "Yes, I am very fond of the blue. I promise I shall take very good care of it."

Mother smiled in approval at Lisbeth. "Show me your patterns," she instructed the seamstress.

"This is the one the Andersons chose," the woman explained, pulling out a drawing. The fabric puffed out over a full-length hoop skirt. The hem of the gown gathered into a series of scalloped rows tied by large bows.

"No. That is too frilly," Mother declared. "I want something more elegant. What did the Cunninghams choose for Emma?"

"I will be taking their order tomorrow."

"That is unfortunate," Mother murmured under her breath.

Mother sorted through the patterns. All the gowns had fashionable hoop skirts and tight bodices. She rejected any dresses with long sleeves and high necklines as unsuitable for an evening event.

"Elizabeth, do you care for either of these?" Mother asked, holding out two drawings.

"I like them both. But this one is lovelier, in my opinion." Lisbeth pointed to the pattern with a single row of shallow scallops across the bottom.

"That is fine," Mother agreed. "We will have this one, with the light-blue silk chiffon as the underskirt. If Emma Cunningham's dress will take away from or conflict with Elizabeth's, please let me know and we will revise our order."

"Of course, ma'am. I will inform you right away if that is the case," promised the seamstress.

Lisbeth slowly reached out a hand to lovingly stroke the blue silk taffeta. It was soft and smooth, so beautiful. "This is so lovely! I am very excited. Thank you, Mother!"

"I trust you will make us proud, Elizabeth. We are going to quite an expense so that you may make a good first impression."

"I will, Mother. I will make you so very proud of me."

Lisbeth burst into Mattie's cabin, too excited to contain herself. After settling into a chair with Jordan on her lap, she spoke in a rush. "Mattie, my first dance will be in three weeks. I am frightened. Mother says I am prepared, but I am still nervous. We have asked the seamstress to make a gown in deep blue. It is almost exactly the shade of my eyes. I hope I will look beautiful. Mother says beauty is not as important as bearing, but I so want to be beautiful.

"Mother says we will not know the song list until the week before. And even then they may change it. I must be prepared for anything. Oh, I shall die if they play a Cumberland reel. I am not so good at the Cumberland. But a waltz or the Virginia reel—those I can do very well. So Mary tells me.

"How do you think I should wear my hair? It cannot be all the way up because I have not had my debut yet—not until I am nineteen, as you know, but still I want it to be elegant. I am trying to decide between sweeping up the front and pulling it all back, or simply pulling back the sides. What do you think, Mattie? Do I look better like this . . . or like this . . . ?"

Mattie replied gruffly, "I don' care how you do your hair, Lisbeth. It just fine either way."

Shocked at Mattie's callousness, Lisbeth exclaimed, "How can you say that? This dance is extremely important. Mother says your first dance sets the stage for the rest of your life. It has to be perfect. My entire future depends upon it."

Mattie sighed. "Ain't nothin' ever perfect, and it hard to believe one dance can change your life."

"Well, it is important. You do not care, do you? How can you be so selfish?"

"Lisbeth, I just worked from sunup to sundown in the fields after bein' up all night with Jordan. Jordan weak from havin' the runs for five days. Wanna know what I care about? I care about my daughter gettin' better."

Lisbeth rolled her eyes. "Then give her some salt water with sugar like you served me when I was ill. She will become better soon enough."

"I ain't got no salt and I ain't got no sugar. How I gonna give my daughter what I don' got?" Mattie stared at Lisbeth.

"Oh," said Lisbeth, instantly deflated. Then, for the first time since walking in the door, she looked carefully at the child resting against her body. Through the dusky light, Lisbeth made out dark circles under the little girl's sunken eyes. Jordan was nearly motionless. The girl was extremely ill and Lisbeth had not noticed. She felt deeply ashamed.

"Oh, Mattie, I am sorry," the young woman said. "Cook will give me sugar and salt if I tell her I have the runs. I shall bring some of each to you."

True to her word, Lisbeth lied to the cook and then sneaked down the rear stairs to deliver the elixir that Jordan desperately needed.

The night after the dance, Lisbeth went to tell Mattie all about it. When she got to her cabin she first asked, "How is Jordan, Mattie?"

"As you can see for yourself . . . she doing just fine now. Thank you for checkin'."

"And you, Mattie? Are you fine too?"

"Yes, hon. I just fine. Whatever Jordan had ain't got to me. How was the dance?" Mattie asked.

"Oh, Mattie, the evening was simply awful," Lisbeth reported. "I cannot believe I have wanted to attend those dances for years. I hated it. Camilla Anderson is no lady, I tell you. She gave me cruel looks from the moment I walked into Willowbrook. I think she still holds it against us because Samuel ran away. I do not blame him one bit. They must be an awful family to have such a daughter.

"First I danced with Matthew Johnson. Matthew behaved very kindly and gentlemanly throughout the entire dance. It was a waltz, so I know I did not embarrass myself. He and I can talk so easily. The time just flew by."

"Well, that sound nice. Me and Emmanuel met at a dance," Mattie said.

"That dance with Matthew was the best part of the evening. If I could have only danced with him the whole night, it would have been much more enjoyable," Lisbeth said. "Matthew has lovely hazel-green eyes, but Mother says I need not concern myself with Matthew's eyes. His family has only ten acres and three slaves. Mother says they are 'not in our league and are practically abolitionists,' although she thought it fine for me to dance with him once as a kindness. As she likes to say, 'it is always proper to show generosity to our inferiors.' I am glad that I shall be allowed to dance with him on occasion, because truly he is the most pleasant dance partner."

Mattie passed Jordan into Lisbeth's arms. Lisbeth sat down with the toddler. She bounced the little girl on her lap as she spoke.

"Next I danced with Nathaniel Jackson, who has horrid breath. I turned my head to avoid the stench. You can imagine how difficult it is to dance whilst trying to avoid inhaling. After Nathaniel, I was partnered with William Anderson, Camilla's brother, who could not dance at all, I tell you. He pulled me entirely too close and stepped on my toes on more than one occasion. As a lady, I had to pretend not to notice. It is difficult to stay quiet with a smile on your face when a large, clumsy buffoon smashes your foot. But I behaved as a lady should."

"Good for you, Lisbeth." Mattie moved through the small room, folding and sorting her belongings while Lisbeth talked.

"My last dance, the Virginia reel, which was not meant to be my last, started with Robert Ford, Mary's brother. He is entertaining. Robert is very accomplished in mimicking the adults. He did a perfect Mr. Anderson, which made me laugh out loud, but I do not think he was bothered. In fact, I think he was pleased I found him so amusing."

"You think he be bothered if'n you laugh?" Mattie asked, surprise written all over her face.

"Mother says I am not to laugh out loud with young men." Lisbeth shrugged.

Mattie scoffed, "That sound like a foolish rule to me. How ya gonna know if you like being with a man if ya can' laugh together?"

"I do not think my liking him matters to my parents," Lisbeth explained. "After dancing with Robert I was waiting for my next dance when Camilla pretended to trip, spilling her glass of punch as well as mine all over my gorgeous blue gown. It was so beautiful. And if I do say so myself, I looked lovely in it. But now it is ruined due to Camilla's cruelty—though Mother says we may get it dyed so I might use it again. I am certain that Camilla did not want me to dance with Edward Cunningham. She already had her dance with him. I do not think she wanted me, or anyone else, to have time with him. Mother says he is going to make the best marriage in the valley. After the incident he attended to me, which I believe made Camilla even more cross. But he did not dare to dance with me so as to not ruin his suit. Instead we sat together, but I was so furious I could not steer the conversation in an amusing or delightful direction."

The young woman asked, "Mattie, do you think I have ruined my chance at the best marriage on the river?"

"Lisbeth, I can' say much 'bout marriage. But I know a good man make life more sweet. Someone to hold you and love you, someone to share your dreams with, someone kind and thoughtful. A good man's a treasure."

"Oh, Mattie, I am sorry. I am being thoughtless again. You must miss Emmanuel very much. It has been two years since he left. Do you think about him and Samuel often?"

"Ev'ry day," Mattie replied. "I pray to God for them ev'ry day."

Tentatively Lisbeth asked, "Have you heard from them at all? Do you know if they are safe?"

Mattie shook her head. "Miss Lisbeth, you know I can' answer such a question. They in God's hands; just leave it at that. You don' want to be knowin' any more. It ain't safe for neither of us to know more'n that." Mattie paused. She looked at Lisbeth carefully, like she wanted to say more. She sighed, shook her head, and went on, "'Nuff about that. Tell me more about the dance. You say you had no fun except with that Matthew? What about Mary?"

"Mother allowed no talk with Mary at all! She ordered me to fetch tea and food to all the old ladies, except for during my times to dance. Then I was to be on the floor for everyone to watch. It was awful having all those eyes on me, waiting for me to make a mistake. I cannot believe I have to do this for years to come."

"You can always say no to the dances," Mattie said.

"Oh, no, I cannot!" Lisbeth said emphatically. "Father and Mother will not let me forgo a season. They have been preparing me for this for years. I shall be fortunate if they allow me to miss some of the dances at lesser estates."

Mattie walked over to the pallet and sat close to Lisbeth. She put her arm around the girl who was on the verge of womanhood. "Lisbeth, it gonna be hard, but you have to find a way to follow your own heart, even if it not what your parents want."

Lisbeth did not really understand what Mattie was trying to tell her. But it was nice to sit close to her with Jordan on her lap. When it was time to part, they had a long hug. Lisbeth did not know why Mattie was extrasweet tonight, but she did not mind it. Being held in Mattie's arms for a good-night hug, she felt little and safe again.

CHAPTER 15

Late that night Mattie sat on her bed with her mind racing, going over every last detail. Jordan, drugged with valerian root, slept soundly next to her. Dried meat and a bladder of water were packed away with other essentials in an old burlap seed sack tied shut with heavy twine. Stolen boots sat under the cot, waiting for Mattie to fit her feet into them and escape. Only three things were left to do: pray to God, say her good-byes, and head out. This night would change her life forever.

"Dear God, please watch over us tonight. Keep us safe and guide us to freedom. I promise once we there we gonna help other folks get they freedom too. Thank you, Lord. Amen."

Her grandfather tied Jordan tightly against Mattie's torso with a heavy cloth.

Poppy whispered, "You go hard, girl, and don' look back. You strong; you can do this. Emmanuel got you a good home in Ohio. You gonna make it." His voice broke, but he looked straight into her eyes. "I don' ever want to see you again, you hear me? You gonna be free. Your family the first ones of us that got away. You makin' me proud."

Blinking the tears from her eyes, Mattie gave him a hug to last a lifetime and left. Quietly making her way to Rebecca's cabin, she worked the latch without knocking and slowly opened the creaky door. Rebecca was sitting up, waiting for Mattie.

"I gonna miss you so much," Mattie said. "You gotta come someday. All of you."

Tears streamed down her cheeks as Rebecca whispered, "Mattie, I ain't got it in me, but you do. You gonna make it. Here you go."

Rebecca handed Mattie traveling papers written in Sarah's distinctive handwriting. Mattie had given up a portion of her rations for six months to trade for the paper and ink necessary to create this ticket to freedom. They declared that "the bearer of these papers, Georgia Freedman, a free African, is traveling to Clarksburg, Virginia, to visit her kin." Mattie folded the forged document carefully and squirreled it in the bodice of her dress.

"Can you do somethin' for me?" Mattie asked as she pulled a black string out of her bodice. On the end dangled one of the shells from her necklace. "Give this to Lisbeth, okay?" Mattie whispered. "She ain't gonna understand why I gotta leave her. You help her, 'kay?" Mattie's tears flowed freely.

The two women embraced tightly. Rebecca whispered into Mattie's ear, "I gonna pray for you every night. For always." As they pulled apart, she looked intently at Mattie and spoke emphatically, "You get word to us you made it, promise?"

"Promise," Mattie confirmed. "Good-bye."

"Bye."

Mattie paused after she closed the door. She looked up at Lisbeth's window. "Good-bye, sweet girl," she whispered. "You smart and strong and you got a good heart. You stay one of the good ones."

Then Mattie journeyed away from her home toward freedom and her family, leaving behind the bones of generations of her ancestors and their captors.

—

Stumbling west through the underbrush in the forest, Mattie made it to Herring Creek in two hours. The heavy boots protected her feet as she waded through the stream for a mile before getting out on the western bank, but soon she felt blisters rise on her heels and ankles. Ignoring the pain, she trudged through a forest of cedars, cottonwoods, and river birches for another mile, then backtracked to the stream, headed two miles north, then west in a crooked path through the dense forest until sunrise. After climbing into the branches of a sycamore tree, she untied Jordan from her back and breastfed her before dosing her again with valerian root . . . and then she waited. Waiting was a hard but very essential part of this journey. Silently Mattie sang and prayed, and imagined. She pictured herself holding Samuel. She thought of the home Emmanuel had waiting. She practiced introducing Jordan to her father and brother. She did everything but think about getting caught. And when images of being captured intruded upon her mind, she quickly pushed them away.

—

That afternoon Lisbeth ventured down to the fields to visit with Jordan, but the baby wasn't with Grandma Washington. "She ain't been here all day," the old woman informed Lisbeth. "Don' know why. Go looky in their cabin. Maybe she sick."

Lisbeth trotted up the dirt path to Mattie's cabin, but it was empty. She resisted rushing down to the fields to check for them. Mattie would get in trouble if Lisbeth bothered her while she was working the fields. Instead she waited on the benches in the back. She stared up at the back of her home and tried to see inside, but the windows reflected all light. Patiently she waited for Mattie and Jordan. Soon folks started returning from the fields, and Lisbeth went to the front of the cabin to look for Mattie. She didn't see her, but she recognized Rebecca's distinctive limp far down the path. She walked over to Rebecca's cabin, where she was waiting when the other woman came near.

Rebecca stopped walking the instant she saw Lisbeth standing by her door. Staring at the young mistress, she shook her head. "Didn' expect you so soon," she said. "Come on in. I got somethin' for you." Rebecca's eyes were moist, and tension filled her shoulders as they entered her home. Lisbeth thought it was strange that she closed the door tightly. In a hoarse voice Rebecca whispered into the girl's ear, "Lisbeth, Mattie left this for you." Pulling a single shell on a string from her pocket, she uncurled Lisbeth's fingers and placed it in her hand.

Lisbeth felt the shell and knew at once. A chill traveled down her spine. "Where is Mattie?" Lisbeth screeched. "Where is Jordan?"

"Shh!" Rebecca rebuked. "Honey, they gone. Mattie gone to be with Emmanuel and Samuel."

Blinking, Lisbeth tried to comprehend Rebecca's words. A sharp arrow stabbed through her heart. "But . . . ? Where . . . ? Why . . . ?"

Rebecca's deep-brown eyes mirrored the panic and confusion Lisbeth felt. "Mattie trusts you. No one know she gone," she whispered fiercely. "Don' go tellin' no one, promise?"

"Where did they go? Will they be all right? Will we ever see them again?"

Rebecca shrugged. “They in God’s hands now. Mattie strong and smart. If anyone gonna make it, she gonna. I pray we ain’t gonna see them again. She be in big trouble if she caught.”

“But . . . but . . . how could . . . ? Where did . . . ?”

Rebecca shook her head. “There nothing else for me to tell you. You gotta keep this quiet. Promise?”

Lisbeth agreed before she flew out of Rebecca’s cabin. She ran and ran, fast and far, running past the fields along the bank of the river until she collapsed in a heap on the ground. Her body heaved with sobs, and tears streamed down her face. They were gone. Just gone. How could Mattie leave her? She did not even say good-bye!

Lisbeth clutched the shell tight in her hand. In a fury she flung it into the tall grass. Her eyes followed the arc of the shell. The moment it left her hand, regret flooded through her. She crawled after it, into the grass. Desperately she pushed aside the green stems as tears poured from her eyes. Sharp blades cut her hands until they bled. Her fingers became red and swollen from combing through the grass.

After nearly an hour, long after her tears had dried up, she found it. Relieved, she collapsed to the ground and clutched the shell and string to her chest. Then she ran inside to get ready for supper before her parents realized she was missing too.

Supper was excruciating for Lisbeth. Neither Mother nor Father spoke of any runaways.

“Elizabeth, why are you so quiet this evening?” Mother asked.

“I have a headache.”

“I am afraid you must be getting ill.”

Lisbeth nodded rather than tell Mother she had been crying all afternoon.

Father said, "You may go to bed rather than come to the sitting room if you prefer."

"Thank you. I think that would be for the best," Lisbeth replied. She was relieved that she wouldn't have to keep pretending.

Kneeling by her bed for her nightly prayers, Lisbeth whispered to God, "Please, God, make Mattie change her mind and return. No one knows she is gone yet, so she would not be in trouble. Tell her I want her back. Amen. Oh, and bless Mattie, Jordan, Mother, Father, Grandmother, and Jack. Amen."

Lying in bed, her head on her soft pillow, Lisbeth clutched the shell necklace tightly in her right hand. She quietly sang to herself, "*Go to sleepy, little baby, go to sleepy, little baby,*" as she drifted off to sleep.

The next morning she sat in the rocker and gazed out the window, hoping desperately that Mattie had returned in the night. When the door to Mattie's cabin opened, Lisbeth stood to get a better view. Poppy came out all alone, looking more stooped than ever as he made his way to his work. No Mattie. No Jordan.

In the breakfast room Mother spoke privately to Lisbeth. "Elizabeth, I have sad news."

"What is it?" Lisbeth asked nervously, extremely conscious of the shell necklace in her pocket.

"Mattie is missing. We fear she has run away. I do not know what she is thinking, taking that baby away from her safe home to go into the woods and heaven knows where. Your father is confident she will be found, but we thought you should know. I know you are quite fond of her. However, it shows you what I have explained before: you cannot trust any of them, no matter how well you think you may know them."

"Yes, Mother," Lisbeth said, pretending to agree. "Thank you for telling me." Lisbeth kept her voice as neutral as possible. "I will pray for them."

"Yes, we must all pray for their return."

—

Mattie and Jordan made the slow trek north and west. By night Mattie walked; by day she hid in trees, bushes, caves—any shelter where she could imagine they were safe. Mattie's dried meat and hardtack ran out after five days, so she foraged bits of food from the forest—elderberries, gooseberries, pawpaws, black walnuts. It was just enough to keep up her milk for Jordan.

After seven days she came upon a dirt road in the midst of the trees. Using the stars as a guide, she followed the road north, staying hidden in the brush, until she came to an intersection. Though it was the middle of the night, she moved more deeply into the forest searching for a cave marked by a faint charcoal star. After finding it, she settled in and waited for what was to come next.

CHAPTER 16

Lisbeth went through each day in a fog. It was hard to concentrate on her studies. At dance lessons she acted terribly, even to Mary. She was disoriented without the anchor in her life. Each morning and evening she stared out the window, looking for a sign of her Mattie and her Jordan. Desperate for news that they were safe, she sought out Rebecca.

"Rebecca, you will tell me if you hear from Mattie?" Lisbeth implored.

"If we hear they safe it not gonna be for a long, long time," Rebecca explained. "If they caught and brought back, you probably gonna know as soon as I do."

Hope rustled in Lisbeth's heart. "Do you think it is possible they will come back?"

"If that happen, they gonna be paraded in front of ever'one before they sold south."

"Sold?!" Lisbeth exclaimed.

"Yeah, sold. To Alabama or Georgia. She ain't gonna get a second chance." Rebecca's voice caught. "They gone from here for good."

"No, that's not true!" Lisbeth insisted. "I will ask Mother and Father. I can get Mattie to promise to never leave again. They will believe me!"

Rebecca shook her head in disbelief, but did not argue with the young mistress of the plantation.

Before the sun had fully risen, Mattie heard the low cry of an owl. She returned the call. It came back doubled. She responded in kind. After the third call, she came out of her cave to look at the road. A tired old horse, hardly more than skin and bones, with open sores showing through its dirty white hair, was harnessed to a creaky wagon. Driving the hay-filled wagon was a middle-aged White man. Small, with narrow eyes and pockmarked skin, he did not look at Mattie as she and Jordan emerged from the forest.

"Hello, I—" Mattie began.

"Don't need to know who you are. Just give me your papers and climb in."

"Yes, sir," Mattie replied. She had no choice but to trust this man, though he wasn't giving her much reason to. She followed his directions and climbed into the back of the wagon. They drove west down the road in utter silence.

Hours later, when the sun was low in the horizon, the driver turned around and spoke in a loud whisper, "Here come some folks." He sounded scared.

Quickly Mattie dug a hollow in the straw. She placed her drugged child in it and covered Jordan over with hay until she could not be seen at all. Mattie lay down against the hay, but she was not entirely hidden. Her heart beat hard as she listened to the sounds of hooves echoing closer, closer, closer. Then the sound passed and Mattie breathed a sigh of relief. She turned her head for a peek. The horsemen doubled back. They were coming right toward her. She tried to make herself small as they passed, but she knew they had seen her.

"Whoa," cried the driver.

The men on horseback had blocked the way forward.

"Looky, looky, looky! What do we have here?" exclaimed the larger, mustached man on the left. "Looks like you be transporting a nigger along with your hay."

Wiping sweat from his red brow, the driver nervously responded, "I don't want no trouble. I got her papers right here. She paid me good money. I ain't looking for no trouble. Just making an honest dollar."

Bile rose in Mattie's throat. She could hardly breathe for fear of what these men could do to her and Jordan.

"Well, I'm the local law, and my job is to make sure everything is legal," replied the sheriff. "Let me jus' take a look at those papers."

After examining the papers carefully, he rode over to Mattie. "Hey, Vern," he shouted to his deputy, "you got that list of runaways? Let's see if she matches any of 'em."

The deputy dug the list out of his bag. "Looks like only two women are taking their chances: Mattie Wainwright and Rose Cuthbert. Can you imagine, Vern? A nigger named Rose? Hah!" Turning to Mattie, he yelled, "Get your ass out of that wagon."

"Yes, sir."

Clammy with sweat and visibly shaking all over, Mattie turned around to climb down from the wagon. With her back to the authorities, she slipped some wild ipecac plant into her mouth and swallowed it.

The sheriff dismounted his horse. He came close, flicked his gaze up and down Mattie's body, and drawled out, "Do you fancy yourself a Rose? No, I guess not; you're too old to be her. But

Miissss Maaattie—now, that might be you." Moving in so close that flecks of his spit hit Mattie, he went on, "Says here this Mattie has herself a pickaninny, but I suppose you might have killed it just so's you could get clean away. Ain't that right? No telling what a nigger will do to her own young. Don't have the same motherly feelings as a lady, now, do you?"

Mattie stared intently at the ground. She did not move a muscle or do anything to antagonize this man.

To his mate, he asked, "What do you think, Vern? Do you think"—he looked at the papers the driver had given him—"that 'Georgia Freedman' is Mattie Wainwright? Let's take a closer look." Back in Mattie's face, he asked, "What brings a free nigger to these parts?"

"My mama been sick, sir. I went to visit afore she dies. She gots the ague," Mattie barely stammered out through a dry mouth.

"Well, ain't that sweet," he replied, a smirk on his face, his voice dripping with sarcasm. "You wanted to see your mama afore she dies."

Vern broke in, "She don't look so good herself, Lucas. I'd stand away if I were you."

"She just scared of getting her neck in a noose." He stuck his tongue out, disdain in his eyes, as he mimicked being hanged.

Mattie shook hard and suddenly heaved as the ipecac took effect. In an instant, a gush of vomit erupted from the depth of her stomach. The men jumped back, disgust on both faces. A horrid stench rose up. Mattie fell to her knees in front of the law officers, expelling the limited contents of her stomach. Vern gagged. Continuing to retch, Mattie emptied her stomach of its bile. With nothing left to vomit, dry heaves violently racked her body.

Rushing to the side of the road, Vern leaned over the grass to throw up.

"You are both disgusting. Looks like maybe you got the ague too," Sheriff Lucas declared, staring down at Mattie with no compassion in his eyes. To the driver he declared, "I reckon you should just leave her here. Don't want a dead nigger on your hands, now, do you?"

"No, sir."

"Okay, then, get on. We gonna take care of her."

"Yes, sir," the driver replied, signaling his horse to move on.

Horrified, Mattie watched as the wagon drove away with Jordan. Shivering and sweaty, she held back screams of protest. Instead she lay curled in a ball while tears of frustration and fear seeped from the corners of her eyes.

Vern returned to peer down at Mattie. Specks of vomit mottled her dress, her skin glistened with moisture, and she shook hard all over like she had a fever. Vern asked, "What we gonna do with her? No reward is worth touching that for! I ain't gonna ride with her on my horse. Suppose she ain't even that Mattie?"

"We ain't gonna touch her, fool." Scorn was in the sheriff's voice. "We just gonna leave her here to die. If she's a free nigger, we don't want her thinking she can just come and go from Cumberland County as she pleases. If she's a runaway, she gonna get hung anyway. No need for us to take a chance on getting the ague taking her anywheres else. Let's go."

They mounted up and rode off, taking Mattie's travel papers and leaving her huddled on the dirt road.

With the sun behind the horizon, dusk soon turned into complete darkness. Mattie wanted to move, willed her body to crawl down the road toward her daughter, but she could not. Every ounce of energy had drained from her body. She lay there, sick and helpless. Entirely spent, she was too weak even to shoo the flies off her gown. She feared she might fulfill the sheriff's desire and die in the night.

But she had the strength to pray. *Dear God, I sorry I runned. I shoulda stayed home, but I only wanted to see my son. I want my baby safe. Please, God. Let me see my baby again. She need me, God. You know she does. Please, God, have mercy on her. Have mercy on me.*

Shivering, parched, and fevered, Mattie prayed, dozed, and dreamed of her daughter through the long night. Screams. Desperate toddler cries of "Mama, Mama, Mama" filled Mattie's dream world. Tears streamed from her closed eyes. She woke with a start, rubbed the moisture from her eyes, the dream still so present she heard the echo of faint cries.

In the pitch-black, nearly moonless night, Mattie heard the faint crunch of wagon wheels. "Please, God, let him be coming for me. Please, Lord. Please, Lord. Please, Lord," she begged.

Mattie listened hard. This was not a dream. Sounds from a wagon drew louder. "Please let it be him, Lord. Let it be him with my Jordan."

She stared hard at the darkness until she made out first the old horse and then the familiar face of the driver. He had come back. The driver steered the horse past her, bringing the rear of the wagon next to her.

The man flew over to Mattie. "Are you all right? I hated to leave you, but I had to go. I couldn't take the chance."

"My baby!" Mattie croaked out weakly.

"I left her at the next house. She cried too loud when she woke up. Are you all right?"

"I all right now that you back. I ate some poison plants. I figured they gonna leave me alone if I got sick all over. I didn' count on them sendin' you away too."

Mattie tried to sit up, but her body shook too hard and her arms did not support her weight. Tenderly the driver helped her up and into the wagon.

Before the sun rose again, the man turned into a small, well-kept farm. He pulled behind the white clapboard house and came to a stop by a door in the earth that led to a cellar. Pointing to the door in the ground, he said, "You wait in there till someone else comes for you."

Mattie replied, "Thank you. I don' even know your name . . ."

"Better that way. Keeps us all safer. Best of luck to you and your little girl. God bless you."

"God bless you, sir."

Mattie's weak arm shook as she pulled open the whitewashed door. Jordan stood frozen in the center of a damp, dark cellar.

She was alone. She looked awful. Terror shone in her deep-brown eyes, and her face glistened with a thick coat of mucus, sweat, and tears. Her small body shook violently.

Mattie squeaked out to her daughter, "Mama's right here, baby girl. I back. You all right now."

Still weak from the ipecac, Mattie cautiously climbed down the steep staircase. As soon as Mattie got into the cellar, Jordan threw her body against Mattie's legs, shaking uncontrollably and gasping for breath. Desperately she clung to Mattie, burying her face into her chest, whimpering in a hoarse voice, "Mama, Mama, Mama."

Mattie held Jordan as tight as a clamp, tears streaming down her face. "Sorry, baby. I so sorry. You musta been so scared. So sorry. I jus' had to do it. We gonna be free. We are. And it gonna be worth it. It gonna be worth it. Someday, it gonna be worth all this."

Jordan clung tightly to her mother through the entire night.

Mattie and Jordan stayed in the small, dark quarters alone for two days. Hardtack, boiled eggs, and water, delivered in the dead of the night, sat inside the door each morning when they awoke. Then, in the middle of the third night, the door opened. A man beckoned them out and directed them to lie down in a wagon. He covered them with a canvas sheet.

They arrived at a new farm just as the sun rose. Before the door to this new cellar closed, Mattie caught a glimpse of the four figures in the cramped room: a bone-thin young woman; a boy who looked to be about six years old or so; a tall, dark man missing his left ear; and a woman so old she had only one skinny tooth left sticking up from her bottom jaw. Mattie did not learn their names, and the man glared her into silence when she started to tell him hers.

The skinny young woman, not once looking at either Mattie or Jordan, occupied herself by biting tiny bits of her fingernails over and over, spitting the small fragments onto the dirt floor. The frail woman hummed lullabies until the man told her to "Hush up!" in a fierce whisper. Every few minutes she would begin humming again, and he would repeat the hushing. The boy, cowering in the corner, watched it all in silence.

In the middle of the night, Mattie awoke to the screams of the old woman. "They gonna get me! They gonna get me!" she cried out as she clawed at the closed door.

"Shut up, old woman!" roared the man before slapping her hard to the ground. He towered over the nail biter. "We got to bring her, you say!" he yelled. "I ain't going without her, you say! I shoulda left you all behind! We all gonna get caught 'cause of her. She gonna get me killed with all her carrying on. Don' she know we got to be quiet?"

He paced in circles like a caged jaguar, mumbling to himself, "Gonna get me killed. We in danger. This the real thing. I the one they gonna kill. You all only gonna lose an ear or get a whippin' or get sold to Alabama, but me, they gonna kill me. They gonna kill me! But before they do they gonna chop off my balls and shove 'em down my throat. I shoulda left you all."

Wedged into their own corner, Mattie clutched Jordan close, silently watching the drama.

Food appeared at irregular intervals, as did other escapees. No words were exchanged among any of the strangers. On the third night, the cellar dwellers continued on their journey to the next safe house. They stayed there for only one day before they moved on to the next station. Weeks passed with the group traveling most nights and hiding during the day in a cellar, basement, or attic. Each night Mattie closed her prayers with a request that the old woman sleep through the night. Occasionally God obliged.

One night, while they were being transported by wagon, the driver woke his passengers. They quickly came to attention, ready to take flight if necessary. As they rolled along the driver pointed and said, "Up ahead. It's the Ohio River. You cross and you in a free state."

They stared ahead, barely making out the dark snake of river in the black night. When they pulled up to the water's edge, Mattie could not believe its size. She had never seen such a river before. It was wide and foreboding, ready to swallow them up.

The driver signaled, and a man dragged a small boat from the bushes by the water. They climbed down from the wagon and organized into groups for the crossing. Mattie and Jordan were to go with the first group of three. Shivering mostly with fear, Mattie eyed the vessel that would take her to the other side. She had never been in a boat before, and she had no idea how to swim. If she or Jordan fell in the water, that would be the end of their journey.

The man standing in the river and holding the boat motioned her group forward. She stood at the edge of the water and watched as the others waded through the water and then climbed into the vessel. A man came to her and reached for Jordan. She looked at him in panic and shook her head. He wanted to take her girl over the water.

He said, "Is okay. I won' drop her."

Reluctantly she relinquished her daughter to his arms. He carried Jordan toward the boat, and Mattie stepped into the cool water to follow. The current tugged at her. She froze, afraid of losing her balance. Soon the man was back for her. He had left Jordan in the boat in someone's arms. He held her elbow firmly as she walked. Stepping carefully in the water, she made it to the side of the boat. She gripped the edge and tried to get in. The boat moved with her. Getting into the boat was even harder than walking through the water. Mattie awkwardly crawled over the side. She stayed on her hands and knees until the boat stopped swaying so much. Then she crept onto the seat and wordlessly took Jordan back. She sat frozen on the wooden bench with Jordan clutched tight. Not daring to look, she closed her eyes to the world and prayed silently: *Bring us to the other side. Bring us to the other side. Dear God, deliver us safely to the other side. Thank you, God, for delivering us to the other side. Please don't let there be no hunters. Jus' get us over to the other side.*

Once they reached the Ohio shore, Mattie thanked God for their safe arrival. As she climbed out of the boat her skirt and shoes got wet again. Huddled on the free side, Mattie sat and watched as others made the nearly half-mile crossing. She prayed that God would get everyone else across safely.

Near the end of the long crossing, she saw the final two freedom seekers on the Virginia side of the river startle and run toward the forest. Mattie's mouth went dry and her palms went moist as adrenaline coursed through her body. She grabbed Jordan and made to run. Then she saw a large deer across the river. There were no bounty hunters, just tight nerves.

Collapsing back down to earth, she worked to steady her heart with a deep breath. She offered Jordan her breast and whispered to her daughter, "We free now. Honey, we free." She thought the air would feel different in freedom land, but it didn't. It was still hard to breathe.

Before sunrise a cart came for the group on the Ohio side of the river and carried them northward. Soon Mattie and Jordan separated from the rest of the group. The others traveling with Mattie were heading north, but she and Jordan turned west to join their family in Oberlin, Ohio. They had made it. After six exhausting weeks of traveling nearly five hundred miles, they were almost there.

Yet another stranger brought Mattie and Jordan to a small lean-to just ten miles from their new home. They were left alone to wait. This was their last day of hiding—tonight they would be reunited with Samuel and Emmanuel.

The dwelling could not even be called a cabin. From the footprints in the dust, Mattie knew someone had used it recently—probably for the same purpose. She rested on the bare floor, leaning against the wall with nothing to do but wait. Jordan wandered around the empty room, looking for something of interest. Toddling over to Mattie, she proudly held out a treasure she had found in the corner: a decomposing mouse. Mattie slapped it out of Jordan's hand, exclaiming, "That dirty!" With a sigh, Mattie dragged herself upright to take a closer look around the room. She found no other dead rodents or anything else warranting removal. After kicking the mouse outside, she sat back down on the floor to resume her wait.

A few hours passed before Mattie ate a little of the dried meat she had been left with. Getting used to small rations had been difficult, but after weeks on the road, her stomach had shrunk to nearly nothing. She hardly ate more than a few bites at a time. She and Jordan had both become so thin; Jordan's eyes had sunk into her sockets and Mattie's arms were skin and bones. They had little energy. Fortunately it didn't take much energy to wait.

On the second day they ran out of the food the driver had given them, and halfway through the third day their meager rations of water were gone. Mattie looked for a source of water or food, but found nothing near the cabin.

Hungry, thirsty, and exhausted, she pondered her options. If no one came, they would die of thirst in a few days. They had little choice but to travel west on their own. She could not gamble away her last bit of energy hoping someone would show.

Exhausted and desperate, she tied Jordan to her back and stumbled out of the cabin into the still-dark early morning. She trudged along through the forest of beech and elm trees, parallel to the only road but out of sight. It was early enough in the day that dew still coated the leaves. Mattie desperately licked the little bit of moisture off the plants, but it did nothing to quench her parched throat. Nor did it help her daughter.

She traveled on and on through the hot, sticky morning, praying with each step that she would find a stream. She journeyed, hoping she was reading the sun correctly and heading in the right direction—toward her son and her husband, toward a town in the midst of this endless forest, toward some water.

When she stopped to rest and offer Jordan her breast, she discovered that her milk had dried up. Mattie had nothing to offer her daughter. She tied Jordan to her back with a ragged, dirty cloth and continued on. The little girl hung there listlessly, making no complaints or demands. Normally that would have been terrifying, but Mattie was grateful for the quiet. She continued on, forced to cut out to the road occasionally when the forest became too dense to pass through.

On one of these forays, Mattie heard the sound of running water on the other side of the road. As quickly as her body would allow, she stumbled to the sound. Water! A small stream cut close to the road from the north. With Jordan still tied to her back, Mattie collapsed to the ground on the bank of the stream and dropped her mouth into the water. Sucking the cool liquid past her cracked and bleeding lips, Mattie drank and drank and drank, forcing herself to stop when her stomach lurched in protest. Then she untied Jordan's limp body and laid her gently on the earth. Filling their leather pouch with water, she brought it to Jordan's lips and poured water into the unresponsive child's mouth. The water dribbled out the sides.

"Baby, you got to swallow this. Come on now, girl," coaxed Mattie.

She dribbled more water slowly into Jordan's mouth, watching carefully to see whether her daughter was swallowing. She did not. Mattie's heart raced.

"Baby, you got to swallow!" begged Mattie.

But the water sat pooled in Jordan's dry mouth. Mattie turned Jordan's head to the side. She hoped that the water would make it down Jordan's throat. Slowly the water lowered. Mattie dripped more cool liquid into Jordan's mouth, praying some of it, enough of it, would get down her small throat.

Eventually they both fell asleep on the damp earth by the stream in the midst of the forest, Mattie's body curled protectively around Jordan.

Waking in the dark, Mattie pulled Jordan close. "Let see if the good stuff flowin' again," she muttered as she checked to see if she had made any milk. A bit of white came to the surface when she squeezed her nipple.

Bringing her breast close to Jordan, she said, "Try this, baby girl. Maybe I got a bunch of the stuff you love."

Mattie squirted a bit of precious white liquid into Jordan's mouth. The girl swallowed the little bit of milk from her mama's breast. Mattie expressed more past her daughter's lips, and Jordan swallowed that too. Mattie pulled her close, but the child did not latch on. She was too weak. Instead Mattie spent more than an hour squeezing a thin stream of liquid into her daughter's mouth and waiting patiently for Jordan to have the energy to swallow.

"Dear Lord, please let this milk be enough to keep my baby girl alive." Then Mattie went to sleep too.

In the morning she woke suddenly, and immediately checked on Jordan. Her chest was moving up and down. She was weak, but still alive. She pulled Jordan close. This time the girl latched on. Relief surged through Mattie.

"Thank you, Lord," Mattie praised. "Thank you, dear Lord."

After a good feed Mattie got ready to go again. As hard as it would be to leave this stream, staying here would not make Jordan better. They needed food and a safe place to rest. With a belly full of water and a full pouch, Mattie and Jordan set out once again.

Mattie stayed at the edge of the forest, passing under huge elm and beech trees. When she heard the steps of a horse coming, she ducked behind a bush to wait for it to pass. But, to Mattie's surprise, the sounds of hooves stopped before it got to her.

"Whoo, whoo, whoo," she heard someone call. Then she heard the horse walking, and then it stopped again.

"Whoo, whoo, whoo," called the voice, followed by more hoofbeats.

The call was the same signal she had listened for so many weeks ago in the forest in Virginia. But she did not expect it here in Ohio. Mattie crouched in the forest, hidden. This might be a driver looking for her, but she wanted to see him before she showed herself. His looks were scant evidence to go by, but that was all she had.

When the wagon moved just past her, she cautiously leaned around the tree to get a better view. She could just make out the profile of the driver as he gazed into the forest. Two large coffee-colored hands held the reins. A straw hat with a low brim threw a shadow over the man's face. She had to decide without a good look at his features. He might be the missing conductor, or it might be a trap. Some bounty hunters were Negro.

The wagon drove on. A plaid work shirt covered the man's broad back. A slight person sat next to him in the wagon. They were both searching the forest. She watched as they moved down the road away from her. She had only moments to decide. The smaller figure turned his head, looking backward. Mattie studied his profile.

"Oh, dear Lord. Thank you, Lord! Thank you!" Mattie cried out.

She stumbled out to the road. "Samuel!" her hoarse voice cracked out. "Emmanuel!"

They did not hear her.

She yelled again, but it came out as a whisper. Her throat was too dry. She collapsed on the ground. Grabbing for her water bag, she removed the stopper with shaking hands. The wagon was moving on. Quickly she drank some water, swallowing hard.

She took a deep breath, summoned all her energy, and yelled, "Emmanuel!" The two figures turned at the sound of her voice.

"Mama!" exclaimed Samuel. He leaped off the wagon and ran back to Mattie and Jordan.

"Oh, baby! Oh, baby!" Mattie cried in joy and relief. "Thank you, Lord! Thank you!"

"Mama, Mama, we found you!" Samuel exclaimed. Mattie opened her arms wide to hold her son. He fell right into her embrace on the ground in the middle of the road. Emmanuel rushed up behind them. Kneeling on the dirt, he wrapped his arms around them all.

Mattie cupped Samuel's face and then pulled him into another tight hug. She could not believe he was here. Right here with her.

They sat in the middle of the road, hugging and laughing and crying. Jordan reached around to pat her mother's head. "Baby girl, you want to be part of this too," Mattie declared.

Mattie turned her back to her husband. Emmanuel untied Jordan from her back. The girl squirmed away from Emmanuel and dove into Mattie's arms. Mattie shifted the toddler onto her left hip. She wrapped her right arm around Samuel. For the first time ever, Mattie held both of her children close. It felt so good she was about to burst. She had done it. They got away. And now they were together.

Jordan pushed Samuel away from Mattie. "Jordan, this your brother, Samuel," Mattie said gently. "And this here your daddy." Jordan stared at the two figures before her, moving her gaze between the two. Her bottom lip quivered a bit. "It all right, honey," Mattie assured her, hugging her close.

"We gonna be a family now," Samuel explained gently to his baby sister.

"We sure are," Emmanuel agreed, embracing them all. None of them wanted to stop talking and hugging to make their way to the wagon, but eventually they did.

"How you come to be lookin' for me?" Mattie wondered as they traveled to her new home.

"Mr. Mattox told me the fellow that was gonna bring you to us was being watched, so he didn' get you. They went a few days later, but you was gone. This the only road between there and town. We figured you be somewhere in this forest and you be more likely to come out if'n you saw it was me and James. You almost made it to Oberlin."

"James?" Mattie echoed, shaking her head. "It gonna take me a while to get used to our new names. Thomas, James, Georgia, and Jennie Freedman."

"I like Jennie," Emmanuel smiled. "You picked a fine name for the baby."

"Hard to imagine, but she ain't never gonna remember being Jordan."

Mattie's heart was full to bursting as they made their way to her new home. She kept looking back and forth at Samuel and Emmanuel, taking them in like water for a thirsty soul.

"Tell me about our home. I want to know ever'thing," she asked.

"Right now we got two rooms," Samuel told her, "but Papa say we gonna add another. In the back we got a shed for buildin'. I help when I ain't at school."

"School! You go to school?" Mattie shrieked in surprise.

"Yep." Samuel grinned and nodded. "I best in my age, thanks to Lisbeth. She a good teacher, it turns out."

"She sure was." Mattie teared up. She thought her heart was already as full as it could get, but she was wrong. There was more to feel. She hugged Samuel. "I sure proud of you, Samuel . . . I mean, James! You got a school. We got a house . . . with a shed for work. God is great. He sure is. God is great," Mattie declared.

"Oh, Mama!" Samuel said.

"And we got you," Emmanuel said. "Both a you. You a strong woman, Mattie. I always thunk that, but now I know for sure. You a strong woman."

CHAPTER 17

SPRING 1851

Lisbeth stood at the window in her room looking out at the quarters and fields. Her treasured twice-daily ritual was unchanged, though Mattie had been gone nearly two years. Gazing at the view in the early evening, she watched as a storm of activity swelled up in the fields. In the distance she made out a group of four anonymous men carrying a collapsed person toward the quarters. Rebecca followed close behind. As they drew nearer, Lisbeth realized they were carrying Poppy. Too soon they disappeared from her sight and into his cabin.

Worried, Lisbeth continued to watch for some time but did not catch another glimpse of either Poppy or Rebecca before Emily arrived to dress her for supper. Lisbeth nodded toward the quarters when she saw her maid. "It looks like Poppy collapsed. Have you any news?"

Emily said, "Cook say they found him at the end of a row of plantin'. No one saw when he went down, so no one know what happened."

"Oh, no." Lisbeth was concerned. "Can he speak? Is he conscious?"

Emily shrugged.

The next morning Lisbeth watched for Poppy, but he did not emerge from his cabin. Rebecca went in carrying food and water and came out alone. Lisbeth went to breakfast with a heavy heart.

Over a meal of soft-boiled eggs, dropped biscuits, and peach marmalade, Lisbeth asked Mother, "May I call on Poppy out in the quarters?"

"Why ever would he want to see you?" scoffed Mother. "He is an ill old man. Let him rest. He does not need a fourteen-year-old girl as his nurse. If they need our assistance, the overseer will inform me. I am sure he will be fine with rest."

Lisbeth pushed back. "Mary goes with her mother to tend to ill slaves." She really wanted to see him, to take care of him for Mattie.

Mother replied sharply, "Each plantation has its own ways. At Fair Oaks the overseer and your father take care of the field hands, while Mrs. Gray and I see to the house hands. You are quite aware of our arrangement by now. We do not need a little girl to tell us how to run the plantation."

Feeling thoroughly chastised and embarrassed, Lisbeth changed the subject. "Mother, I saw the first crocus of spring yesterday. Can we have a picnic to celebrate?"

"What a lovely idea. Who do you wish to invite?"

"I thought it would be for us, you and me, this afternoon," Lisbeth said out loud, but in her mind she added, *Like Mattie and I used to do.*

"This is a wonderful opportunity for you to practice hosting," Mother declared, ignoring Lisbeth's suggestion. "We shall hold it a week from Saturday. Invitations can go out today. Ten days is adequate notice." Mother went on, mumbling to herself, "A small group—a dozen at the most. All three of the Ford children; Edward and Emma Cunningham, of course. I believe it would be in poor taste to pass over Camilla Anderson, so she must be on the list too. But we shall do our best to make certain she is paired with . . . Matthew Johnson." Mother nodded confidently. "What shall you serve?"

"Perhaps some fruit and corn bread."

"No. Something nicer is in order—scones with clotted cream, pickled cucumbers. It is too soon for berries. Cook will have ideas." Mother added, "What a wonderful plan, Elizabeth."

Lisbeth did not reply. This was not her plan at all. She had hoped for a picnic with just her mother. But there was no point in saying so.

Ignoring her mother's advice, Lisbeth went down to the quarters at the end of the day. Lisbeth did not visit as often as she used to, but she was not entirely a stranger. Rebecca did not look surprised to see her when she answered the door to Poppy's cabin.

"How is he?" Lisbeth asked.

"He real bad off," Rebecca admitted to her. "He ain't sittin' up or swallowin'. We takin' care of him best we can, but . . ." Rebecca's voice broke and tears welled up in her eyes.

"What are you saying?" Lisbeth cried. "He is not going to die, is he?"

"Hard to know. Some folks recover from such things, and other don'. Just add him to your prayers; that about all we can do." Rebecca sighed.

"Does Mr. Wilson know? Is the doctor coming?" Lisbeth queried the weary woman.

"No overseer gonna call the doctor for an old man." Rebecca sounded resigned. "He already lived longer than most folks. Besides, ain't much a doctor gonna do for him now."

Lisbeth swallowed hard. "I can bring him some salt and sugar if it will help."

Rebecca smiled at the young woman. "A little bit of sugar water might be just the thing his body need. You go get some from Cook and bring it down to me. I make sure he get a taste of it. You know how he loves sweets. That gonna be a nice treat for him."

Lisbeth delivered the sugar, but did not know if Poppy got a taste of it. If he did, it did not help. The next morning she stood alone at the window and watched in sorrow as Rebecca's husband and sons, Lawrence, Henry, and Frank, carried a cloth-bound body out of Poppy's cabin. They brought him up the path by the river to the slave cemetery. In the distance she could see dirt piled up by a gaping hole in the ground. Poppy was placed into the earth. Songs and cries filled the air as dirt poured over his body. Marked by a cross of branches, Poppy's grave rested between his wife's entombed body and his daughter's empty grave. After the burial was over, the mourners trudged to work.

As they spread out into the tobacco plants, Lisbeth spoke out loud: "Mattie, your Poppy died today. I thought you would want to know. Now he is going to watch over you with your mama. He was very sick. Rebecca and I tried to help him. I gave him sugar and salt just as you would have wanted. I am sorry."

"What you say, miss?"

Lisbeth turned her tear-streaked face toward Emily's placid one. "Nothing. I was not speaking to you. You may dress me now."

Lisbeth was sullen when she saw the overcast sky on the morning of her picnic, but the weather transformed into a beautiful spring day, brightening her mood as well. Mother had made all of the arrangements, though she gave Lisbeth credit for it. Two days earlier at comportment lessons, Mother bragged to her peers, "Elizabeth planned every last detail of the gathering."

As the first guest arrived, Lisbeth told her mother firmly, "I shall take care of the picnic from here on."

"Are you certain?" Mother inquired. "I am happy to supervise Emily while you enjoy yourself."

Wanting to take on this responsibility, to prove to herself and to her mother that she was growing into a fine lady, Lisbeth insisted, "Yes, I am certain. Please go inside."

Excited and nervous, Lisbeth greeted her friends. After all the guests had arrived, Lisbeth announced to the group, "I shall drive with Emily in the wagon with the food. Jack will lead the rest of you on the path."

Jack broke in, "Past the graveyards, ooh! You better be careful of the spooks—a fresh nigger is in the yard."

Annoyed with her brother, Lisbeth declared, "Do not mind him."

"Never fear, ladies, I will protect you," Edward Cunningham shouted.

"Then you are all in trouble. Go home while you can. Stay away. Stay awaaaay," teased Robert Ford.

Edward shoved Robert, who collapsed to the ground. Rolling around, wrestling with an unseen ghost, Robert yelped, "Help me, Edward, help me. I am being attacked."

"Enough, you two!" Lisbeth shouted. "Start walking."

Mary Ford asked Lisbeth, "Shall I come with you to assist?"

"Yes, Mary. Thank you."

Matthew Johnson spoke up eagerly, "I would be happy to assist you as well."

"Thank you for your kind offer, Matthew." Lisbeth smiled at him. "But Mary and I will be fine. You enjoy the walk with the others."

From the wagon, Mary and Lisbeth waved to the energetic group of teens. As they drove past, Matthew nodded, but disappointment showed on his face.

"Matthew is entirely in love with you," Mary declared when the group was out of earshot.

"I suppose," Lisbeth replied. "He is very nice . . . but I am not in love with him. He will simply have to suffer. I am not certain why Mother put him on the list. Mother and Father have their sights set on either Edward or your brother, Robert, though they swore me not to tell even you."

"It would be grand to have you as my sister. Do you fancy either of them?"

"Robert is amusing, and Edward is handsome, but so far I am not in love with anyone. Matthew is the most interesting. I like dancing and speaking with him far more than any of the other boys, but I am still waiting for Cupid to shoot an arrow at me. Who do you fancy?" Lisbeth asked. "Jack, perhaps? We would be sisters twice over if you marry Jack and I marry Robert."

"Your brother is entirely too wild!" Mary laughed. "Not that mine are any less so."

Lisbeth rolled her eyes and nodded in agreement. "If not Jack, then who?"

"Daniel Bartley has the kindest eyes."

"Oh, no," Lisbeth declared. "If it is eyes you are after, Matthew's are the loveliest."

"You are wrong! Daniel's eyes are the most lovely—such a bright blue."

"I prefer Matthew's hazel eyes. Much more interesting than plain old blue."

Mary teased, "It sure sounds like you have taken a fancy to Matthew."

"I like his eyes and I enjoy talking to him. That does not mean I have taken a fancy to him," Lisbeth insisted.

Lisbeth instructed the driver to stop the wagon at a grassy spot just past the slave cemetery on top of a rise. They would have a lovely view of the James River for their meal.

Emily and the driver pulled out navy-blue wool blankets and spread them on the bright-green grass. The picnic basket they took from the wagon produced a delicious spread that included scones with clotted cream, crumpets, sweet potato buns, canned peaches, and pickled cucumbers. When they were finished setting out the treats, Lisbeth and Mary waited demurely on the blankets.

Though Lisbeth had imagined a mature, adult meal eaten in leisure and punctuated by quiet conversation, the boys had a different plan. They quickly devoured the food, and then set out to test their strength against one another. Drawing a circle in a patch of dirt on the ground, Edward shouted, "King's Domain."

Robert leaped up and yanked hard on Edward's arm, unseating him from his "throne." The boys lined up to play as the girls watched from the blanket and whispered to one another.

Lisbeth leaned in close to Mary. "Look, Daniel is trying to get Jack out. He looked at you to make certain you are watching."

"He did it!" Mary clapped as Daniel pulled Jack out of the ring.

Daniel kept the throne through three more turns, but Matthew finally unseated him. Daniel smiled at Mary as he walked past.

"His eyes are definitely more beautiful than Matthew's," Mary whispered into Lisbeth's ear.

"Absolutely not!" Lisbeth replied, smiling at her friend.

Mary's other brother, Albert, took a go at Matthew but walked away in defeat. Neither Jack nor Nathaniel Jackson was able to unseat him. Finally it was Edward's turn.

"Watch how a true man does it," Edward said as he strutted over to Matthew.

The two young men locked eyes. Matthew planted his feet wide and firm on the ground. He did not break eye contact as Edward grabbed his arm and gave a strong tug. Matthew did not budge.

Edward pulled harder and harder, but still Matthew did not move. Though Edward was the taller of the two, Matthew was strong and muscular. Matthew's legs shook as Edward used all his strength to pull. Matthew bent slightly at the waist, and a small smile crept over Edward's face. Matthew suddenly bent over farther, throwing Edward off balance, and then pulled back quickly while twisting his wrist to break free of Edward's grip. Edward stumbled backward and nearly fell to the ground. He caught himself at the last moment by stepping back and crossing out of the boundary. He had lost the game.

Smirking at Matthew, Edward turned to the group and shouted, "Enough of this!" He challenged the boys, "Who can hit the river with a stone?"

Following his lead, the boys gathered rocks and pitched them downhill at the moving water. Matthew smiled and shrugged at Lisbeth before he joined the gang of boys in competition.

"Mary?" Robert shouted to his sister. "Whose stone went farther, mine or Albert's?"

Always the diplomat, Mary responded, "I cannot say. They both went in the water; how can one judge?"

Edward turned away from the water and toward the slave cemetery. "Aim for that cross," Edward declared, pointing in the distance.

Lisbeth's breath caught. It was Poppy's marker. She watched him pitch a stone and strike the cross. Robert, Albert, and Jack immediately followed suit. Hard rocks smashed it over and over again. The cross jerked back with each blow. Lisbeth watched in disgust as the horizontal arm sagged downward until it was hanging to the right.

Unable to control her outrage any longer, she leaped up and shouted, "Stop! You are being disrespectful."

"To whom? The niggers?" scoffed Edward. "Since when do we have to be respectful to niggers?"

"It is wrong to be rude to the dead." Lisbeth turned to Mary for support, but her friend shrugged.

All eyes were on Lisbeth. She searched for the right words, but her mind was blank. Flooded by shame, embarrassed to have spoken up, she wanted everyone to stop staring at her.

"Too easy," Matthew said, casually breaking the uncomfortable silence. "Anyone can hit that cross. The cottonwood takes skill," he challenged.

He lobbed a stone at a faraway tree. All eyes turned away from Lisbeth. Stones started flying toward the cottonwood.

Grateful to Matthew for deflecting everyone's attention, Lisbeth stared at him until he looked over at her. She smiled and nodded across the distance. He smiled back shyly. She sank down to the ground and tried to enjoy the rest of the picnic, pretending not to care so deeply.

CHAPTER 18

JUNE 1856

"I do not care if you have scarlet fever, you will be in attendance at White Pines this evening. Now get dressed," declared Mother. "My goodness, Elizabeth, you act as if this dance is inconsequential. It would be the gravest of insults to Edward and the Cunningham family—if you do not go this evening we would be publicly declaring our rejection of a match. We certainly do not want to leave that impression," Mother said sternly. "I fear you are taking dangerous risks with your future. While it may seem assured that Edward will ask you to marry him, your position is not guaranteed until the engagement is announced. I promise you Camilla Anderson has not given up her intention to be his bride."

Lisbeth retorted, "If he wants to marry Camilla rather than me, then let him. I do not care."

Mother stiffened and stared at Lisbeth in outrage. "You should care! You know very well that this marriage will ensure your social standing for the rest of your life. While Robert Ford would be an acceptable match, your father and I would much prefer you marry into the Cunningham family. I know you find the idea of Mary as a sister-in-law romantic, but romance will not ensure your happiness as easily as the finer things in life. Going to a dance with a chill is a sacrifice worth making for your future happiness."

"Do you really believe I will be happy with Edward as a husband?" Lisbeth asked.

"Absolutely. He has everything a woman needs. He will be inheriting the largest estate in the valley. White Pines is as grand as any home in England, and I am certain they have at least seventy-five workers."

"But is he a good man?" Lisbeth asked.

"A good man?" Mother sniffed. "What a question, Elizabeth. Of course he is. He comes from one of the oldest families in Virginia. Honestly, I do not know where you get such ideas. It must come from reading Jane Austen. You are not a character in a romantic novel. You are nineteen years old. You need to stop being childish and start acting like the young lady you are.

"Emily!" Mother shouted loudly to Lisbeth's maid, who waited in the next room.

"Yes, ma'am?" responded Emily.

"Please help your mistress get ready. I want her in the second hairstyle we tried yesterday, the one with the triple upsweep."

"Yes, ma'am. As you wish."

Lisbeth supposed she should feel flattered and excited at the prospect of marrying Edward. His home was grand, and he was handsome. But she found nothing inspiring about him. He talked of nothing interesting and was always distracted. He hardly ever looked at her while they were dancing. She did not believe that he cared for her at all; he was simply going along with their parents' wishes. Lisbeth desired to be in love with the man she would marry. What could Mother possibly understand about love? Lisbeth had so hoped to be a target of Cupid's arrow, but it seemed that was not to be.

White Pines contained the grandest ballroom in the valley, built specifically to accommodate long lines for the Virginia reel.

Women in floor-length, colorful silk gowns with plunging necklines packed the room. Bone corsets constricted their capacity to breathe and their appetites. Plates of untouched food sat on laps. Dresses twirled to the music and voices interspersed with the notes from the chamber orchestra.

As Lisbeth danced with Edward, the blurry swirl made her dizzy. She told Edward, "Please stop. I feel faint." But he did not hear her. He was busy scanning the room and was not looking at her.

"Edward, I must stop," she said louder—and then she collapsed.

Fortunately Edward caught her in his arms so she did not fall to the ground. He grabbed her under her legs and carried her off the dance floor. If fainting were less common at these events, she might have drawn more attention, but women regularly collapsed while dancing. She returned to consciousness as Edward placed her on a chair close to the veranda. Mary Ford and Matthew Johnson rushed to her side. Mary began fanning her friend.

Edward said, "That was fast. You look better already."

"Yes, I am, thank you. I have a slight chill. It must have left me light-headed," Lisbeth replied.

"I am glad to see you are well again. You shall understand if I go on to my duties as a host," Edward declared while he looked around the room. "I would not leave you, but I have a dance. You will look after her, will you not?" he asked Mary and Matthew.

"Please, go ahead," replied Lisbeth. "I would hate to spoil your evening in any way."

"You could never spoil anything," Edward replied. "Matthew, will you see to it she gets punch?"

Mary broke in, "We will both stay with her. I do not dance again until the waltz."

"I will be more than happy to take care of these lovely ladies," chimed in Matthew.

Edward parted with a kiss on Lisbeth's right hand, then crossed the floor to greet his next dance partner. Lisbeth watched Edward escort Camilla to the dance floor, bow, and take her in his arms.

Mary broke into Lisbeth's thoughts. "Lisbeth, do not worry. He has to dance with Camilla, but I know it is you he is most fond of. No one is more beautiful than you."

Lisbeth smiled at her friend. "You are a dear to worry on my account, but it is of no concern to me. I understand the duties of a good host."

"Lisbeth?" Matthew asked.

"Yes."

"She called you 'Lisbeth.' I have never heard you called that name before."

"It is my childhood name. I wanted everyone to call me that when I was young. My parents never went along with it, but many of my girlhood friends still call me Lisbeth."

"How sweet. It suits you."

"Why, thank you kindly, sir." Lisbeth beamed at him. "That is one of the nicest things a gentleman has ever said to me. But I have adjusted myself to being known as Elizabeth."

"A rose by any other name would smell as sweet."

"Now you flatter me with Shakespeare."

Surprise registering on his face, Matthew asked, "You are a fan of the old master?"

"Oh, yes. I have read nearly all his work. *Hamlet* is my favorite."

"Not *A Midsummer Night's Dream*?"

"No, I prefer tragedies to comedies."

"Do you care for any contemporary authors?" Matthew inquired.

"I adore Jane Austen."

Matthew nodded. "I find her portrait of British society so accurate, and yet so dreadful."

"I agree. It must be awful to be so bound by what society expects," Lisbeth answered. "I am so glad to have been born in America, where one has freedom."

"I am glad to be an American too," Matthew agreed. "Though one has to wonder how much freedom exists here. But enough about literature. I am failing in my responsibilities. Now, if you will excuse me, ladies, I will fetch you both punch."

As Matthew walked away, Mary scolded Lisbeth. "Lisbeth, you know a lady does not talk about books with a gentleman."

"He broached the subject," Lisbeth defended herself. "A lady must follow where a gentleman leads," Lisbeth mimicked Miss Taylor. "Besides, he is hardly a true gentleman. As Mother puts it, he is 'barely more than a farmer.' Although he truly is one of the kindest men I know. Can you imagine Edward noting that you call me 'Lisbeth'? Do you think I would be happier with Matthew than with Edward?"

"Oh, Lisbeth, you are ridiculous!" Mary declared. "Matthew will not be inheriting any of his family's land, as the third-born son. Edward will be getting all of this. You could not possibly refuse."

Mary went on, "It will be wonderful for you to be the mistress of White Pines. Look at this grand ballroom! It has no rival in the valley. You shall host the most wonderful dances. And Edward is so handsome. How can you put all this at risk by flirting with Matthew Johnson?"

Shocked, Lisbeth declared, "I was not flirting with Matthew. I was only making pleasant conversation."

"That is not how it appeared to me," Mary scolded.

"I simply find Matthew Johnson interesting," Lisbeth protested. "I always have. That does not mean I am flirting with him. Besides, it is harmless fun. Edward is everything I should want in a husband, but he is not interesting or amusing. He does not care about what I am thinking; nor do we converse about books—or anything else for that matter."

Mary reassured her friend, "I am sure when you are married, you and Edward will have plenty to speak about."

"I suppose. I certainly hope you are right," Lisbeth said. "Shhh. Here comes Matthew."

After drinking the punch, Lisbeth returned to the dance floor to fulfill the obligations on her dance card. Her last dance of the evening was with Edward.

In his arms she asked, "Edward, do you believe a rose by any other name would smell as sweet?"

"Actually, I have never cared for the scent of roses," he said. "They give me a headache. So it hardly matters to me what they are called.

"Mother has made the final arrangements for your tea tomorrow," he went on. "Remember, she is quite old-fashioned. She prefers young ladies who are pleasant and not outgoing. You can manage, can you not?"

"You need not worry. I shall thoroughly impress your mother with my ladylike demeanor."

"That is a good girl." Edward patted her on the back. "I will not be present, of course, but Emma shall be. I have asked her to assist you, to treat you as a sister."

"I shall be glad of her company."

CHAPTER 19

"Tell me everything. I want to hear absolutely every last detail about your tea with Edward's mother," Mary commanded Lisbeth a few days later as they strolled through the gardens at Fair Oaks.

Lisbeth was excited to tell her friend about her wonderful day at White Pines. "The event was so lovely. Edward made his mother out to be stern, but she is charming and sophisticated."

"Where did you eat and what did they serve?" Mary asked.

"We had a delicious spread out on the veranda overlooking the gardens. The teacakes were the best I have ever eaten, with a tasty clotted cream. The watercress-and-cream cheese sandwiches were dainty with no crust. We had tea, of course, but they also served the most wonderful hot chocolate. I believe they make it with cow's milk; it was rich and delicious. At Fair Oaks we serve hot chocolate only on Christmas Eve, made with water. It is not nearly as rich. But Emma did not remark on it, so I imagine they have it at many special occasions. Watermelon, peaches, and strawberries were presented on a beautiful silver platter."

"That sounds so elegant."

Lisbeth continued, "It was all extremely tasteful. Their hands are so skilled that I did not notice when they replenished our plates, but they must have, for each plate was full at all times. I noted that Mrs. Cunningham does not acknowledge them as they come and go, so our conversation was not interrupted in the slightest. Mrs. Cunningham put me entirely at ease. She asked me about my friends, my family, and my favorite styles. She knows ever so much about the latest fashions. We compared the merits of silk and velvet."

Mary wondered, "Did you get a tour of White Pines?"

"Nearly all of it. It was dear and clever how they found an excuse for me to see the private rooms of the house. It felt very natural, not forced in the slightest. Emma pretended to break a hair comb; then she asked me to accompany her to get another. Of course, she could not find one in the first room, so we had to go on a hunt from room to room. We did not go to all of them—there are so many—but we went into quite a few. All the while Emma was speaking to me as if it were the most natural thing for me to be accompanying her through sleeping chambers.

"The house is lovely and has beautiful decor. It is a nice balance of traditional and modern. Mrs. Cunningham has remarkable taste. All the beds are new four-posters in deep cherrywood and the spreads are the latest in silk damask. But the washstands are old-fashioned with inlaid wood and marble tops. Each bedchamber has a fine Persian rug. Emma even devised a means for showing me the kitchen. She found a dish in one of the rooms and decided to return it. They must have planned the route for days. It was so thoughtful to give me a thorough tour in such a natural fashion."

Mary beamed. “Oh, Lisbeth, I am so excited for you. You are the most fortunate girl to find such a good husband with such a dear sister and mother. His mother was not distasteful at all?”

“Quite the contrary; I think I shall learn much from her. And Emma and I shall be dear friends,” Lisbeth replied. She quickly amended, “Not dearer friends than you and I, of course.”

Mary smiled at Lisbeth, then asked, “Did you see the grounds?”

“We took a walk in the gardens after tea. Casually I suggested we take a turn that would lead us toward the quarters, but Mrs. Cunningham replied that nothing of interest lay in that direction. Apparently they do not think I need be concerned with the field hands. I can infer that they will expect me to oversee the house slaves. Eventually, of course—not right away. We have the same arrangement at Fair Oaks, so I am comfortable with it.”

Mary commented, “Lisbeth, only a week ago you wondered if Edward would be a good husband simply because he does not converse about books.”

“Yes, I do feel rather foolish,” Lisbeth agreed. “Thank heaven for you, dear Mary. I can speak such foolishness out loud and see what it is worth. How could I even consider not becoming a Cunningham and the future mistress of White Pines?”

“Hard to imagine you thought Matthew Johnson could possibly be a more suitable husband than Edward Cunningham,” Mary agreed. “Have you heard? He is moving to Ohio to farm. Daniel says he has become an abolitionist.”

“An abolitionist!” Lisbeth burst out. “I declare, I am so tired of hearing that awful word! It is all anyone speaks of these days. I wish we would simply secede and end all this tiresome conversation.”

“Father believes it will mean war.”

“I cannot imagine why,” Lisbeth replied. “Who cares if we are one country or two? What is there to fight over?”

CHAPTER 20

APRIL 1857

Lisbeth woke with a start. She did not remember her dream, but adrenaline rushed through her body from something that had disturbed her in her sleep. She lay in bed for a few moments, steadying her breathing and thinking about this day. Today would seal her life forever. Today she would be presented as Edward's intended bride. Twenty years old, and her life was set. Her family was hosting a gathering to celebrate her birthday and announce the engagement.

Lisbeth acknowledged Emily, who arrived with the tea tray. Emily set it upon the table by the divan and returned to her small chamber. Lisbeth rose, poured herself a cup of the hot beverage, and added two teaspoons of sugar and a splash of cream. Taking the cup with her, she went to the window to gaze out as she did every morning. The workers were already in the fields. She could barely see the pen of babies at the end of a row. Sarah, who was only six months older than Lisbeth, had two children now. Grandma Washington was long since dead, and Lisbeth no longer tracked who cared for the children of the field hands.

She had a year to plan for the most lavish wedding of next spring, but it still seemed too soon. Mother had already given birth to Lisbeth and was pregnant with Jack by the time she was twenty. Lisbeth knew she should feel ready to be married, but she did not.

"Emily," Lisbeth called out, "I am going to wear the cream linen dress. Get it ready."

"Yes, miss," Emily replied.

Emily pulled a corset and hoop skirt from the wardrobe. Lisbeth slipped the corset over her head and lay down on the bed. Emily bent over Lisbeth and pulled hard on the strings, bringing the edges of the corset closer and closer until they finally touched. Lisbeth rose, taking a few small breaths to accustom herself to the constriction. With a sigh, she put on cotton bloomers and then stepped into the four-boned hoop skirt. She raised her arms to allow Emily to lower the linen dress over the underskirt.

Lisbeth sat in front of the vanity while Emily slicked down her hair and arranged it in a hairnet.

"Emma will be bringing her maid this afternoon. I believe her name is Margaret. You will spend time with her while she is here. She will start to familiarize you with the routines at White Pines."

"Yes, miss."

Lisbeth explained, "We are both fortunate to be moving to such a grand estate."

"Yes, miss."

"Do you not agree?" Lisbeth demanded.

"It is not my place to agree or disagree, miss."

"You do not believe I am making a good marriage?"

"Miss, it is not my place to say."

"Please, Emily," Lisbeth cajoled. "I want you to speak the truth to me."

Emily replied in a steady voice, "You do not seem pleased."

"That is not true!" Lisbeth protested. "I am delighted at this match. This is all I could have dreamed of. White Pines is a beautiful home. Emma is the kindest sister I could have hoped for. Mr. and Mrs. Cunningham have done everything imaginable to extend a welcome into their family."

Emily ventured carefully, "And young Mr. Cunningham?"

Lisbeth's eyebrows furrowed. "What do you mean by that question? Edward is a handsome gentleman. His manners are impeccable. I am finished with this conversation. Have you completed my hair?"

"Yes, miss."

"Then leave me be!" she scolded.

Emily stepped back, but Lisbeth did not rise. She sat in stony silence, staring at her reflection. A fury that she did not understand buzzed through her veins.

"I do not know what is the matter with me!" she declared out loud.

Emily stood by silently. Lisbeth rose and crossed over to the window. She watched the scene before her, hoping it would calm her as it had on many other occasions. But today it did not help. She paced the room, which only served to agitate her further.

"I am sure these are just premarital nerves," Lisbeth declared. "Mother says everyone has them."

Emily nodded.

"I believe I need a rest. I will lie down for a few minutes."

"As you like, miss. Shall we remove your clothing?"

Lisbeth sighed. "No."

Tears of frustration worked at the edges of Lisbeth's eyes. She did not have time to undress and redress, so she would not get the rest she hoped for. She sat on the edge of her bed, careful not to muss her clothing. Without thought, her hand snaked under her pillow to find the comfort of Mattie's shell. She rubbed it between her fingers until she was relaxed again.

Instead of returning the shell to its hiding spot, she reached up to tie it around her neck. She carefully tucked it under the high neckline of her dress, then examined herself in the mirror over the fireplace. The cream-colored fabric hid the shell, but she could feel its comfort against her heart.

"Emily, is this visible to you?"

"No, miss. No one would think you were wearing it," Emily replied.

A few hours later the group of celebrants were gathered in the garden. Old women and men perched on chairs around small tables with bouquets of wildflowers. Young men and women sat on blankets, enjoying boisterous conversations. Lisbeth sat on a blanket next to Mary. Mary's beau, Daniel Bartley, was entertaining a large group with an amusing story. Lisbeth was surprised when she saw Matthew Johnson walking toward her. She smiled across the distance. He came right up to her.

"How lovely you look today, Elizabeth," Matthew said.

"Thank you. You are too kind. Please sit with us," Lisbeth invited. Matthew sat a respectable distance from her.

Daniel Bartley finished his story and turned to Matthew. "I understand you may be moving."

"I am considering a move to Ohio," Matthew responded. "Land is more affordable."

"But workers are not," Daniel countered.

"I prefer to have paid hands," Matthew replied. "At a different price."

All eyes turned to him.

"I do not understand how you can abandon your home and your family," Daniel said.

"Ohio!" Edward said. "It sounds positively barbaric. Elizabeth, promise me you will never insist we leave White Pines."

Mr. Wainwright spoke from behind Lisbeth before she could give an answer. "Elizabeth and Edward, come with me. It is time."

Lisbeth gave a shy shrug to Matthew before walking away with Edward and Father. A horseshoe of people gathered around Lisbeth, Edward, and their parents.

Mr. Wainwright spoke. "It is with great pleasure that we announce the betrothal of our only daughter, Elizabeth, to Mr. Edward Langston Cunningham."

The crowd gave polite applause.

Mr. Cunningham then addressed the gathering. "We are delighted to welcome Elizabeth into our family. As a token of our pleasure we present her with this necklace."

Edward opened the jewelry box, exhibiting it in a slow arc to the crowd, who responded with obvious approval. He then turned it toward Lisbeth. A large, deep-blue sapphire hung down the center, with smaller sapphires marching up the sides of the necklace. It was too large for her taste, but her eyes shone with the delight she knew he and everyone else expected. Edward stared at her with anticipation.

"Thank you so much. It is lovely," Lisbeth spoke loudly enough for all to hear.

Edward continued to stare expectantly. Finally he jerked his head and motioned in a circle with his finger.

"Oh!" Lisbeth said as she twirled around to present her neck to her fiancé.

As Edward stepped close, Lisbeth became extremely aware of the shell at her heart. She resisted the temptation to touch it. Edward reached around and fastened the sapphire necklace at her throat. She felt a small tug on the string of the shell. He knew it was there. She turned around and the crowd clapped once again. Lisbeth smiled at them and then at Edward, but he did not return her gaze.

As the crowd broke up Edward hissed in her ear, "What are you wearing?"

"Oh, this?" asked Lisbeth. Feigning indifference, she fingered the string at her neck. Thinking quickly she made up a story. "I always wear it on my birthday. It is an old gift from a dear friend who moved away."

Edward scolded quietly, "Well, it is not at all suitable for an event such as this. A string around your neck! Honestly, sometimes I do not know how you get by at all."

"No one can see it," Lisbeth countered. "It is entirely private."

"I know it is there," Edward insisted.

"Yes, Edward. Of course; I do not know what came over me," Lisbeth acquiesced. "I can be overly sentimental sometimes. I shall not wear it around you again."

"Thank you. Now let us greet our guests as betrothed."

First they circulated to the small tables, making polite conversation and accepting the best wishes of the elders and married adults in their community. When someone asked for a closer look at her jewels, Lisbeth made sure to hold the sapphire out against the palm of a hand so that no one would notice the bump of the shell under her gown.

Eventually the newly engaged couple was able to sit with their friends. After showing off the necklace and discussing wedding arrangements, the conversation turned to their honeymoon.

"I would love to go to Paris," Lisbeth said. "Or perhaps London. Europe sounds beautiful and intriguing. I would go anywhere in Europe, even Rome!"

"I would be afraid to travel so far!" Mary declared.

"Not I," Lisbeth replied. "I should love such an adventure."

"New York City will be adventure enough for me," declared Edward. "I see no need to leave the shores of this country. I certainly have no need to listen to people speak French or Italian."

"French is a beautiful language," Matthew interjected.

"It may be beautiful," Edward replied, "but I have no need of it!"

"Sounds like you will be going to New York on your honeymoon," Mary observed.

"I suppose," Lisbeth nodded.

She discreetly rubbed at the fabric over the shell.

CHAPTER 21

APRIL 1858

A year of vigorous planning passed quickly. The ceremony would be at Mt. Vernon Christian Church at two o'clock in the afternoon on May 14, 1858. Four hundred guests were expected to attend both the ceremony and the reception. After much debate, the families decided to follow tradition and hold the reception at the home of the bride. Lisbeth's trousseau was nearly finished, though none of it would ever be used: her handiwork would be stored away, since much finer linens were in use at White Pines. But protocol required a lady to bring a trousseau to her marriage, so hers would be complete. She had two more napkins to finish by May.

Lisbeth arrived at White Pines to celebrate her twenty-first birthday with a tea for her friends and family. Emma greeted her with an eager embrace. "Elizabeth, the seamstress has brought my gown for your wedding! Come see. Mary, you come as well."

The three young women ascended the stairs to Emma's bedchamber. With a flourish Emma produced a pale-green silk gown. The low neckline, trimmed with deep-green ribbon dotted by small pearls, would draw special attention.

"It is beautiful, Emma," Lisbeth told her friend. "You shall outshine me on my own wedding day!"

Mary protested, "No, Lisbeth. Your wedding gown is the most beautiful dress I have ever seen. The sheer layer of silk over the skirt shall set the fashion trend for next year. I wish my mother would allow me to wear something as stylish for my wedding."

Emma responded, "'Lisbeth'—what a silly name. I much prefer you as Elizabeth. It is ever so much more elegant. You need a fashionable name to go with your fashionable dress."

"You are correct. I shall become entirely Elizabeth, starting at the wedding." Lisbeth nodded. "Mary, you must remember only to call me by Elizabeth once I am married. I shall be Elizabeth Cunningham and no longer Lisbeth Wainwright."

The tea was characterized by the elegant simplicity Lisbeth had come to expect at White Pines. Naturally the conversation centered around wedding and honeymoon plans. Lisbeth's expressed desire for an extended trip to Europe had been vetoed without any consideration or conversation; instead the newlyweds would be taking the train to New York City for the month of June. Lisbeth looked forward to walks through Central Park and visits to museums. Having never traveled to a city more glamorous than Richmond, she told herself that it would be adventure enough.

Mrs. Cunningham asked her future daughter-in-law, "Elizabeth, dear, would you please go see what is taking Edward so long? I told him to return in time for tea. He is in the back garden, doing heaven knows what."

"Certainly, Mrs. Cunningham."

"You shall not be allowed to call me that much longer. I expect to be Mother to you after the wedding."

Lisbeth beamed. "And I look forward to calling you Mother," she replied as she kissed the elder woman's smooth cheek before she departed to find her betrothed.

Lisbeth refused Emma and Mary's offer to accompany her in order to have a few minutes alone with Edward. As she walked through the front garden, she felt at peace. This home and this family would soon be hers. She had come to understand that this was the mature choice.

Mattie's necklace was in her pocket. It would be childish to wear the necklace in public, but carrying it as a reminder of Mattie on her birthday seemed safe enough. She touched the shell as she took in the beautiful grounds.

Lisbeth broadcast a silent message while she walked: *Mattie, wherever you are, I hope you are safe and happy. I am. I want you to know I am to have a wonderful marriage. You would be happy for me.*

In the back garden Lisbeth noticed a particularly grand willow tree, larger even than her favorite at Fair Oaks. Long branches reached all the way down to kiss the ground. Straying from her path, she parted the fine branches and took in the cool air, the smell of moist soil, and the hazy light. Oh, this place was a treasure, a large, private umbrella. Soon she would be able to come here whenever she wished. Perhaps she would have a bench placed by the trunk so she could read in this protective shelter. This would be her haven. Someday she would bring her own daughter under these branches to take naps, learn to read, and share stories.

She heard the rustle of an animal on the other side of the trunk. Undaunted, she moved forward, counting—one . . . two . . . three . . . four . . . five—as she walked from the branches to the trunk of the tree. Walking slowly around the trunk, being careful not to approach the animal too quickly, she stopped when she saw what was making the noise.

She stared at the confusing sight before her. Her eyes took in the length of Edward's body, his pants around his ankles, his knees slightly bent, his naked buttocks, his thighs covered in thick black hair. His entire body pounded up and down with his head arched back and his eyes closed tight, shutting out the world. He was mounted on a field hand, fiercely thrusting himself into her. He was so intent on the pleasure of his own movements that he did not notice his fiancée watching him. Lisbeth's incomprehension slowly transformed into horror.

She shook as a wave of anger and hatred flooded though her. Her stomach lurched, leaving the acrid taste of bile in her mouth. She put her hand on the trunk of the willow to steady herself.

Lisbeth looked past Edward into the eyes of the girl underneath him. The child stared up, her terrified, caramel-brown eyes boring intensely into Lisbeth. Pain and shame filled her young face. She turned her head away and hid her eyes with her hands.

Lisbeth screeched, "Get off of her!" Then she ran from the shelter of the willow, desperate to get away from the vile scene.

Sobbing and shaking, she was stumbling along the garden path when Edward grabbed her from behind and spun her to face him. She jerked her arm free and screamed, "Do not touch me. You are despicable!"

"Elizabeth, calm down," Edward soothed. "Let me explain."

Outraged, she stepped back and yelled at him, "Explain? What explanation can you possible provide? I saw all too clearly the act you were engaging in!"

"I am not the first young man, nor will I be the last, to take pleasure before I am married. This does not affect the way I feel about you or the plans for our marriage. Nothing need change."

"For you perhaps, but not for me!" Lisbeth shouted. "I cannot imagine life with a man such as you."

"A man such as me?" he scoffed. His lip curled up. "Do not be foolish. All men are like me."

"All men? How can you say such a thing?" Lisbeth was further enraged at his accusation. "Not my father! Not my brother!"

"Do not be so naïve." Edward smirked. "You really are such a child." He looked at her with pity and shook his head. "How did you imagine so many light-skinned house slaves came to be? I assure you they are not the product of two niggers. As I recall, you have your share at Fair Oaks."

Emily's face swam before Lisbeth, and a numbing horror filled her soul. Her anger was instantly deflated and replaced with shame and sorrow. She stared at Edward, blinking away tears, entirely stunned. After a few moments, Edward slowly put his arm around Lisbeth. Meeting no resistance, he turned her back toward the house. She let him lead her as thoughts whirled through her head.

Gently, as if speaking to a toddler, Edward instructed her, "Elizabeth, we will tell everyone that you became ill. This is not such a falsehood. I understand you are quite shaken by this. You are so innocent, and I treasure that in you. You must go straight home. Rest. You need tell no one what transpired here. Once you are over this shock, you will understand everything is fine. You are so dear to me. It would not do to call off the wedding at this late date. Everything has been arranged."

Lisbeth unconsciously nodded along to Edward's soothing voice.

CHAPTER 22

Lisbeth stumbled up to her room and fell into bed. She burrowed into her feather pillow and replayed the events of the afternoon. She imagined what she could have done differently to prevent this horrible experience. She berated herself for being so impulsive. She wished that she had simply called out for Edward rather than straying from the path and taking the liberty of parting the branches of the willow. She struggled to forget all that she had seen. More than anything, she wanted to get out of her mind the image of the girl's desperate caramel eyes pleading for release.

Lisbeth claimed to be too ill to come downstairs to supper, so Emily brought parsnip soup to her in bed. She scrutinized Emily's face. It was unmistakable: Emily's hazel eyes were identical to Jack's. How had she not seen it before?

Lisbeth asked, "Emily, did you ever live in the quarters?"

Clearly surprised by the question, she replied, "I'm told I was born out there, but I have no memory of it."

Lisbeth nodded, but did not ask any further questions, though many swam around her head. Did Emily know? What about Lisbeth's parents? Did people keep track of such things?

She felt her entire understanding of her world come apart. She wondered if she could ever put it back together again. Eventually a troubled sleep, filled with chaotic dreams, overtook her.

When Lisbeth did not rise from bed by the next afternoon, Mother arrived to chastise her. "Elizabeth, whatever is the matter? Clearly you have been crying. I believe you are only pretending to be ill. I cannot imagine what has caused these kinds of theatrics. Do tell me what happened between you and Edward."

Grateful to be able to speak of it, Lisbeth blurted out, "Mother, at my birthday tea, when I went to find him in the gardens, Edward was . . . he was . . . he was with one of the slave girls. As a man is . . . with a woman."

"Is that all?" Mother scoffed. "Well, of course you were traumatized if you saw the act. It truly is unpleasant to contemplate involvement in such an endeavor. But it is not as terrible as it appears."

Lisbeth stared at her mother.

"Elizabeth." Mother sighed as she explained, "Men have needs that must be met before they are married to a lady. Ladies do not meet such needs before a wedding, so men turn to the hands. It is quite flattering for a girl to have the attention of the young master of the house. You need not be concerned." Mother patted Lisbeth's hand.

"Does Father . . . ? Has Jack . . . ?" Lisbeth stammered in confusion.

Fury burning on her face, Mother snapped, "It is not my place to know such things! Nor is it yours. Their relations outside this home are not our concern."

"But is it not unchristian to behave in such a way?" wondered Lisbeth. "I thought the hands need our protection?"

"It is not as if they are true Christians," retorted Mother. "Most of them are eager for such attention. They use it to earn special treatment. You cannot imagine they have the same moral standards we do, Elizabeth."

Unconvinced, Lisbeth argued back, "She did not appear to be eager, Mother. Not in the slightest."

"Elizabeth, I realize it is difficult for you to understand." Impatience filled Mother's voice. "But you are about to be a married woman. You must stop being so naïve and idealistic. The world is not always kind, but every person has their place in it. Edward has his place, and the young slave has hers. You have yours. We may not choose our place, we may not enjoy it, but we must accept it."

Feeling unrestrained, Lisbeth asked, "Mother, is Emily my sis—"

Mother struck her hard on the cheek. Lisbeth's head jerked to the side. Mother's furious eyes burned into Lisbeth.

Mother yelled, "That is enough, Elizabeth! I am finished with this conversation. You have two more days to lie in bed and feel sorry for yourself. I expect you to be at dinner on Friday, dressed, with a smile on your face, ready to charm our guests. Have I made myself clear?"

Lisbeth's face burned and throbbed. She rubbed it with her hand. Feeling entirely chastised, Lisbeth nodded.

The next day, after another night of troubled sleep, Lisbeth accepted a visit from Mary.

"What beautiful flowers!" Mary exclaimed.

"They are from Edward. And that garnet necklace as well," Lisbeth replied, shaking her head with a frown on her face. Then she added, "Sent as peace offerings."

"Did he do something for which he is sorry?" Mary asked.

"I do not believe he is sorry for what he did. Though he wants me to believe he is. I am greatly troubled by it."

After recounting the story of what occurred under the willow, Lisbeth asked her dear friend, "Mary, did you know such a thing was common?"

"Yes, I suppose so, though I have never heard anyone talk of it directly," Mary admitted. "Light slaves are born on every plantation. My brothers often tease one another about whose seed made the harvest. I knew they were talking about sexual matters. I do not think it makes Edward so awful."

"You think I should still marry him?" Lisbeth wondered, eager for her friend's advice.

"Certainly! What alternative do you have?" Mary pointed out. "No one else is available for you to marry. Everyone is engaged. Robert would not break his engagement to marry you at this date. Do you imagine you would be able to find a match next year if you did such a thing? No one would find that an acceptable reason to end an engagement. Would your mother and father support such a choice?"

"Mother told me young men have needs that young ladies cannot satisfy until a wedding has occurred. She believes I am being overly dramatic and naïve. I feel so sad for that little Negress. She was no more than a child. I am so ashamed to have seen what they were doing. Mother believes I have been traumatized by seeing the act, but that I will get over it soon enough."

Gently Mary replied, "I cannot see that you have any choice but to marry Edward. You would have to leave if you did not. Where could you possibly go?"

"I do not know," Lisbeth admitted. "I have never heard of someone breaking their engagement. Have you?"

Mary shook her head. "Not directly. Though I have heard whispers."

"Perhaps my mother's sister would take me in. But only for a short time." Lisbeth eyes stung. "Oh, Mary, I am so confused! I must decide soon."

Mary reminded her friend, "Lisbeth, remember when you wondered if it would be romantic to marry Matthew Johnson because you share a fondness for Shakespeare?"

Lisbeth nodded.

"You realized in time how childish it would be to make a marriage based on such an idea," Mary lectured Lisbeth. "This is no different. You cannot possibly choose a husband based on the literature he cares for; nor can you reject a husband for how he treats the hands. You would be giving up everything. For what? It changes nothing."

Lisbeth sat in stony silence, taking in her friend's wisdom. She nodded slowly.

Mary went on, gently this time, "I know it is selfish of me, but I cannot bear the thought of you living anywhere but here. I imagine us drinking tea on the veranda at White Pines while we hear our children play in the garden."

"I dream of that too."

Mary pleaded with Lisbeth, "Please put it out of your mind and continue with your plans."

"I am trying to put it behind me," Lisbeth assured her friend. "I promise."

After Mary departed, Lisbeth sat in her rocking chair and gazed out the window at the landscape below—the cookhouse and smokehouse, the willow tree, the quarters, and the fields dotted with bent workers. She wanted to make out someone familiar, Rebecca or Sarah or Henry. But no one stood out. It had been so long since she had visited any of them. She hardly knew them anymore. The habit had slowly slipped away. She had given it up in preparation for her new life.

Lisbeth watched her brother Jack giving directions to the overseer. He spent more time outside since he turned nineteen, preparing for his eventual role as master of Fair Oaks. Watching the way he spoke to the overseer and interacted with the hands, she knew with sudden, painful certainty: Edward spoke the truth. Yes, her brother too. He would use any of these workers for his personal satisfaction. Indeed, most likely he already had—perhaps under her very own willow tree.

Suddenly overcome, Lisbeth bent in half, sobbing. She cried so hard she could not breathe. Her lungs clamped in tight; she gasped for breath. Squeaking sounds rushed from her throat. Sobs racked her body, harder and harder, until saliva poured out of her mouth. She gagged. Running to her washstand, she spit bile into the bowl. Too tired and overwhelmed to return to the rocker, she collapsed onto the floor. She took a towel from the stand and wiped her face; then she sat on the floor, leaned back against the shiny cherry-wood washstand, and cried until she ran out of tears.

Before Lisbeth went to sleep that night, she prayed for guidance: "Please, Lord, show me what you will for me. If I am to marry Edward, then take these images out of my mind and heart and return me to innocence. If I am not to marry Edward, then guide me to another path. Please, God, show me what to do."

More troubled dreams filled Lisbeth's sleep. She was being chased through willow branches. She cried out as long green vines slapped at her legs and tugged at her hair. She ran, gasping for breath with every step, then suddenly fell hard, landing on top of a small body. She looked down. The girl Edward had mounted lay on the ground. "No," Lisbeth cried out, fighting to look away, but her eyes locked onto the girl's. Suddenly the girl transformed into Mattie, then baby Jordan. Horrified, Lisbeth flailed against the ground, struggling against gravity to stand. But her legs would not cooperate. She had to stay in this position. A crowd watched, cheering her on. Mother, Father, Edward, and Mary yelled indecipherable words of encouragement. Lisbeth struggled to hear what they were telling her. Then she looked down at the Mattie/Jordan person under her, who shook her head and said, "You had such a good heart."

Suddenly Lisbeth was in front of a group of dark-skinned women lined up against a bright-white wall. Walking back and forth across the row, she examined each one. Edward shadowed behind her so closely that she felt his warm breath against her neck.

"You choose, Elizabeth," he whispered seductively into her ear.

It was hard for Lisbeth. She wanted to please Edward by making the right choice, but she did not know any of these slaves. Suddenly Lisbeth recognized Jordan, no longer a baby, but clearly the girl Lisbeth had carried on her hip so long ago.

"Her," she pointed.

"Good choice," Edward confirmed.

He took Jordan by the hand. *She can walk now*, Lisbeth thought to herself in the dream. As Edward led Jordan away, Mattie suddenly appeared and started screaming, "Not my baby! Don' take my baby!"

"Mattie, it is all right," Lisbeth soothed her old nurse. "We shall take care of her. We would never hurt Jordan. See . . ." Lisbeth turned her attention to Edward and saw him leading Jordan toward the willow tree.

"No!" Lisbeth screamed because she realized what she had chosen the girl for. "Not Jordan. No, not her. Not there. No!"

Lisbeth yelled out and woke with a start. She sat up, shaking and gasping for air. Alone and scared, she reached under her pillow for the shell necklace. She breathed in deep and rubbed the smooth shell.

"Oh, God, oh, God, oh, God," Lisbeth panted.

For the first time in two days she allowed herself to focus on the face of the enslaved child, a girl with eyes so similar to Mattie's that it hurt. Lisbeth felt the child's fear. She imagined the feelings of the girl's mother, the pain of knowing such a thing was being done and yet being unable to protect her daughter from it. Lisbeth knew with absolute certainty that if Mattie had stayed, someday it would have been Jordan lying on the ground under a White man. Had Mattie known such treatment? It was devastating to think about, but Lisbeth allowed herself to consider life at Fair Oaks from Mattie's perspective. She finally understood that Mattie left to protect Jordan.

Mother and Father insisted slaves were children who needed guidance to survive. They argued fervently against emancipation as being entirely unfair to the Negroes. But how could Mother consider the incident under the willow protection? If Lisbeth married Edward, she would be agreeing that such treatment was acceptable.

I cannot do it, she realized. *I cannot marry Edward.*

Adrenaline rushed through her body. She clenched her eyes tight against a dizzying wave. Her hands turned icy as blood rushed away from her limbs. It would be the end of her life as she knew it. She would be giving up all hope of having any social standing along the James River, but Lisbeth could no longer pretend enslaving Negroes was for their own protection.

She lay down, gripping her shell, and a peace settled over her. She felt free. Though she was frightened and confused—in some ways more than ever—it was done. She was not going to marry Edward.

Now she needed to make a plan for her life.

She thought late into the night. She recalled all the women she knew who were not married: Mrs. Gray; Aunt Beatrice; and Miss Taylor, the comportment instructor. She considered following each of their paths. She thought of all the young, and not young, men who were available for marriage. She thought and she weighed, imagining a future for herself with each option. Finally she chose the best, though still unlikely, possibility.

CHAPTER 23

The next day, Lisbeth led Mother to believe she was taking the buggy to visit Mary, though she never stated it outright. Her parents would be dismayed if they knew where she was actually heading. After driving for nearly an hour, she pulled up to a modest but well-built home. Roses and marigolds in full bloom formed a colorful border along the edge of the front yard. Green paint covered the stairs leading up to a large porch with white wicker furniture. Lisbeth slowly climbed the stairs, counting with each step—one . . . two . . . three—until she reached seven. She willed herself to breathe along the way. Fearing the rapid pounding of her heart was making her face flush, she paused on the porch to fan herself with a handkerchief. She opened the screen door to reveal a shiny front door painted to match the stairs. After striking the wood three times, she put her arm at her side to wait through the eternity it took for the door to open.

A large Negress peered out at Lisbeth. "Yes, mistress, may I help you?"

"I am looking for Mr. Matthew. Is he home?"

"Yes. Come sit down while I fetch him."

She escorted Lisbeth to a small living room with a plain couch, two chairs, and a grand piano. The room was comfortable, not intimidating. Lisbeth was still standing, gazing around the room, when Matthew arrived. His hazel eyes popped wide, and a small grin tugged at the corner of his mouth.

"Elizabeth? What a surprise. How lovely to see you," Matthew called out. Delight shone in his face. "To what do I owe the pleasure of your visit? Do you perhaps need a favor for your wedding? Whatever it is, I will be happy to be of service."

"Oh, Matthew," Lisbeth replied. "I truly hope you can help me." She breathed deeply to prevent tears from seeping out.

Matthew, seeming to sense her distress, invited her to sit while he went for lemonade. When he returned, Lisbeth was pacing in front of the couch.

"Please sit," she implored. "I realize it is unconventional for you to be seated while I am standing, but I must walk while I talk. I have come to realize that . . . I am not so conventional. I have a question for you. As you can see, I am nervous about it. It is not seemly. I hope you will forgive me. Actually, I have more than one question."

"Elizabeth, you can ask anything of me. Do not be concerned about being offensive," Matthew replied as he hovered on the edge of his seat. His own emotions mirrored Lisbeth's. He looked nervous; he shook his leg and tapped on his knee. His eyes followed Lisbeth as she paced in front of him.

Lisbeth wiped her sweating palms on her gown, stopped pacing, swallowed hard, and finally stammered out her first question, stumbling for the correct language, "Have you ever been . . . as a man and woman . . . with a slave . . . ?"

Full of shame, she looked at the carpet, unable to be more articulate. Biting her lip, hoping he understood, she waited for a reply.

"Are you asking me about relations?" asked Matthew, sounding incredulous.

"Yes!" Lisbeth exhaled. She was relieved that she need not say more. Her cheeks burning with humiliation, she confirmed, "Relations."

The room pounded with silence. Lisbeth did not look up because she did not want to see the look on Matthew's face.

Shock in his voice, Matthew replied, "That is your question of me?"

Lisbeth nodded.

"I am surprised. No, I cannot say I have . . . had . . . relations."

Lisbeth was relieved. Her instinct had been correct.

"My next question may be more shocking," she told him. "Give me a moment."

On the drive to Matthew's, she considered how she would ask him this. She rehearsed what she would say. But now no words seemed appropriate. She took a drink and a few deep breaths. The tension built, but the perfect words did not come to her. Eventually she stammered out, "I . . . I am not going to marry Edward Cunningham." Those words were like a dam breaking inside Lisbeth. She looked directly at Matthew. His eyes opened in shock. She asked in a rush, "May I come with you to Ohio? As your wife? I need a husband. You are not engaged. We both enjoy Shakespeare."

Matthew collapsed against the back of his chair. He stared at her, confusion written on his face. "You cannot possibly be serious?"

The adrenaline rushed out of Lisbeth's body. Suddenly she was unable to hold herself up any longer and sank down into the couch. Trembling on the sofa, she wanted to curl up into a ball and disappear.

Mustering up her last bit of energy, she politely responded, "I hope that you can forgive me for being too forward. I see now that I am being foolish. It was my best idea. But I understand you would not want me for a wife."

She stood to leave.

"Good-bye, Matthew," Lisbeth stated. "Thank you for your time. I apologize for placing you in this uncomfortable situation. I would appreciate it if you would keep this conversation in strictest confidence."

"Elizabeth, you misunderstand me," Matthew replied.

He moved to the couch to be closer to her. He reached up and lightly rested his fingers against her arm. She sank back down to the cushion. She was acutely aware that her shaking knee was only inches away from Matthew's.

He looked intently at Lisbeth and went on, "I did not mean to say that I do not want you as my wife. What I cannot understand is why you want me for a husband?"

Desperate to make her case, Lisbeth blurted out, "I saw Edward . . . lying with a slave. I am ashamed to say I did not realize such things went on before, but I found that afterward I could not pretend any longer that slavery is beneficial to the Negroes. My parents have always insisted that we are kind to our slaves, that they needed us to give them a good life on earth, and they need us to help them be Christian so they can have salvation for eternity." Anger rose in Lisbeth's voice as she spoke more adamantly. "But it is not Christian to lie with a girl against her will. I cannot pray to God each night married to him. I believe I can if I am married to you. To be honest, I want a good man more than I want a good husband. I believe you are such a man."

Lisbeth searched Matthew's face, looking for any sign of understanding. Matthew slowly nodded his head.

"I can only hope to prove your faith in me justified," Matthew said. He laughed, and then with a bemused grin on his face he asked, "You are entirely serious? You want to marry me? You understand I am going to Ohio to farm? I will have no bondsmen, only paid field hands. I will not have a house even as large as this one, only four bedrooms and no study."

"I understand. I am willing to go if you will have me," Lisbeth replied.

"Are you free to marry? Will your parents approve?"

"Yes, I am free," Lisbeth replied, though she had not yet spoken to Edward, "and no, my parents will not approve—but they cannot force me into a marriage of their choosing. I am willing to marry you without their blessing. I am of age. They can do nothing to prevent it if I have my birth certificate."

Matthew went down upon one knee and took Lisbeth's hand in his. He was trembling. Staring into her eyes, he spoke clearly, "Elizabeth Wainwright, will you do me the honor of becoming my wife?"

Lisbeth gazed at Matthew's gentle and hopeful face, his beautiful hazel eyes. A chill traveled down her spine. This was more than she had hoped for. Matthew was such a kind man.

Tears of hope and relief glistened in her eyes. "Yes, Matthew, I will."

Impulsively she leaned in to hug him. But then, suddenly feeling shy, she pulled herself back. Her improper question was bold enough. She did not wish to risk further diminishing his respect for her.

Clearing his throat, Matthew returned to the couch. "When shall we do this? Would you care for a wedding?"

"I would like to get married as soon as possible, if you are willing, by a justice of the peace."

"Whatever you would prefer is fine with me."

Having given this thought in the midst of the night, Lisbeth suggested a plan. "I prefer that we go to Charles City on Monday. Afterward, when it is too late, I will inform my parents."

Of course, she would inform Edward as well, but she would not speak of that with Matthew. They agreed to carry on with their lives as they had been until Monday morning. Matthew walked Lisbeth to her buggy and carefully assisted her into it.

She felt his eyes upon her as she drove away.

Lisbeth reveled in her good fortune. She had done it; she found a way to salvage her life.

Detached from all that was going on around her, Lisbeth suffered in silence through dinner that evening. As always the conversation was filled with speculation about the ongoing disagreements with the Northern states and the arrogance of abolitionists. There were long-winded arguments in favor and against secession from the Union. Lisbeth paid little attention to the talk. Soon she would be living in a free state and would not have to be concerned with the politics or morality of slavery. She was leaving all this behind.

Misinterpreting Lisbeth's quiet mood, Mother noted, "I am so glad to see you have fully recovered, Elizabeth. You are remarkably at ease this evening. It bodes well for your ability to take your place at White Pines."

After her nightly prayers, Lisbeth did not climb into bed. Instead she sat in a chair reading by a dim oil lamp. She refused Emily's offer to fetch warm milk. She waited, struggling to stay awake, until well into the night, when she could be certain the entire household was deeply asleep. At two o'clock in the morning, she left the sanctuary of her room.

Carrying the oil lamp, she carefully crept along the hallway, down the front staircase, and into Father's study. She crossed to his desk and started pulling open drawers. She was seeking her birth certificate. She had no idea where it might be. The top drawers held ink, pens, a knife, and other odds and ends. The bottom drawers held ledgers and papers. There were records from crop sales going years back, but no birth certificates.

She turned around to search the bookcase behind the desk. The upper shelves held leather-bound books. A wrought-iron chest sat on the bottom of the case. She opened it and found stacks of papers. She brought the documents to Father's desk and stood sorting through them, careful to keep them in order. Partway through the stack, she found a meticulous family tree going back for decades.

She examined this record, looking for her own name. There she was: Elizabeth Ann Wainwright, April 14, 1837, live birth. Two neat lines connected her name to her parents. Next to her name was a record of Jack's birth, followed by three more entries: Baby Boy Wainwright, August 20, 1840, stillborn; Baby Boy Wainwright, September 30, 1841, stillborn; and Baby Girl Wainwright, April 27, 1842, stillborn. Lisbeth was shocked. She had no memory of her mother being pregnant, and had never heard that her parents had lost so many children.

To the left of her name was another entry: Emily. A line interrupted by a thick question mark ran from Emily's name to Father's. "Dear God!" Lisbeth gasped. Another line ran from Emily's name to Uncle Alistair's name. It too was interrupted by a dark question mark. There was the proof that in some way she was related to Emily. Emily was either her half sister or her cousin. This information further confirmed her choice to leave.

She renewed her search through the papers with vigor. She found her own birth certificate in the pile of papers below the family tree. Lisbeth returned everything else to its place and sneaked back upstairs undetected. She hid her birth certificate in the back of her wardrobe and then slept soundly.

CHAPTER 24

After two long and nerve-racking days of pretending nothing was amiss, Monday morning came at last. Lisbeth lay in bed anticipating the events of the day. She imagined standing before the justice with Matthew at her side. She tried but could not picture his face. Panic started to rise, but she pressed it back down. *This is the correct path!* she insisted to herself.

She thought through what she might say to Edward after the ceremony. She imagined telling her parents that she was married.

Getting dressed was complicated. She did not want to raise her parents' suspicions, but she wanted to look nice on her wedding day. While Emily waited, Lisbeth spent considerable time sorting through her gowns. In addition to wanting an attractive dress, she needed one that she could remove herself. She did not know if someone would be available to help her undress. She did not allow herself to think about where or with whom she would be undressing that night, but she would have to get used to dressing herself in the future. Her new life was beginning today. Eventually she chose a Swiss dot with a light-blue background and bright-blue dots that buttoned down the front. It was not particularly tight in the bodice, so she could wear a corset that laced on the side.

Emily looked surprised but did not comment when Lisbeth took the same care in choosing a hairstyle. She tried a tight bun, then an upsweep, before finally settling on a loose chignon. To finish the outfit, Lisbeth wanted to wear the shell necklace. Her trembling hands made it difficult to tie. Noticing Lisbeth's struggles, Emily wordlessly completed the task.

"Thank you, Emily. You are very kind."

"Are you all right, miss?"

"I will be. I am very nervous. Something important is happening today. I will tell you about it when I get home."

Lisbeth tucked the shell beneath her gown before rising from the vanity.

She told Mother she was calling on Mary, but instead she guided her horse to Matthew's parents' home. He was waiting for her on the porch. She was glad to see him dressed in a nice suit for the occasion—for their wedding. It was hard to believe, but it was true. She was about to get married. He nodded a greeting, and a bemused smile crossed his face as he assisted her from the buggy. She smiled back at him.

"I am glad to see you," Matthew said. "You look lovely."

"Thank you," Lisbeth replied, looking down, feeling quite nervous.

"Are you certain you want to do this?" he asked, lowering his head so that he could see her face.

Lisbeth raised her head, nodded once, and confirmed, "Yes."

They drove to Charles City in Matthew's carriage. Lisbeth longed for something interesting to say. In the past, it had been so easy to speak with Matthew, but today she had to think of something appropriate. She harked back to Miss Taylor's lessons.

"We are fortunate the weather is so mild today," Lisbeth said.

"Yes," agreed Matthew, "it is mild."

Wanting to keep the conversation going, Lisbeth asked, "Is the weather similar in Ohio?"

"I understand the summers may be warmer and the winters cooler."

Lisbeth nodded, but could not think of anything more to ask.

"I had been planning to move in early May so I can oversee the planting. Is that suitable to you?"

"Yes, Matthew. Anytime will be fine."

"The land I purchased does not have a home. I am having one built. We will live in town until it is finished. You can decide how you want to set up the kitchen," Matthew said. "It can be however you wish."

"Oh, dear. I am afraid I have no experience in a kitchen. I cannot cook at all," Lisbeth voiced with anxiety. She had not even thought about cooking. There were so many things she did not know how to do: laundry, cooking, housekeeping.

"I did not mean to concern you," Matthew rushed to say. "We can have a cook, of course. I only meant that you can plan it however you like."

"Well, thank you, Matthew," Lisbeth said, relieved. "I think a cook would be wise. At least to start with. Perhaps she can teach me how to prepare meals."

As they traveled the road toward the life-changing ceremony, they cautiously made plans for their future together. In Charles City everything happened very quickly. Lisbeth had been afraid that the justice would refuse them a marriage license, but there was no problem once she showed her birth certificate proving she was of age. The ceremony was simple and over in less than ten minutes. Pausing before his buggy after it was all over, Matthew leaned in to kiss Lisbeth. She turned her head to give him her cheek, but then realized, too late, she should offer her lips to her husband. She turned her head back, and his lips landed at the edge of her mouth.

"Excuse me," he stuttered.

Lisbeth blushed. Embarrassed that she did not know how to behave with Matthew now that he was her husband, she did not speak very much during the ride back. She was so grateful to him.

She hoped he would not regret his choice.

Lisbeth drove away from Matthew's childhood home, though she supposed it was her temporary home now too. Matthew offered to accompany her, but she wished to face Edward and then her parents by herself. She had been practicing her speech for two days. She asked Matthew to come for her at Fair Oaks at suppertime. He would either join the family for supper or she would leave with her husband before they ate. That would be up to her parents.

At White Pines, Lisbeth breathed deeply to settle her nerves. She left the buggy with the livery boy, a large, middle-aged man. Though he had been waiting in front of White Pines the many times she had visited, she looked at him and wondered about his life for the first time.

"Thank you, Francis," Lisbeth said, hoping she remembered his name correctly. "Good afternoon."

Surprise registered on his face. "Good day to you, miss. It is a lovely day."

"Yes, it is," she confirmed. "An especially lovely day. I shall not be long, so you need not unhitch Shadow from the buggy."

"Yes, miss. Thank you, miss."

Ma'am, Lisbeth thought to herself. *I am now a ma'am*. But she did not correct him.

Lisbeth was shown into the elegant parlor. She stood by the davenport nervously waiting for Edward. He looked relieved when he saw her.

"Elizabeth, I am so delighted at this unexpected visit. You look wonderful. I see you are fully recovered from your 'flu,'" Edward fawned, with only a slight hint of irony in his voice.

Lisbeth did not reply or move toward him.

Crossing to her, Edward asked, "Did you receive the necklace I sent? Mother assisted me in selecting it. She wanted it to be simple and to your taste." He glanced at Lisbeth's neck. "Oh, you are not wearing it. You have that old thing on. You must be feeling sentimental today. Shall I call Mother and Emma to join us for tea?"

He reached for her, prepared to kiss Lisbeth's cheeks. Twisting away from him, she sat down upon the divan. He sat close, reaching for her hand. Clasping her hands tightly together, she moved away from him and looked him in the eye. Her heart was racing, but she was determined to speak clearly and firmly.

"Edward, I have come to speak with you and you alone. This is not easy for me." She paused, cleared her throat, and then went on, "But . . . I came to inform you that I am not going to marry you. I have prayed for guidance every day since the incident, and I know now I cannot possibly be your wife."

"Elizabeth, have you gone mad?" Edward exclaimed, indignation filling his voice. "If this is about the episode under the willow, I can assure you it will not happen again. Once we are married, you will be the only woman with whom I shall lie. I can hold off until our wedding night. You need not worry about it again." He reached over and gently stroked the back of her left hand with one finger.

Disgusted, she pulled her hand away. "Edward, I have come to realize that this is not about you and me. It is about the little girl who was lying on the ground beneath you. At night when I close my eyes, it is her face I see, in pain, hoping for release. It is wrong for her to be in such a position. I suppose, if I am being honest with you and with myself, I have become an abolitionist." Edward looked as if she had slapped him. She paused for a breath and then went on, "On my birthday, I realized . . . it is wrong to own another person. I will not be a part of it anymore. I am moving to a free state, to Ohio."

"Now I know you are mad!" Edward screeched with contempt. "You have nothing! You are not a woman of independent means. Your parents will have none of this. You are being childish over one small matter. Do you expect me to beg? What are you hoping to accomplish by making such a threat? This is no way to begin a marriage! I am to be your husband. I will not grovel before my future wife. That is enough. I do not want to hear any more about it. It is over."

"It is over," Lisbeth agreed, intentionally keeping her voice calm, "because I have made my decision. This is not a threat, Edward. I will not be marrying you."

"How can you ruin both of our lives?" Edward yelled.

"I am not ruining my life. I am saving it. As for you, I have grown fond of you this past year . . ."

"Fond?" Edward snorted in disbelief. "That is little consolation to me. This is outrageous."

"Please say good-bye to your mother and sister for me," she said with a composure that belied the frantic beating of her heart. She rose and handed him a red velvet pouch filled with the gifts he had given her.

She quickly crossed to the door to escape. Several house servants were standing in the foyer. They watched as Edward followed close behind Lisbeth, his hot breath on her neck, screaming, "When you change your mind, do not bother to return to me! You are ruined!"

She reached for the doorknob and gave it a firm turn. Her moist hand slipped. Cowering away from Edward, she wiped her hand and then turned the knob successfully.

Once she was out of the house, crossing the front porch, she heard the door slam hard, followed by the sound of breaking glass from one of the panes above the door. A sharp shard bounced off the porch floor and struck her ankle, cutting a thin line on her skin. She cried out but did not turn around. She did not want to see Edward.

Grateful that the buggy was still in front of the house, she rushed down the stairs toward it. After she climbed into the safety of her transportation, she looked over at the porch. The door flew open. Edward stormed out in a rage, his eyes burning and his face red. He reached back his arm and hurled something directly at Lisbeth. A necklace flew through the air. Lisbeth ducked and it sailed past her. She urged her horse forward. Edward continued to hurl his gifts at her, hatred in his eyes, yelling with each movement of his arm: "You . . . will . . . never . . . be . . . accepted . . . again!"

One of the missiles, a sapphire ear bob, landed in the buggy next to Lisbeth's foot. She stopped the horse, tossed the jewel onto the ground, and turned for one last look. Edward sat bent over on the top stair, his head buried in his hands, fingers entwined in his dark-brown hair, his body shaking. In the foreground, Francis bent over, slowly gathering the scattered jewels.

"I made the correct choice, I made the correct choice, I made the correct choice," she panted to herself, tears streaming down her cheeks as she continued on her path.

Rehearsing along the way, Lisbeth prepared for the ordeal that was to come. She did not expect her parents to understand her choice, but she hoped they would let her go without behaving like Edward.

"Lisbeth, whatever is the matter? You look as if you have seen a ghost," Father commented when Lisbeth came into the sitting room.

"You must be tired from your excursion, dear," asserted Mother lightly. "Have a rest before supper. We shall eat in one hour."

"Mother, Father, I have something to tell you. It cannot wait." Her voice shook as she spoke to them.

Lisbeth studied her parents, then looked around the room. She might never be allowed in it again. She noticed the final napkin for her trousseau peeking out from her basket, the texture of the velvet curtains, the mingled scent of smoke and perfume. Memories flooded in: listening to poetry while stitching by the fireplace, singing at the piano, memorizing scripture, Father arguing with the newspaper, Grandmother Wainwright picking out her sewing. She took in every corner before returning her gaze to her parents. She wanted her bearing to convey strength and confidence, but her glassy eyes betrayed her.

"Elizabeth, you are frightening me," Mother said forcefully, but there was no disguising the anxiety in her voice. "Stop being dramatic and tell us what you have to say."

"Go on, Elizabeth," Father prodded.

"I am not marrying Edward," Lisbeth blurted out.

"Oh, that nonsense again," said Mother, clearly relieved. "You are only having premarriage concerns. Every young woman has them. You had me overwrought. Go have a rest. You will feel better when you are not so tired."

"No, Mother. Truly, I am not marrying Edward," Lisbeth insisted. She paused and then she told them, "In fact . . . I am already married . . . to someone else."

Father leaped up, outrage and confusion in his eyes. "What do you mean 'already married'? Elizabeth, this is not a joking matter!"

"Mother, Father, I am sorry, but I will not marry Edward and be the mistress of White Pines," she choked out through a tight throat. "I married Matthew Johnson earlier today. We will be moving to Ohio. I do not expect you to understand, but I hope you will accept him."

"Matthew Johnson!" screeched Mother, her face scarlet. "You expect Matthew Johnson to be the father of my grandchildren, in Ohio? Absolutely not, we forbid it."

"It is too late, Mother. We were married this afternoon in Charles City."

"We will have it annulled," declared Father.

"I do not want my marriage to be annulled." Lisbeth stood firm. "I am Matthew Johnson's wife."

Father stormed around. He paced at the edge of the sitting room, moving between the globe and the piano. Unable to contain himself, he turned to Lisbeth and glared with undisguised fury burning in his eyes. He hissed, "I do not think you understand the implications of your decision. Your reputation will be ruined. My reputation will be ruined. You will disgrace yourself, this family, and all of Fair Oaks. I absolutely forbid you to do this."

"It is done," Lisbeth said, shaking all over. "I am an adult. You cannot stop me. I am leaving with Matthew. The only decision you have to make is whether we leave before supper or after. I am going to pack. Please inform me if you wish me to leave behind any of my personal belongings."

Giving her parents a wide berth, she walked to the sewing basket, removed the nearly finished napkin, and slipped out the door. Behind her, Mother's sobs echoed in time with Father's pounding on the top of the piano.

Lisbeth shook as she ascended to the second floor. In her bedroom, she collapsed into her familiar rocking chair and bent over, sobbing. Her body heaved uncontrollably as all the emotion of the day came pouring out in this safe, familiar place. Then she felt a gentle hand on her shoulder.

"Here you go, miss," Emily said, handing Lisbeth a glass of water.

Lisbeth tried to take the water, but her hands were shaking too hard.

"I just gonna leave it here. You let me know if you need anything else. Sorry you so sad."

Lisbeth took in a gasping breath to calm herself. After three tries, she was able to stammer out a weak "thank you" to Emily. Emily stood quietly next to Lisbeth, patting her back, murmuring soothing words. Finally, when no more tears came, Lisbeth took a sip of the cool water, wiped her damp face, and told Emily she needed to pack her belongings.

"So soon, miss? The wedding not for two weeks."

"Actually, though it is hard to believe, I am a married woman already. I ended my engagement with Edward Cunningham. I am now Mrs. Matthew Johnson; we were married this morning. I will be leaving with him this evening. Can you please fetch my trunk?"

"Yes," Emily replied, then went to get Lisbeth's luggage. At the door she turned back and quietly said, "Congratulations."

"Thank you, Emily. Thank you very much."

"Do I ready myself to leave tonight as well, miss? I mean, ma'am."

"No, Emily. My parents will no longer be giving you to me as a wedding gift."

—

While Lisbeth and Emily were sorting through items to pack and items to leave behind, Mother came into the room. Her eyes were puffy and red. She looked concerned and exhausted. She sat carefully in the chair by the fireplace.

"I will not change my mind, Mother," Lisbeth preempted.

"You are clearly upset by your decision. Your father and I are as well. I want to understand what you are thinking. Edward's actions were harmful to you. I can see that, but is it worth throwing your life away over his behavior? I do not believe you understand what you are giving up. You will be the wife of a farmer, very far from home. You have the opportunity to stay so very nearby, to have holidays with us. To have the better things in life, to maintain your friendships. Do you truly want to give all that up? You are naïve and romantic if you believe Matthew Johnson will be devoted to only you. Yes, Edward hurt you, but you are hurting yourself even more."

"I will tell you what I told him, though I do not expect you to understand either," Lisbeth asserted. "I did not cancel the wedding because Edward hurt me. I ended my engagement because of the girl he hurt."

"Whatever are you talking about?" Mother exclaimed.

"That is exactly the problem, Mother! You do not even see the trauma he caused the girl he mounted. I, on the other hand, cannot stop seeing it! Every night when I close my eyes, her image is floating in my mind, desperation in her eyes. What did she ever do to deserve such treatment? She was hurt, far worse than I will ever be. And you try to convince me, and yourself, that she would be flattered by such an experience!" Lisbeth said with contempt. "Well, I do not believe you, Mother! She was not flattered. She was in pain. That is why I will be moving to Ohio, a free state, where I will not have to be a part of the evil of slavery."

"You are naïve, Elizabeth," Mother scoffed. "Slavery will be a part of you wherever you go. It is as much a part of you as your hair color or your blood. It is a fundamental part of this country. It will not be going away anytime soon. Throwing your life away for a nigger. I am ashamed of you."

Lisbeth had no response. Her mother's lack of understanding and compassion was predictable. She saw no reason to persevere with this conversation. The women were silent as Lisbeth continued to pack her belongings while Emily, who had heard every word, scurried in the background, attempting to be both helpful and invisible.

Eventually Lisbeth broke the silence. "Mother, I would like to take the rocker, if that is acceptable."

"You may take anything from this room except Emily." Mother rose with a deep sigh and stared at the pile of belongings gathered on the bed. She walked slowly to the door. From the threshold, tears glistening in her eyes, she spoke softly, "Let me know when you are finished. I will send William to fetch your belongings. You and Mr. Johnson are not welcome at my table."

Lisbeth took a deep breath to steady her nerves. She looked over at Emily and gave an awkward smile before resuming her packing. She heard the front door open and close. Curious about the visitor, she went downstairs. The entryway was empty. She heard voices coming from Father's study and started to walk toward it.

"Elizabeth, move away from that door," Mother commanded.

"Who is Father speaking with?" Lisbeth asked.

"He is talking sense into Matthew," Mother replied.

Lisbeth pushed past her mother. She turned the handle on the study door and pushed. It didn't move. It was locked. She knocked on the door and yelled, "Father, let me in!"

Mother commanded, "Elizabeth, stop! Your father and I only have your best interest in mind. We cannot stand by and let you do this."

Lisbeth put her ear to the door. She heard voices, but could not make out any words.

"You cannot intimidate us, Mother. I am not changing my mind. Neither is Matthew." She knocked on the door again.

"Your Father is offering Matthew a thousand dollars to annul this marriage. He is also making it very clear that neither of you will ever receive any money from us in the future if you continue with this disgrace." Mother explained, "He married you for your money, Elizabeth."

Lisbeth was stunned. She knew her parents would be unhappy, but she did not anticipate outright bribery. Anger and fear flooded through her, and she pounded on the study door again. Finally it opened. Father stood there with a check in his hand. Matthew looked imploringly at Lisbeth.

Matthew said, "Is it true? Your father says you have changed your mind. I had to hear it from you. I do not want any money, but we can annul our marriage if you wish."

Lisbeth crossed over to him and took his hand. She looked right at him and said, "No. Matthew, it is not true. He is lying to you." She turned to her parents. "I chose Matthew. I choose Matthew. I am not going to change my mind. We do not need your money."

Before her parents could reply, the front door opened and closed. Father left the study.

"Who is that, Mother?" Lisbeth asked.

"The sheriff is here to uphold our rights."

Panicked, Lisbeth exclaimed, "What about my rights, Mother? I am an adult. You cannot force me to marry Edward!"

The door to the study opened. Father walked in with the sheriff and Jack behind him.

"Sheriff Hughes has some questions for you, Matthew," Father said. "Elizabeth, go wait in the sitting room."

"I do not want—" Lisbeth started to say.

The sheriff broke in, "I will speak with you next, miss."

"Ma'am," Lisbeth corrected the tall man. "We are not making a mistake," Lisbeth whispered to Matthew. She smiled at him nervously and squeezed his arm. He smiled back and patted her hand. Lisbeth and Mother walked out of the study while the men stayed behind.

Mother watched as Lisbeth paced around the sitting room just as Father had earlier that evening, moving between the globe and the piano. Lisbeth felt ready to jump out of her skin. This was taking too long. She went over to the door and peered down the hallway. The door to the study remained closed.

"Stay in this room, Elizabeth," Mother commanded.

Lisbeth did not reply. But she stayed in the doorway, looking down the hall. A few minutes later the sheriff, Jack, and Father came out of the study. Matthew was not with them. They chatted as they walked down the hallway. Once in the sitting room, the sheriff accepted Father's offer of a drink, and then he turned his attention to Lisbeth.

"Where is Matthew?" Lisbeth asked.

"I am speaking with each of you in private. Your father tells me that Mr. Johnson has pressured you into marrying him. The boy denies it, but of course he would," Sheriff Hughes said. "You do not need to be afraid of angering Mr. Johnson. We can protect you."

"He is not pressuring me. In fact, I am the one who proposed marriage," Lisbeth corrected the sheriff.

"I understand that you are too young to make that decision," Sheriff Hughes replied. "You need your parents' permission to be married and they have not given it to you. The law is very clear."

"I am of age," Lisbeth declared.

The sheriff looked at Father with a question on his face.

Father laughed. "Elizabeth has no proof of her age. So it is her word against mine. My memory of her birth is better than hers."

"I have proof," Lisbeth told the sheriff. "My birth certificate shows I am twenty-one."

"We will be not able to get our hands on your birth certificate, Elizabeth. I am so sorry," Father said snidely.

"I have it, Father."

Father looked surprised. "What?"

"My birth certificate is with my belongings. It states that I was born on April 14, 1837. I am twenty-one. I am of age. This is my decision."

"Well, go get it," the sheriff directed Lisbeth.

She rushed upstairs and returned with the document from her room.

The sheriff looked it over. "This her birth certificate?" he asked Father.

Father nodded with a scowl.

"Then she is of age to marry without your consent," Sheriff Hughes told Father.

Mother insisted, "Matthew Johnson took advantage of Elizabeth. She was pressured into this mistake."

"Is that true?" the sheriff asked.

"No. I told you that already," Lisbeth replied. "Matthew did not force me to marry him. I did so of my own free will."

"I'm sorry, Mr. and Mrs. Wainwright, there is nothing I can do for you legally. The judges are clear on this matter," the sheriff said. "I'll be on my way."

The four of them stood in stony silence after Sheriff Hughes left them. Lisbeth felt like a rag doll that had been tossed around by a huge storm. She hoped it was over, but feared a harsh wind would start blowing again. She slowed her breath and thought carefully before she spoke.

"My husband and I will leave now," she told her parents. "We will return in the morning for most of my belongings."

"Elizabeth, you must know we only have your best interest in mind," Mother said.

"So you have said. I believe that you believe you know what is in my best interest. But you do not know my mind or my heart. Nor are you interested in knowing them. In time you will see this is best for me."

Lisbeth walked down the hall to find Matthew. He leaped up from his seat when she opened the door. She crossed to him.

"He is gone," Lisbeth told him. "Can we leave now as well?"

"We are free to go?" Matthew asked.

"Yes, Matthew. We are free." Lisbeth smiled at her husband.

He smiled back and shook his head. "Are they finished fighting?"

"I cannot be certain, but I believe that once I drive away with you, they will lose all hope," Lisbeth said. "You did not know I would cause you such trouble when you agreed to be my husband."

"I fully anticipated your parents' behavior. Everyone in this valley is afraid of the changes that are coming. This way of life is going to be over soon. I have no interest in fighting to preserve it. And I am very glad you will be with me rather than staying here."

"Thank you, Matthew," Lisbeth said, filled with tenderness. "I will go get my things for tonight. Would you like to stay here?"

"I will come with you, if you do not mind," Matthew said.

"I will be very glad of your company."

It felt very strange to have Matthew in her room. No young man had ever been in here. Emily arrived within moments.

"Matthew, this is Emily," Lisbeth said. "Emily, this is my husband, Mr. Johnson. We will leave with the essentials tonight. I will fetch the rest of my belongings tomorrow."

"Congratulations on your marriage, sir."

"Thank you," Matthew replied.

Lisbeth walked over to the window looking over the quarters. Matthew followed her. Emily packed Lisbeth's belongings into a case.

"I have watched out this window every day, twice a day, for as long as I can remember," Lisbeth told him. "When I was little my nurse and I looked for her son and the rest of her family. I never stopped the habit, though she has been gone for nine years."

There was not much to see outside. The hands had left the newly planted fields of tobacco for the night. A few people darted in and out of cabins, or were cooking food over kettles outside. Lisbeth did not see Rebecca or anyone from her cabin.

"I think this ever'thin' you need, Miss Elizabeth. I mean, Mrs. Johnson," Emily broke in.

"Thank you, Emily. For everything. I wish you the best," Lisbeth said. "Can you please say good-bye to Cook and to Rebecca and her family for me? I fear I will not see them again."

Emily nodded. Matthew grabbed the case and they went downstairs. Standing in the entryway, Lisbeth was torn. Mother, Father, and Jack were probably still in the sitting room. She wanted to say good-bye, but was not interested in a scene. She started to walk out the front door and then changed her mind.

She opened the door to the sitting room. "We are leaving now."

Father and Mother stared at Lisbeth. Lisbeth considered going to them to hug good-bye, but decided not to.

"I will be back tomorrow for the rest of my belongings. Will you be here?" she said.

Mother said, "Once you drive away there is nothing, absolutely nothing we can do for you. That will be it. Your life will be over."

"I understand the choice I am making, Mother. Good-bye," Lisbeth said. Then she shut the door tight before her parents could say anything else.

Lisbeth studied her childhood home as they drove away from Fair Oaks. A jumble of emotions and thoughts filled her. Her throat ached and her eyes burned. She stayed alert for any signs they were being followed, but she did not see anyone. Perhaps they had given up. She was grateful to have gotten away, yet sad to be leaving the only home she had ever known. Once again she felt so naïve. She had somehow thought her parents would accept her decision. She realized that the shame she brought on them would be overwhelming, and she was sad to cause them such pain and disappointment.

Lost in her thoughts, she did not talk or pay attention to the journey. When Matthew turned off the road, she became aware of her surroundings.

"I am sorry, Matthew. I am not pleasant company," she said.

"I cannot blame you for being preoccupied," he replied. "You have been through many changes today."

She could hardly comprehend the enormous shift her life had already taken. And yet there was still more to come. She grew nervous as they drove closer to her new home, where she would greet her in-laws, eat in a strange room, and lie with Matthew for the first time.

Matthew broke into her thoughts. "If you prefer, we do not have to share a room tonight."

The offer was tempting, because Lisbeth was so tired. But she was determined to be a good wife. It was the least she could do for the man who had given her a way out. She said, "No, Matthew. I am your wife. I shall sleep in your room."

They drove on in silence for the rest of the ride.

Matthew's parents greeted them warmly at the door.

"Welcome to the family," Matthew's father said as his wife gave Lisbeth a shy hug.

"Thank you, Mr. Johnson," Lisbeth replied.

"Elizabeth, you must call us Mother and Father Johnson now. We are your family," Matthew's mother said.

"Yes, ma'am," Lisbeth agreed. "That would be nice . . . Mother Johnson. Will you please call me Lisbeth? It is my preferred name, though not many use it."

"Certainly," Father Johnson said.

"You too, Matthew," Lisbeth said to her husband. "Please."

"I imagine I can adjust myself to calling you by your childhood name," he said.

Lisbeth was shocked and pleased. "You remember?"

"I remember every word that has ever passed between us," he said with a shy smile.

Lisbeth smiled at him.

"Come, we have supper waiting," Father Johnson said. "You can tell us more about your day while we eat."

After supper the foursome enjoyed playing whist in the living room. Lisbeth was delighted that Matthew liked card games. She was glad they would have something to do when it was just the two of them in Ohio. Soon it was time for bed, and Mother and Father Johnson excused themselves. Lisbeth was alone with Matthew again. She followed him to her new bedroom. Her legs felt weak as she climbed up the stairs.

Lisbeth made a request. "May I please get changed and under the covers in privacy? A man has never seen me in my nightclothes."

"Certainly," replied Matthew. "Do you wish to have Mother or Fanny help you undress?"

"No, thank you. I can manage on my own. Please just let me know where to put my things."

Matthew opened a door to their bedroom at the end of the hall. "It is simple compared to what you are used to. I hope you will be comfortable here, though it is only for a few weeks. You can place your belongings in this wardrobe. It is for your use alone; I moved my clothes to another room. The water on the washstand should be warm and the towel is for your use," Matthew informed her and then left the room.

Lisbeth took a deep breath. *You can do this*, she told herself. She had planned for items she could remove herself, but her hands were shaking so, it was difficult to unlace her corset. She wondered whether Matthew was waiting for her right outside the doorway. She felt exposed and vulnerable at the thought, even though she was alone in the room. After slipping on her nightgown, she opened the oak wardrobe and pulled out a hanger. Her dress slipped off to the right. She tried again. It slipped off again. There was a skill to using a hanger. She felt like a child. Finally she got her garment placed just right in the middle and it did not fall to the ground. When she hung it up, it looked lonely in the center of the wardrobe. She considered hanging up her underthings in the wardrobe but decided instead to fold them and place them in the drawers. Her shoes and case went in the bottom of the cupboard. She unbound her hair and carefully brushed it. She washed her face and then climbed under the blue-and-brown log cabin quilt to await Matthew.

After an eternity of waiting—she supposed he wanted to give her adequate time to undress—he returned. He was dressed for sleep. She looked at his head, wanting to avoid looking at his nightclothes, but her eyes flickered down his body against her will. In a flash she saw a bit of dark hair on his pale leg below the white cotton sleeping gown. As he climbed into bed, Matthew's foot touched hers. She flinched. Though her heart was racing, she lay still on her back, arms at her sides, looking up at the wooden ceiling.

"We do not have to—" Matthew started to say.

"Yes, we do," Lisbeth interrupted. She was scared, but she did not want to have it hanging over her head for yet another day.

Matthew leaned over her and gently kissed her lips. She wanted to kiss him back, but her lips would not move. He abandoned her mouth to softly kiss her across one check and then the other before returning to her lips. This time she returned the kiss. Her lips opened as she began to relax, meeting his open mouth.

He made a trail of kisses across her chin, traveling down her neck, and pulled away the neck of her gown to reach the hollow where it met her shoulders. She shuddered with pleasure as he tasted her skin with his tongue. Every bit of her attention was focused on the movements of his mouth across her body.

When he came to an obstacle of fabric, she watched as he fumbled with the buttons of her gown, muttering to himself when he had difficulty. She jumped in sudden pleasure when he touched her again.

Matthew pulled away from her. He exclaimed, "I am sorry."

"No, no, you mistake me. Please go on," Lisbeth whispered.

One hand was twined in her hair, and his other hand traveled across her body, starting at her shoulder, moving down to her waist, only to be met by another obstacle of fabric. He pulled the material up and reached his hand under her gown, gaining full access to her smooth, warm hip. He slowly moved down her thigh, coming to the end of his reach at her knee. She opened her leg; his hand moved to the inside of her knee.

His hand froze for a moment before it started its ascent up the inside of her thigh. The tips of his fingers meandered along, up, up, up, ever so slowly, crisscrossing back and forth and from side to side. He froze. She was quivering. Why did he stop? She turned to look at him. He was staring at her intently. Was she doing something wrong? Was she supposed to do something besides lie here? She looked at him with a silent question in her eyes.

He whispered so quietly that she barely heard him, "I do not want to hurt you."

"Oh, Matthew, I am fine," she said. "Whatever comes next, I will be all right."

A shiver went down her spine. This truly was wonderful. She did not know it could be so lovely. She turned to him and ran her fingers across his back. She hoped his fingers would continue where they had left off, and soon enough they did.

Quivering with desire, Lisbeth pressed her body against him until he entered her. He cried out. She cried out too, in pain and longing.

After a few minutes, Matthew froze then shook all over. She feared that he was hurt. Just as she considered asking him if he was all right, he exhaled deeply and collapsed across her chest. Matthew lay there, panting. Then he rolled to the side and hugged her tight. It was finished. She had done it. She lay in his arms, pressing her body close to his, astonished by her own yearning.

Overwhelmed with a flood of emotions—joy, shock, excitement, and relief—she wept against Matthew's chest.

CHAPTER 25

JULY 24, 1858

Dearest Mary,

Thank you ever so much for the news from home. You wrote in such detail, I feel as if I were present at your wedding. My biggest regret about my sudden move to Ohio is that I was not in attendance. I am delighted you and Daniel are having a lovely honeymoon. I am certain New York is wonderful. I know you do not understand my decision, and I am truly sorry for that. I am also sorry for the shame and confusion I have brought on my family. I miss you and regret that we will not be watching our children grow up from a veranda in Virginia. But I am pleased you have forgiven me enough to write. I promise to return each letter faithfully.

As for us, we are well. The house is progressing satisfactorily. You would be astonished at how many decisions must be made every day. We have chosen cherrywood trim in the entryway, living room, and dining room, along with oak flooring. We will not be having a study—apparently it is not in fashion out here—but will have a "sunporch" off the living room. It will have windows on three sides. That is in addition to a standard porch that will wrap the house on the other three sides. We shall only have four bedrooms upstairs, in addition to the servants' quarters off the kitchen. The fortunate part of a small home is that decorating it will not be a burden. We are building servants' quarters, though we may not ever use them for that purpose. In Ohio, most help choose to live "away." It is actually wonderfully convenient not to be responsible for servants at all hours of the day. Matthew and I spend enjoyable, quiet evenings in each other's company. We have agreed on most everything, which is fortunate.

Oberlin is lovely. The weather is sticky right now, but they say that the leaves will turn the most beautiful shades of red, yellow, and orange in the autumn. I am preparing myself for a cold winter. We hope to be residing in our new home by Christmas. It shall be odd to have the holiday with only the two of us, but we are not in a position yet to entertain.

Well, I am running on, so I shall close. In the strictest of confidence, I shall share with you my sincere feeling that I may be able to confirm news of an addition to our family in the New Year. Please give my best regards to everyone in Virginia.

Your dear friend,
Lisbeth Johnson

CHAPTER 26

FEBRUARY 1859

Lisbeth was gathering eggs from the chicken coop in the early morning when she felt the first labor pain. Even though it was uncomfortable, she smiled. Her baby was coming, possibly today. She wanted to be sure this was not false labor before she shared the news with Matthew. So she said nothing and went about her morning, stopping to breathe slowly whenever a strong pain came.

Over the midday meal Matthew noticed she was uncomfortable. "Are you in labor?" he asked.

"I am having some pains, but it is early yet." She was touched that he was so observant about her needs. He had been so attentive and kind to her throughout the pregnancy. Lisbeth was confident that he was going to be a wonderful father.

"Are you certain?" he asked, looking excited and scared.

"The pains only come about ten times in an hour. Mrs. Williams says they will be more than double that when it is time."

"Shall I fetch her?" Matthew asked.

"She asked me to wait until I have twenty pains in an hour," Lisbeth told him.

"You trust her?"

"After eight children, she knows about birth. And she assures me that the Negro midwife is better than a doctor if there are any problems. You agreed when we spoke of this before," she teased him.

Matthew sighed. "Yes, you are right. My mother believes midwives are best for childbirth as well."

"I will be fine, Matthew. I am excited to meet our child. Please do not worry about me." Lisbeth understood his concern, though. Many women and babies did not survive childbirth. It was a risk each time, but especially with the first.

"I am excited as well," Matthew replied, "but I cannot help my concern."

Lisbeth paced around the house throughout the afternoon, stopping to lean on a wall whenever a labor pain came. By late afternoon the contractions were coming every three minutes, so Matthew asked the cook to fetch Mrs. Williams. The bag of waters broke soon after she arrived.

"Looks like your baby will be here any minute," Mrs. Williams said. "Soon the urge to bear down comes."

Lisbeth continued pacing. The pains came and came and came, but the urge to bear down did not. Instead she threw up until nothing was left in her stomach. Thoroughly spent, she lay down in bed and rested between contractions. Matthew and Mrs. Williams wiped her forehead with a cool cloth and offered her small sips of water, but she threw that up as well. Hours passed as the evening turned into night. Lisbeth lay in bed as if she were asleep, but she listened as Matthew spoke to Mrs. Williams.

"Is this normal?" Matthew whispered.

"Nothing to be concerned about," she replied. "First babies take a long time. We just need to keep her comfortable and let her body keep at it."

Lisbeth began to be afraid. Something was wrong. Her baby was not coming out. Her body labored well into the night, but sometime before morning, the contractions started to spread out. By the time they were eight minutes apart, Mrs. Williams was concerned.

"Mr. Johnson," Mrs. Williams said, "I am sorry, but this is not normal. That baby should have been out by now. We need to fetch the midwife right away. I pray that she can get labor going again."

Lisbeth barely heard the woman's words. She was exhausted and dehydrated. Soon she slipped away into another world.

The midwife awoke at once. After so many years of welcoming babies, she responded immediately to a knock on the door.

She left the warm bed she shared with her husband to make her way to the door. Grabbing a robe from a peg by the door, she was barely presentable when she opened it. A slight White lady shivered before her in the night.

"We got a difficult birth over at the Acres. They sent me to fetch you."

"Let me change and get my things. I gonna be ready in a moment. Wanna wait inside?"

"I'll wait in the wagon."

In less than ten minutes, Mattie was ready to head out the door. She roused Emmanuel to let him know she was going. He wished her an easy birth before he returned to his dreams. Moving to Jordan's bed, she kissed her sleeping daughter on the forehead. She went to kiss Samuel, but he was not in his bed. Her heart sank a bit. The previous night he had gone out with his friends and had yet to return.

Nearly ten years had passed since Mattie and Jordan joined Emmanuel and Samuel on the outskirts of Oberlin. All vestiges of their former selves were gone, except their memories. Colored folk in the area knew better than to ask too much about the past. White folks too. It was a welcome relief that the Whites in this part of the country showed very little interest in the Negroes, though they were willing to purchase and sell goods and services across color lines. Mattie had built a reputation as the best midwife in the area—even White folks used her services if it meant the difference between life and death.

Mattie and Emmanuel were proud of their house, their work, and their children. Their home was comfortable and large, with two bedrooms added onto the main room. Everyone knew Emmanuel made the best furniture around; his ladder-back chairs were the finest in the county. After three years of saving, he bought a lathe to craft round-spindled as well as square-spindled chairs. Between growing corn, furniture making, and midwifing, Mattie and Emmanuel made a good life.

Jordan still went to the colored school when she wasn't working. She was as good a student as Samuel had been. He was the best in his class when he graduated. He was so good that he went back each week to teach the younger children. The teacher, a Quaker woman, kept saying he should go to Oberlin College, but Samuel did not know if he wanted to keep going to school. He liked working with his father in the shop. Emmanuel would just as soon have Samuel follow in his path, but Mattie hoped he would go to college. College! Her son could go to college. It was still hard to believe they had come so far from their life in Virginia. She was grateful to God and to Lisbeth that her son was free and had the chance to be a teacher or even a lawyer.

Mattie was proud of her boy, but he was a constant worry to her. He liked going out with his friends more than being at home. Emmanuel assured her their son was a good boy and that being out all hours of the night came naturally to a young man. But she could not help wondering, even in Ohio, if he would come home hurt one of these nights.

She pushed her thoughts about her family aside and left her home to help bring a new life into the world.

Less than an hour later, time enough for night to have turned to morning, Mattie entered the birthing room. Before asking any questions, she went straight to the bed to study the mother. A shiny layer of sweat glistened on the pale woman's swollen cheeks; her sunken eyes were closed. The movement of her eyeballs showed through thin eyelids, and her breath was shallow.

As Mattie studied the face, a chill crept up her back. She knew this woman. This was Lisbeth! Her face had changed in ten years, and it was swollen after many hours of hard labor, but Mattie knew she was right.

"Dear Lord," she whispered to herself.

It seemed impossible, but the shell around the young woman's throat erased any doubt. Reaching her hand out to touch her, Mattie brushed damp hair away from Lisbeth's face. She was acutely aware that the other eyes in the room were on her. Reeling with this turn of events, she worked to hide the onslaught of feelings, steadying herself by taking deep breaths in and out.

She studied Lisbeth's face. She was so far gone into this birth, she no longer existed only in this world. The young woman was entirely unaware of the people around her.

Mattie knelt by the bed and quietly whispered into Lisbeth's ear, "I here now. Mattie here with you, strong woman. You gonna be all right." Before rising she touched the shell at the base of Lisbeth's neck and felt its companion under her own dress. Then she said the prayer that started all her midwifing: "Dear Lord, please guide me in gettin' this baby born and savin' this precious woman's life." Then she added something extra for Lisbeth: "God, thank you for letting me take care of her one more time. Please get us both through this safely, and the baby too. Amen."

Then she turned to the others in the room and introduced herself to the man who was hovering anxiously nearby. "Georgia Freedman. I glad you called on me to come."

"I am Matthew Johnson. This is my wife, Lisbeth Johnson. Can you help her?" He looked at Mattie desperately.

Matthew Johnson. That name tickled a memory in Mattie. She smiled to herself. Lisbeth had done it. She picked a good man and found her way out of that nasty place. *I proud of you, girl*, Mattie thought.

Out loud, Mattie said, "Mrs. Johnson needs to get somethin' in her. Mr. Johnson, I want you to get some sugar water with salt brought up. Mrs. Williams, can you help me with examinin' her?"

"But she keeps throwing it up," Matthew said.

"We just gotta hope some stays in her," Mattie told him. "Sugar water with salt, Mr. Johnson. That the first step. That how you gonna do good for your wife right now."

Matthew stared at Mattie, desperation in his eyes. She wanted to reassure him that Lisbeth would be fine. She wanted to reassure herself that she had the skills to save both Lisbeth and her baby. But things did not look good. Lisbeth already had the swelling that was the sign a bad turn may be about to come. She needed to find out why this baby was not coming down. And she prayed that whatever the cause, she had the ability to do something about it.

She stared at Matthew until he finally left. Mattie started her exam. Her experienced fingers felt around the perimeter of Lisbeth's swollen belly, muttering the names of body parts to herself as she went. Then she reached deep into Lisbeth to learn more. This confirmed her fear.

When Matthew returned with the prescriptive brew, she told him, "Mr. Johnson, this here baby ain't turned proper to come out."

"Please, you must do something," Matthew pleaded. "Just take the baby out. Anything to save her."

"I wish I could, Mr. Johnson. Can't just take a baby out. I gonna have to reach in and turn it right, then see if she can get this baby out herself. You and Mrs. Williams got to help me while I do the turning. If you too scared, go get someone else, but I need two folks to hold her up."

His face riddled with anxiety, Matthew started to say something, but then stopped himself. He looked at Lisbeth, then back at Mattie. Looking back at Lisbeth, he took a breath and nodded his head.

"No. No need to get someone else. I can help you. I can help my wife." Seeking Mattie's assurance, Matthew asked, "She is not going to die, is she?"

"Not if I can help it, and if God be willin'. I ain't gonna make you a promise that I don' get to keep, but I done this a few times," Mattie said. Sharing the potential danger of this situation was not going to help the panicked father-to-be, Lisbeth, or herself. They just needed to get to work.

"We gonna move her so she lyin' with her legs down over the side of the bed. You two stand by while I reach in. When I say, you pull her standin' up."

The midwife crossed to the head of the bed. Leaning in close to Lisbeth's unconscious form, Mattie whispered, "I gonna reach in you to turn this baby. It gonna hurt—a lot. But it gonna save you both."

They each got into position. Lisbeth was lying down on the bed with her legs dangling over the side. Matthew and Mrs. Williams each held one of her arms while Mattie knelt between her legs.

Mattie reached deep inside Lisbeth's body, stretching open her cervix, to find the baby's shoulder. Lisbeth screamed, her face contorting in pain. Pushing on the baby's shoulder, Mattie turned the child, rotating her hand to bring the infant's head above Lisbeth's pelvis. Mattie directed her assistants to pull Lisbeth into a standing position to get gravity's aid in engaging the infant's head in the proper spot. Mattie withdrew her hand from the cavity between Lisbeth's legs.

"We did it," she declared. "Lay her down gently."

Matthew grinned wide and breathed a sigh of relief. They lowered Lisbeth back down to the bed. When she was settled, Mattie reached inside Lisbeth to check the infant's position again.

"Damn!" Mattie said under her breath. "The baby turned back. We have to do it again. This time we ain't gonna lay her down when we done. She gonna have to squat. Hopefully that gonna get the baby to stay in place. Mr. Johnson, go get a milkin' stool," she commanded.

On his return, they got into position to do the procedure again. Mattie reached deep into Lisbeth. She pushed the baby into a head-down position. Mattie held the head in place as she directed Matthew and Mrs. Williams to lift Lisbeth to stand. Then she told them to lower her into a squat onto the milking stool. They tucked pillows and bedding around her. Lisbeth was squatting on the stool with her back against the bed and her legs bent up. Mattie withdrew her hand.

"That better," declared Mattie after she examined Lisbeth. "The baby staying in the right place."

"Now what happens?" inquired Matthew.

"Mostly we wait and hope she start laborin' soon. You give her the sugar water in tiny bits. Mrs. Williams, will you brew up some tea with this black cohosh? I hope it gonna get the labor pains comin' again."

Matthew looked at Lisbeth's pale, clammy face. Panic shone in his eyes. He started to pace around the room. Mattie shared his fear, but pacing was not going to help anything. The room needed to be calm and supportive if Lisbeth and this baby were going to make it.

"Mr. Johnson, you gonna be feeding that to your wife or do I need to do it? I know you scared. But if you want to help her, you got to make sure her body has what it need to push this baby out once the pains get going again."

Matthew gave a single nod and sat down next to Lisbeth. Taking the warm cup of liquid in hand, he carefully brought a spoonful of it to her parted lips. He poured it in slowly, but not slowly enough: most of it dribbled right back out.

"Tell her what you doin'. She not so far gone she don' know you. Talk to her."

"Lisbeth, it's me, Matthew . . . your husband. We are trying to help you, and our child. You have to drink this to make you strong. You need to be strong to get this baby out. Please be strong. I do not want to lose you." Matthew went on, "I have loved you ever since I first danced with you when you were twelve. You were so amusing and talkative, not like the other girls, and so beautiful too. I wanted that dance to last forever. I never dared hope you would become my wife someday. This year has been so wonderful. I have begun to believe you might be truly happy with me." Then Matthew begged, "Oh, Lisbeth. Drink this, please."

"That real nice, Mr. Johnson. You keep talking to her like that and she gonna get through this just fine," Mattie encouraged him.

He brought the half-filled spoon to her lips again. He tipped it slowly. The warm liquid he poured made it down her throat. Spoonful after spoonful he fed her, alternating the sugar water with the black cohosh tincture, until, at last, there was a strong contraction. Mattie was so relieved. They still had a long way to go, but at least things were moving in the right direction.

"Oh, that just great," Mattie said. "We get a few more of those and then we gonna start seeing the top of the head."

"She is still unconscious. How will she ever manage to get the infant from her body?" inquired Mrs. Williams.

"I seen it done before—animal nature takes over. But we gonna have to work hard to help her."

The contractions built in intensity. Lisbeth moaned in pain with each one but never opened her eyes. Her mind was in a different world while her body worked in this one. Matthew sat close, whispering encouragement in her ear, giving her spoonfuls of liquid between the pains. Hours passed before Mattie saw the top of the head between Lisbeth's legs.

"This baby ready to come on out. You two gonna have to help with the squeezin'. When the pains come big, you pull up her legs. I gonna push around the head, see if we can get it out without her rousin'."

A large contraction grasped Lisbeth's body, the assistants pulled Lisbeth's bent legs toward her chest, and Mattie stretched Lisbeth's perineum as the baby's head crowned.

"It comin', it comin'. Keep goin', keep goin'. Here it come, here it come," Mattie cheered along the incremental movement of the infant until the contraction ended. "It over. Rest her legs now till the next one come."

The next contraction came, and the next, and the next. With each one, the baby's head came down a little more, but then retreated up the canal when it ended. The top of the baby's head turned blue with each contraction. When it stopped going back to pink between the pains, Mattie's concern grew again. The baby was getting tired. It needed to come out soon, before it was too late.

"She gonna have to help," Mattie declared. "This baby need pushin'."

Mattie came around to Lisbeth's head. She bent close to the laboring woman's ear and spoke quietly, firmly, "Lisbeth, listen to me. You gotta help here. Your baby ready to come out. You gotta push. I know you so tired, but you can do this. Jus' a few big pushes and you gonna have your baby. Find your strength, Lisbeth. You got it in you. You the only one that gonna save your baby's life." Mattie rubbed Lisbeth's clammy forehead and stroked her damp hair. Though Lisbeth never once opened her eyes, Mattie prayed the words penetrated through her fog. "You got it in you, girl. I know you do."

When the next contraction came, Mattie commanded from between Lisbeth's legs, "Push, Lisbeth, push! Right here where my hand is. Push!"

Lisbeth stirred, made a feeble effort to push, then quickly collapsed back.

"That a good girl, that a girl. Do it jus' like that, but even more," Mattie instructed. "With the next one, you two push her head forward while you pull up on her legs. Talk her through this, Mr. Johnson. Encourage her."

Along with the next contraction came quiet words from Matthew: "Push, Lisbeth, push."

Lisbeth's eyes blinked open. She looked directly into Matthew's scared eyes. He leaned in close. "You can do it, Lisbeth. We will do this together. Here comes another one. Push, please push," he begged.

Lisbeth weakly squeezed Matthew's hand, gazed at him with glassy eyes, curled up her body, and pushed. Harder, harder, harder, steady, steady, steady, pushing, pushing, pushing until at last Mattie cried out, "You did it! The head out. You did it, baby, you did it!"

Lisbeth collapsed onto the bed; a small smile passed across her lips before she lost consciousness again.

Matthew whispered, "Lisbeth, you have done it." He covered her face with kisses, and his tears left trails of moisture on her cheeks. He kissed the top of her head. "Thank you. Thank you. Thank you."

The next contraction came fast. Mattie grabbed around the jaw and pulled. The baby came the rest of the way out. He was bright blue. Mattie knew she needed to work fast. She laid him facedown on her lap and pushed on the cord, moving the blood from the placenta into the baby, with her left hand. With her right hand she massaged the baby's back. The room was silent.

"Do it," Mattie encouraged the baby. "Take a breath." She kept rubbing hard. Finally, the baby jerked back his head and gave a loud cry. Mattie sighed and a chill of relief ran through her body. "You tell us all about it, little one."

The baby screamed and screamed. At this moment, it was a joy to hear. Lisbeth's baby was alive and well. Mattie looked up at Matthew. Tears glistened in her eyes. "A boy!" she exclaimed. "Mr. Johnson, you got a son."

Matthew looked at his child in Mattie's hands. Tears of joy and relief streamed down his cheeks.

"Thank you. Thank you so much. You saved them. You saved them both!"

"Yes, I did, Mr. Johnson," Mattie said. "With a lot of help from God. And just enough from you and Mrs. Johnson, and Mrs. Williams. We saved them all right."

Mattie had never been so relieved at the end of a birth. There had been harder ones, of course. But never one that mattered so much to her. She did not fully relax until Lisbeth delivered the afterbirth and Mattie cut the cord.

Lisbeth and her baby boy were just fine.

When the infant was clean and wrapped, and Lisbeth was sleeping soundly in her bed, Mattie asked, "Mr. Johnson, do you have a name for him?"

"We did not choose any names before. Neither of us wanted to tempt fate," Matthew replied. "But if Lisbeth agrees, I would like Samuel, after my grandfather."

Mattie's breath caught. "A lovely name. I knowed a baby Samuel once."

"Do you have any children?"

She nodded. "Yes, James—he just twenty-two—and eleven-year-old Jennie."

"They must be a great joy to you."

"It sure is somethin' how much you love your children. It took me by surprise with the first one. Thought I knew what I was gettin' into for the next, but I gave my heart to each one I brung to my breast."

"I know I have said thank you many times already, but truly, I am so grateful to you for what you have done here today. I cannot possibly thank you enough. You are an angel, sent from heaven to save my wife."

"You done a mighty fine job yourself at her laborin'. Most men woulda run the other way," she said.

Matthew shrugged shyly. "I have been at many births with livestock. When I was scared I reminded myself it was not so different."

"She one lucky girl to have a man like you. You a good man."

"Thank you, but I am the one who is fortunate to be married to her. I am the luckiest man alive, thanks to you. I know this might have been the worst day of my life. Thanks to you it is one of the very best," he replied, and smiled at her. "Thank you for everything."

"It my pleasure. It surely was," she replied with a satisfied nod.

Mattie took in the scene. She had wondered about Lisbeth so many times over the years. Every night she said a prayer for the child she left behind. And here she was in person, in the sweet home she had made with a lovely young man far away from the nastiness of the James River. *God is great*, she thought to herself. *God is great.*

—

A few days later, Lisbeth, still in bed recovering, was beaming at the sleeping child nestled in her arms. Matthew sat nearby.

"He is so wonderful, Matthew," Lisbeth declared. "He is a gift from heaven."

She studied the baby: the curve of his ear, the pink of his tiny fingernails, his nearly translucent eyelashes. *Samuel*, she thought to herself. *You are my very own Samuel.*

Out loud she said, "I grew up with a Samuel. He was my mammy's son."

"I did not know. Would you prefer a different name?"

"No. I am pleased my son will have the same name as Mattie's son. Do you suppose he is growing enough?" she wondered. "He still looks so small."

"He is only three days out of your womb. Give him time to adjust. However," Matthew suggested, "if you are terribly concerned, we can hire a wet nurse. Your body may be spent after your ordeal."

"Absolutely not!" Lisbeth snapped back. "No wet nurse for our Samuel. If I cannot provide him with what he needs we shall use cow's milk."

Matthew came close. Stroking Lisbeth's arm, he spoke tenderly and cautiously. "I apologize. I meant no offense. My only consideration is that you might be tired after such a difficult labor. Cow's milk, of course, though I do not think we have anything to be concerned about." After a long pause he went on, "I thought you remember your wet nurse fondly."

"I do. I loved her dearly, more than my own mother. I cannot bear the thought of Samuel loving another woman more than he loves me. I cared for Mattie so much, she is who I always wanted when I was frightened. In fact, I dreamed of her the very night of Samuel's birth."

"I imagine the midwife might have reminded you of her. She was very gentle with you."

"Have you sent the payment yet?" asked Lisbeth.

"No," responded Matthew. "Mrs. Williams said that two chickens is sufficient payment for a standard birth."

"Then we shall give her four, because this was anything but standard. I am certain she saved my life, as well as Samuel's." Lisbeth was struck by a sudden idea. "Matthew, I will bring the payment to her myself, as soon as I am recovered."

"Do you believe that is prudent?" he asked.

"I am perfectly capable of driving chickens across town. It is the only proper way for me to meet this Negro midwife to express my gratitude in person. I will be fine, but if you wish, we can go together."

CHAPTER 27

Weeks later, Lisbeth was well enough to travel. Perched atop the wagon, she sat next to Matthew as he steered a pair of deep-black horses through the fresh spring morning. The warm sun shone down upon them, and a gentle breeze swept across their faces. Clucking sounds from three hens and a rooster accompanied their journey past their neighbors' fields into town. Samuel, filled with his mother's milk, was wrapped tight in a flannel blanket, asleep in a box at Lisbeth's feet. On his head sat a pink cap, a gift from the former Mary Ford, now Mary Bartley. Along the muddy road, Lisbeth spotted a bright-yellow flower in front of a white farmhouse. A crocus! What a surprise. It felt like a blessing from Mattie from across the years.

"Matthew, look . . . a crocus! It is the sign that spring is surely here. Next year I wish to have crocus blooming in our yard."

"That would be lovely," Matthew replied, smiling at his wife. "Though the bulbs are quite expensive . . ."

"It is a luxury we can afford," he assured her.

"Thank you, Matthew." Lisbeth smiled back. "Can you believe we have lived here for nearly a year?"

"It has passed quickly." They drove on in silence, each following the trail of their own thoughts.

"Lisbeth," Matthew broke the silence, "are you very sorry to be in Ohio?"

She was surprised at such a forthright question. She shook her head and replied, "Not at all. You need not wonder for a moment, Matthew. I do not regret my decision in the slightest. Quite the contrary, I thank God each night for you and for Samuel. I love our home, Matthew."

Lisbeth slid across the wooden bench until she sat right next to her husband. She looped her arm through his, leaned against him, and rested her head against his shoulder. She looked up at him in time to see him nod his head with a satisfied smile on his face. She squeezed his arm, confident she had conveyed all that was in her heart.

They stopped in town to get supplies—ground flour, sugar, and cloth—and any letters brought west on the train. Afterward they set out to the other side of town to the midwife's house to make their payment for Samuel's birth. Lisbeth slowly tore open an envelope addressed in her mother's precise hand. Reading silent as they drove along the dirt road, she sat back with a sigh when she finished.

"What does she say?" wondered Matthew.

Lisbeth read out loud:

Dear Elizabeth,

Thank you for the news of Samuel. Congratulations to you and your husband. I imagine you are proud to have a son. Thank you for the invitation to visit your home, but I am unable to travel at this time. Perhaps you and the baby can come to Virginia in the summer. You both will be welcome. Your father sends his best wishes.

Sincerely,
Your Mother

"I am not surprised," Lisbeth said. "But I held a small hope that Samuel's birth would be enticing to her."

"Perhaps my mother will convince her it is not as wild as she imagines. I am certain your mother will visit us one day. She is slowly making peace with your decision."

"I suppose," Lisbeth agreed. She shook her head. "Whatever she does, I shall not let her ruin my happiness."

Past the town, fallow fields eager for the spring planting surrounded small homes. Lisbeth noticed laundry hung out to dry and chickens milling around yards. Occasionally a dark-skinned person with a wide-brimmed hat broke from labor to stare up at the passing wagon.

Carefully reading Mrs. Williams's directions, Lisbeth told Matthew, "This is the turn. It will be the third parcel on the left. Below the road, in the gully."

Past the first and second farms, Lisbeth told Matthew to slow as they came to the third farm. The house was set back a hundred feet or so down a driveway.

"Here it is," Lisbeth said. "Turn here."

Matthew was guiding the horses into the top of the driveway when something caught Lisbeth's eye.

"Matthew, stop!" she whispered urgently.

Matthew stopped the wagon and looked over at his wife.

A gasp escaped from Lisbeth, and she went cold. "Oh, dear God," she whispered. "It cannot be."

"Lisbeth, you look as if you have seen a ghost!" Matthew exclaimed. "What is the matter?"

She scrutinized the scene before her. Two figures were hanging laundry on the clothesline. A child with a head of bouncy braids handed pieces of wet clothing to a woman. The woman, her head wrapped in a dark cloth with bits of gray hair showing through, efficiently hung the clothes upon the line.

"Lisbeth, what is the matter?" Matthew pressed again.

Without taking her eyes off the scene, Lisbeth replied, "That looks like Mattie."

"Who?"

"My nurse, Mattie."

"In Ohio? That is hard to believe." Matthew shook his head. "When did you see her last?"

"It will be ten years on June fourteenth."

"Are you certain that is her?" he asked.

"No."

Lisbeth stared as the twosome went about their chore. The daughter, teasing her mother, snatched away a piece of offered cloth at the last minute. The mother caught the end. A tug-of-war ensued, ending when the mother tickled her daughter to gain possession of the shirt. Laughter echoed up to Lisbeth.

"Her laugh . . . that is Mattie. I am certain." Lisbeth was stunned. "The girl must be Jordan. She is so big. So very big. They look good . . . so happy."

Lisbeth looked over at Matthew, tears running down her face. "I know I am foolish, but I have wondered for so many years . . . if they were even alive. To finally see them, and see that they are so well . . ."

Gazing at the pair in the distance, Lisbeth was transfixed. She took in their clothes, their hands, their faces. As hard as it was to believe, Mattie and Jordan were alive and well in front of her, only one hundred feet away.

"Should I leave them in peace?" Lisbeth wondered out loud. She turned to Matthew. "Mattie must have known me at Samuel's birth. She did not tell you she knew me?"

"No," he said. "But it is extremely dangerous for fugitive slaves right now. She does not know if she can trust me."

"She can," Lisbeth said.

"Yes, she can, but she does not know that."

"Do you believe she would wish to see me?" wondered Lisbeth.

"She was tender toward you at Samuel's birth. It was very apparent. I was surprised at how worried she was and how kind she was toward you. Once she even called you Lisbeth. I imagine she cares deeply for you."

Tears streamed faster down Lisbeth's face.

Eventually Mattie noticed the White folks hovering in her driveway. Recognizing Lisbeth at once, she rushed to pick up the basket of wet clothes.

"Come on. We goin' in now," Mattie commanded.

"But, Mama, we got more to hang out," Jordan insisted.

"See that White lady?" Mattie gestured with her head.

"Uh-huh." Jordan nodded.

"I got to tell you somethin' about her."

Rushing into their cabin, Mattie explained to her daughter, "'Member how I told you 'bout the little White girl I used to care for? The one that made your baby quilt? Well, she up there on the road. Look like they came to bring me somethin' for helpin' her get her baby out. You got to call her Miss Elizabeth if'n she comes round. They may just drive off. She might have known it was me. It was her family we runned from."

"She gonna tell on us?"

"No," Mattie replied with certainty. "We gonna get ready in case she comes down."

"No White lady ever come in before," Jordan said with wonder in her voice.

—

Finally Lisbeth decided. "Matthew, I will do what I set out to do this morning. Please bring me to Mattie's home."

A flick of the reins brought the horses to the house below.

Drying her cheeks, Lisbeth told Matthew, "You wait here with Samuel. I will come get you if I need anything."

Lisbeth cautiously climbed to the ground, mindful of every movement of her shaky legs as she went. Crossing to the door, she was acutely aware of the sounds around her: the clucks of the chickens in the wagon and the crunch of gravel under her shoes. She counted her steps from the wagon to the front door of Mattie's cabin—one . . . two . . . three—up to twelve.

When she got to the door, standing in the bright sunlight, Lisbeth hesitated to knock. Maybe Mattie did not want to see her. Her heart beat furiously. This was foolish. Perhaps Mattie did not care to have her past dredged up, to risk the danger.

Then Lisbeth heard a voice cut through the wooden door: Mattie's deep, warm voice, the voice that had soothed her when she was little, the voice that still sang in her dreams. That was her Mattie inside.

She raised her hand and knocked.

—

Mattie opened the door. She had planned to invite Lisbeth in immediately, but instead she stood in the doorway, taking in the woman before her. Tall and strong, so transformed from the little girl that Mattie loved, and yet, those eyes, they were the same. Mattie's breath caught, her throat closed tight, and tears rushed to her eyes. Motioning with her hands, beckoning Lisbeth in silently, Mattie closed the door tight before she pulled Lisbeth into her strong, warm arms.

EPILOGUE

I wish I could tell you that Mattie and I were like family to one another from that day on, but I cannot. As I told you, this is a true story. The only proper way for me to have Mattie in my home is for me to hire her, and I am not willing to order her about, and I do not suppose that she would agree to take directions from me. The only proper reason for me to visit her home is to provide assistance, charity to a family in need. Which I would provide, without hesitation, if she ever needed me to, but she does not need me. She has Samuel and Jordan, her real children, to care for her.

Every Christmas I bring a package to Mattie's family, a small token that does not begin to repay her for all that she gave to me. I pray that she feels the love and appreciation I pour into every muffin or quilt or jar of jam. Occasionally we see one another in town. The last time was in the spring, when my Samuel was seven. He ran from me, down the side of the general store, as we were going to make a purchase of flour and sugar for a cake. I followed, ready to chastise him, when Mattie came around from the back. Too stunned to speak or move, I froze and stared at Mattie. She stared right back, looking at me as if she knew my soul.

Then Samuel shouted, "Look," breaking our attention from one another. "The first crocus of spring!"

Mattie and I gazed in the direction he pointed.

"Why, looky at that. Yellow too—how lovely," Mattie said.

Samuel announced proudly, "Yellow crocuses are my mama's favorites. My mama and I will have a picnic with black-eyed peas today to celebrate."

"That right?" Mattie said with a shake of her head. "In my family we do just the same thing. Imagine that."

Our eyes met again. I gazed intently at Mattie, hoping she understood all that was in my heart. More than anything, I wanted to rush to her and feel the embrace of her loving, familiar arms; to laugh and hug; to introduce Samuel to her, and have him know that this was the very person who taught me to hunt for crocuses. I wanted my Samuel to meet her, to know her, to love her. But I did not rush or introduce or laugh or hug; I simply smiled, a tender, moist-eyed smile across the vast distance between us.

Mattie smiled back at me before we went our separate ways.

APPRECIATIONS

Writing this novel was a sheer act of strength for me. I needed much encouragement just to keep going. I am deeply indebted to all those who read the many drafts along the way, giving me the feedback that gave me the courage to keep going. Thank you to readers Sheri Prud'homme, Mo Morris, Rinda Bartley, Kathy Post (x 2: one of the first and one of the last!), Catherine Fisher, Kyle Fisher, Julie Scholz, Carolyn Hand, Bonnie Richman, Susan Pence, Cathy Cade, Heather MacCleod, Michelle Berlin, Darlanne Hoctor, Anne-Lise Breuning, Niall O'Regan, Kate Hand, Pat St. Onge, Jody Savage, Melanie Curry, Mary Bartley, RuAjna Kai, Hannah Eller-Isaacs, Fran Bartley, Charlotte Dickson, Carmen Bartley, Laura Prickett, Alisa Peres, Janne Eller-Isaacs, Rob Eller-Isaacs, Skot Davis, Cambron Williamson, Ann Hecht, Jill Miller, Jean Weiss, Mona Ibrahim, Jamie Ibrahim, Sarah Moldenhauer-Salazaar, Mike Jung, Cathy Rion, and Kalin Ibrahim-Bartley. I am grateful to Laura Klynstra for the beautiful cover. Thank you to the editors who greatly improved the story: Janis Newman, Jane Cavolina, Renee Johnson, Tiffany Yates Martin, and Michael Townley. And thank you to Gogi Hodder for being the biggest cheerleader of all by readily making copies, reading nearly all of the numerous drafts, and being absolutely certain that this story needs to be in the world.

Thank you to all the Woolsey School kids who have brightened my life and to their parents for letting me love them.

Thank you to the readers who helped me know I had done justice to Mattie and Lisbeth's story and helped spread the word about it.

Thank you to Terry Goodman and Amazon Publishing for their desire to bring *Yellow Crocus* to a wider audience.

ABOUT THE AUTHOR

Laila Ibrahim's expertise in multicultural developmental psychology provided ample material for the story of Mattie and Lisbeth. The founder and director of Woolsey Children's School, Laila had firsthand experiences loving children who were not her own, and as a birth doula, she is privileged to witness the intensity and joy of childbirth. She loves working as the Director of Children and Family Ministries at the First Unitarian Church in Oakland, California. Laila lives in Woolseyville, a small co-housing community in Berkeley, with her wife, Rinda; their dogs, Bella and Lucie; and on occasion their young-adult daughters, Kalin and Maya Ibrahim-Bartley. *Yellow Crocus* is her first novel.